Breach of Trust

Other Five Star Titles
by Melinda Rucker Haynes:

The Eternal Trust

Breach of Trust

Melinda Rucker Haynes

Five Star • Waterville, Maine

First Edition
First Printing: June 2003

Set in 11 pt. Plantin by Myrna S. Raven.

Printed in the United States on permanent paper.

ISBN 0-7862-5168-9 (hc : alk. paper)

Eternal thanks to my editor, Russell Davis, for his continuing support, encouragement and superb editing.

Eternal thanks to four gifted writers and my dear friends, Darcy Carson, Carol Dunford, DeeAnna Galbraith and Lisa Wanttaja for their generous help, excellent guidance and cherished friendship.

Prologue

Between the stone paws of the Great Sphinx of Giza and far below the crowds of prowling tourists, Majid Sawaya wiped the sweat dripping into his eyes with his shirtsleeve. He glanced away from the monitor and peered over the shoulder of the technician operating the robotic video camera. The long telescoping tube slowly retracted from the 2.5cm hole drilled through the rectangular stone slab. The door sealed a secret chamber that the Director of the Egyptian Antiquities Trust had publicly sworn didn't exist.

The tiny camera transmitted a shadowy image of a large dark mass sitting in the center of the chamber's floor, possibly a stone sarcophagus that served to inflate the Director's hopes of discovering an intact mummy or treasure of knowledge and, of course, priceless artifacts.

The Director was crouched on the stone floor of the cramped, sharply sloped passage in front of the door. His voice rose with excitement as he commanded the technician to secure the camera and move out of the way. While Majid and two of his best workmen pried at the door's smooth edges with steel bars, the Director couldn't stop himself from forecasting the wonders that he expected to find within the chamber.

"There are hieroglyphs and beautiful wall decoration, of course, perhaps even funerary artifacts, but the sarcophagus will hold the best secrets, I am certain," the Director enthused.

Once the seal of millennia was broken, the stone proved to be the width of a man's hand. As if on hidden hinges, it opened easily, wide enough to allow a man to slip through. The Director proclaimed the chamber hadn't been breached since first sealed by the ancients and ordered everyone back up the passage.

When all had withdrawn, he motioned to Majid. "Set up the digital mapping camera. I estimate it will take about seven hours for the camera to record the entire chamber, then I'll enter and you will film my great discovery. Hurry now, set it up and come right back. I will wait here for you. Then we will close the door. The guard will maintain security while the camera is doing its work and we will continue ours topside."

Majid nodded and unpacked the digital video camera, struggling to contain his excitement at being the first human to see what had been buried for thousands of years. Even though he wouldn't get a chance to see much in the minute or so it would take to set up the camera, Majid, who was driven by reckless curiosity and the need for money to satisfy his proclivities, would still be the first. He hefted the camera, pointing a large handheld spotlight into the chamber, and followed the bright beam into the dark.

Well after sundown, Majid took an 8mm video camera out of his truck. "Tell the Director we're ready," he said to one of the workmen and reentered the canvas enclosure screening the dig from public view.

Inside, after dismissing the guard, the Director instructed Majid, "You will follow me with the camera as I go."

Majid nodded and moved where he could capture the Director's best side as he posed to open the door. It swung open noiselessly at the Director's tentative touch as though it were floating in the stone wall.

The Director's eyes rounded in surprise and he gave a

muffled titter. "Majid, you must now agree that I have made a great discovery! It is a wonder, an ancient wonder that will prove the best artifacts are only discovered by Egyptians. It's in our blood, our heritage. Our divine right to rediscover what our ancestors have left for us."

Majid, who was Lebanese, grunted assent because the Director had no interest in conversation. He was performing for the camera, and for himself. He would no doubt spend many hours reliving this fabulous unedited moment of personal triumph, which had been made possible by years of study, research and hundreds of man-hours —all put in by other people who would receive only the smallest acknowledgment for their contribution. The Director would get the majority of the credit for this find when the time was right to go public.

The Director hesitated in the doorway then motioned for Majid. "Shine your light inside so I can see."

Majid took a deep breath and moved forward into the darkness. He aimed the camera's high intensity light ahead while he watched the image on its swing out LCD screen and strove to hold the camera level while keeping one eye on the uneven stone floor. He turned the camera on the Director who switched on his spotlight and stepped further into the chamber.

Majid edged around to profile the Director as he began to speak and flash his light around. Majid wanted to survey the room too, but didn't dare—he must record the Director's great triumph.

"Beautiful! Exquisite! Yes, this chamber has never been breached. It has remained secret from the time the Sphinx was constructed. What great mysteries does this room hold? What ancient kings and priests conducted their secret rituals here?"

The light glowed across the walls of the square chamber. The four sides at angles shot upwards, narrowing to intersect at an apex twenty feet above. In addition to hieroglyphics, the walls were decorated with unusual pictographs and quasi-geometric symbols that Majid determined from his twenty years of research and study were not Egyptian, ancient or otherwise, in origin. The Director ignored this anomaly.

"Ah yes, these hieroglyphs are definitely a marvelous and unusual example of secret funerary rites and practices, possibly."

The Director moved further into the chamber and swung the light to the center. "Unfortunately, no sarcophagus. Perhaps an altar where they conducted ceremonies to the gods. This could be another temple of the God's Wife where she performed her functions for Amun here . . ." His voice trailed off as he neared the stone table.

"Not an altar of the usual sort. Possibly a preparation table. I judge it to be about five feet long, by about four feet high . . ." He leaned forward, careful to not touch the side of the structure and pointed his light at the top. "By four feet wide. Very strange. It's a kind of polished stone like obsidian, but harder, metal-like. The top is . . . there seems to be a long channel in the center." He spanned the rectangular depression with his hand, stretching the fingers wide. "About ten inches across and there's something down in there." The Director shined his light into the dark canal.

"It can't be!" he exclaimed and reeled back, bumping into Majid.

"What is it?" Majid stooped nearer, as the Director's light bobbed wildly along the top, dipping in and out of the depression.

"It's a joke! No, an abomination! Who would do this?"

Majid's gaze followed the Director's horrified stare and his own breath whooshed out of him at the sight. His knees went weak and he began to chuckle as he pointed the camera downward, panning across the cord-wrapped handle of a Japanese samurai sword in four pieces beside a spiral-carved black lacquer scabbard lying on the bottom of the channel. Next to it lay a flattened metal rod-like piece that was hooked on one end and two thirds the length of the scabbard.

Light filled the opening and illuminated three-inch high cuneiform-like characters carved into the stone between the metal hooked rod and the side of the channel. Majid turned the unblinking camera's eye upon them. A disincarnate voice resonated from the chamber's shadows:

Return to the Forge of Balance and the two shall be made whole.

The viewer hovered near like a ghost and watched them empty the chamber of its two aberrant relics. The authority figure's disappointment was raw and angry as the subordinate nailed the top on the rectangular crate that held the target and a flattened metal rod, one end bent to a U shape. He ordered the subordinate to lose the unmarked wooden box among the thousands of other dusty, uninventoried artifacts in the museum's warehouse and forget them.

The subordinate had other thoughts, the viewer perceived. The pieces would indeed be lost to the archeological world. He had a private collector in mind for the Japanese sword and its strange companion. The buyer would want a copy of the digital camera's survey of the chamber, and would get it, at an exorbitant premium and whatever else the subordinate could extort, of course.

The viewer shuddered at the avaricious lust in the man's mind and withdrew from the scene, integrating her energy body within the physical once again.

The sword had been found.

Chapter One

The clanging of metal on metal woke Jonathan Spencer out of the few minutes of fitful sleep he'd been able to achieve in the last two hours. His bare feet hit the cold hardwood floor and he stood, pulling his .45 automatic out of the bedside table drawer. He thumbed the safety off on the always-loaded weapon and eased to the window, plastering his naked back against the clammy wall. He peered sideways through the bank of floor-to-ceiling windows that comprised the west side of his bedroom loft.

That sound he'd heard had to be someone trying to break into this last window opening on the fire escape or downstairs in the shop or offices—again. It was impossible, but some idiot had tried just about every night for the last couple of weeks. Spence hadn't been able to catch them or find evidence of their attempts—no scarring on the bars of the windows, no jimmy marks on the steel back downstairs or on the rollup door in the shop. No unusual images on the security cameras' tapes.

Nothing but the harsh metallic sound that he had come to dread after giving in to his body's need for sleep.

Maybe someone was screwing with him, trying to drive him over the edge.

The problem was he was so damn driveable these days, so close to the edge.

Spence pulled away from the windows and gripped the pistol with both hands, locking his elbows into his sides and made his way across the floor to the loft's framed glass railing. He shielded himself behind a support girder and surveyed the downstairs for a moment, listening to the silence before he stepped down the steel stairs to the main level. He peered around the moonlit interior of the huge open room that served as his living quarters.

Satisfied that no one was lurking behind the few crates and boxes that still held most of his old stuff and antique weapons collection, Spence went straight to the row of security monitors and terminals opposite the wall of bulletproof windows overlooking Lake Union. He tapped in the dynamic sweep code and watched as the networked cameras brought ultra sensitive audio and active infrared online to scan every meter inside and out of Integrity Security's 25,000 square foot building, all revealing nothing unusual. He accessed the tapes for the last thirty minutes and began to replay them while the cameras continued their obsessive surveillance of nothing unusual.

Sweat collected between Spence's shoulder blades, rolled down his spine and caught at the waistband of his shorts. He shivered, eased the hammer down on the Colt, then laid the gun beside the keyboard, grabbing the sweatshirt he'd thrown on the chair earlier in the evening and pulling it on. Blotting his damp face with the sleeve and keeping his eyes on the monitors, he sidled a few feet to the freight elevator, grabbed the handlebars of his Harley sitting in front of the door and swung into the saddle.

It felt good—skin against leather. The Harley was the perfect tranquilizer and turn on, with the right woman behind him, of course. But there was nobody right or otherwise these days.

Everybody and everything was totally messed up.

Things should be good. Hell, they should be freaking fantastic, like when he was able to get some sleep.

And he could . . . if they would leave him alone.

If they would stop trying to get to him and stop trying to drive him back into the shadows.

If they—

What *they?* He wiped the sweat out of his stinging eyes with the heels of his palms. Focusing on the normal, uncorrupted images on the monitors reassured him there was no *they*. He could believe there never had been if he controlled his thoughts well enough.

Most people ignorantly claimed you couldn't change the past, couldn't banish life's horrors into Never Happened Land. The hell you couldn't. However it happened, a big chunk of his memories beyond ten years ago were either nonexistent or indistinct impressions. It was like trying to see your fist in a dark cave. He didn't tell anyone he couldn't remember whatever might have been because it would mean he was heading down the same road his dad had gone.

Alzheimer's.

He didn't want to go out that way—one day strong and sharp and the next not even remembering how to wipe your ass. The shrewd reserve his dad had been well known for had mutated into a crafty evil that tortured his wife and every other caregiver until he finally died when Spence was one hundred twenty days short in the Navy. He was sorry he hadn't been there to help his mom, but grateful, too. Dad had always been a real special son of a bitch toward his only child who, as Mom said, never knew when to keep his mouth shut and duck.

Spence hadn't missed him one second, but he would always yearn for Mom's happy laugh and quiet strength. Why the hell she'd curled up and died after Dad went, he couldn't figure. How could she care that much about the man who'd made their lives hell in every way possible?

It was insane to outlive the bastard who had treated you

15

like dirt for a lifetime, then waste away from loneliness, killed by love.

Forgive your dad. I know he loves us—loves you. Forgive and love him because he needs you to, she'd told him in those last moments before she'd given in to congestive heart failure.

Never. Jonathan Spencer would never forgive. He might forget—for a while, but forgiving meant it was okay, understandable or a *human* frailty for someone to betray, abuse or even try to kill him or those he cared about.

Never! He'd remember when he needed to, when the time was right, then he'd deal.

Spence unclenched his jaw and climbed off the Harley, wiping his smudged handprints off the chrome with his sweatshirt bottom. He headed to the refrigerator and pulled out a Dr Pepper, his tenth or maybe twelfth today, but who was counting? Besides, there was no way he was getting back to sleep now.

The doc had suggested too much caffeine was the root of his insomnia.

Not insomnia. He wouldn't use that word. It was counterproductive to think that he *suffered* from insomnia. There was no suffering to being awake because then he was making money, building his empire instead of tearing up the bed trying to achieve something that *they* were going to snatch away from him in a few breaths. Like some sort of Chinese water torture, but with noise instead. Metal clanging against metal.

They.

There was one person who might know who *they* were— if he would tell.

The target's anguished memories and exhaustion were

too much to bear. The viewer broke off, hovering a moment in the shadows then withdrew.

He was a good man and she couldn't keep doing this to him. Driving him to the crumbling edge of sanity couldn't be the best approach for this operation regardless what they'd told her. Despite all the process safeguards and prohibitions, she'd become connected to him. She felt his thoughts, his emotions and frustrated dreams like her own and more. She knew what he did not—his past.

The next Saturday afternoon Spence rode thirty miles out of the city to the gentleman horse acres and yuppie ranchettes in southeastern King County to attend his godson's fifth birthday party. Besides celebrating with the closest thing to a son he'd ever have, he looked forward to seeing his best friends, the boy's parents, Mike and Dorel Gabrielli.

"Come on, Uncle Spence, you said you'd give us rides for my birthday party," Marty Gabrielli called and climbed on the bike after the mountain of gifts was opened.

"You guys ready?" Spence answered and set down the half-empty can of Dr Pepper with a wink to the boy's mother who was telling the kids not to bother him. The Gabriellis' Airedale terrier, Katana, leaned against his leg, resting his wet muzzle on Spence's knee. He gave the old boy a good scratch behind the ear and stood up.

"It's fine, I'm okay," he assured Dorel.

"You look tired," Dorel said and shook her head, turning back to the kids' mothers grouped around a table under a large market umbrella, sheltering from late September intermittent sprinkles and sun showers.

The big black and tan dog followed Spence across the rain-damp lawn toward the little kids gathered around his

Harley. "Okay, the birthday boy first, then I'll catch the rest of you. Watch how Marty puts on his helmet and hangs on to me. You have to do the same, understand?"

Everyone nodded as his godson hefted his own helmet, a smaller version of Spence's, over his strawberry blond hair. Spence lifted him out of the saddle to the back seat and climbed on. Marty clamped his little arms around his waist and Spence started the bike. He commanded Katana to stay then eased down the pine needle carpeted path through the bordering forest and followed the fence line separating the Gabrielli property from the Christmas tree farm next door.

Once they turned onto the two-lane blacktop, Marty tugged on the back of Spence's leather jacket, their signal to stop. He pulled to the side of the road, put his feet down and turned, lifting off his helmet. Marty had slipped off the seat and stood in the dirt staring up at Spence.

"What's up, M-Man, you okay?" He kicked the stand down and turned off the bike as concern rolled in his belly. He'd vowed five years ago to guard Martin Everly Gabrielli with his life. Every scrape, every *owie* as Dorel called the bumps and bruises the boy had experienced in his short life, Spence felt more than his own. The boy and his parents were the most important things in his life, whom he cared for above his thriving business or anything else.

"Uncle Spence, you got problems," the five-year-old pronounced with conviction. He crossed his arms over his new leather jacket with an Integrity Security logo that Spence had given him today.

"Oh, yeah, says who?" Spence smoothed his hand over his moustache and goatee, squinting down at the serious-looking boy, then pulled his famous wise ass smirk, but his guts went cold. He should have guessed that Marty would know he was in trouble.

Marty dropped his gaze and kicked a rock with his new black boot, a shiny miniature of Spence's own worn motorcycle boots. "Nobody, just me."

"Okay, that's good. So, you think I've got trouble, huh? What kind of trouble would that be, exactly?" Spence asked, casually flicking the long fringe on the handlebar's right grip with his fingers.

Marty looked into Spence's eyes. "I've been hearing the sounds, too. I don't know what it is or who, but you better ask Dad to help you. He'll do it, but they're real careful about that stuff now. You know how they are," he added, then pulled his helmet back on and stepped up on the exhaust pipe to settle in behind Spence.

Spence let out the breath he'd been holding as he put on his helmet and restarted the bike, turning back for the house. Yeah, he knew how they were—they were like him. Pretenders to ordinary existence when their shared and not so long ago past was everything but normal. He was torn between wanting to press Marty further and pretend the kid didn't know what he was talking about.

There was no denying that Marty knew things he shouldn't, weird things. He was *way* too old-man wise for his years. Seemed like he'd shared Spence's interest in weapons and warfare since he could talk, quickly going from baby sounds to full sentences that made so much sense it was scary—to everyone but Spence who had clicked with the kid the first time he saw him. When he hadn't known Dorel for very long, he'd thought maybe because she was jealous of Marty's and his bond, she'd begun to say how much the boy resembled her grandfather, Martin Everly. But he soon learned that Dorel wasn't jealous; she believed Marty could be the reincarnation of her grandfather. Mike hadn't disagreed with her. That one offhanded statement was made so long ago that Spence didn't know if it was a real memory or not. Dorel and Mike were the only ones he could turn to for help and get it without question.

Long after Dorel had said goodnight and gone to bed, Mike and Spence were still working on the purchase agreement for their leasing company's latest acquisition, a 747-400 airliner coming out of passenger service in Miami. The airplane would be their fourth purchase that they would have converted to a freighter. Avion Aircraft Leasing had been Dorel's idea soon after she married Mike and left Boeing. It was a huge gamble for the three of them, but they'd leveraged the financial backing to buy the airplanes and then found customers to lease them with an excellent return. They kept overhead to a minimum with Spence and Mike ferrying the airplanes to the modifications center and Dorel coordinating the engineering and modifications packages.

Their aircraft leasing business was growing faster than they'd thought possible. Accountants and financial advisors reported that Avion's income could quadruple if Spence and Mike gave up their other jobs to focus exclusively on building the business. But Integrity Security's recent plant construction and client base expansion had Spence so in debt and busy he couldn't spare the time or take any income loss. As a senior captain for TransAsia Airlines, Mike was in the best position to go full time with Avion, but he and Dorel were waiting on the time to be right for Spence.

Up to now Spence had ignored Mike's big yawns and longing glances at his watch, but he was beginning to feel guilty because Mike had an early morning flight to Singapore. He better bring up the subject quick before he was talking to wide-eyed asleep Mike.

Spence clicked save and exit on his machine and leaned

back while it shut down.

"Thank God," Mike groaned and began to shut down his computer. "I thought you were never going to quit. Don't you sleep anymore?"

Spence rubbed his burning eyes. "Not so much." He grinned sheepishly, "Got people to screw, revenues to overstate. You know, the usual Machiavellian corporate mogul stuff."

Mike snorted. "Same ole bad, huh? Guess things were simpler when you were a broke but sometimes honest arms dealer, right?"

"Hey! I'm an antique weapons collector now, if you please," Spence answered with a wry grin. He shifted on the leather executive chair and rubbed his moustache. "Say, speaking of antique weapons, whatever happened to that Tadatsuna you guys had me cut up? God, what a waste to ruin a one of a kind sword like that." Why the hell did he say that? Spence silently berated himself. Of all ways to approach the subject that Mike wouldn't want to talk about— he'd just opened with the sure-to-fail worst.

Mike's blue eyes narrowed into a mean squint and he pushed back from the keyboard. He took a deep breath and replied, "Where did that come from? After all these years, why that? And why now?" He walked to the French door to the deck and opened it, leaning on the jamb, his back to Spence.

Spence heaved himself to his feet and tossed off the last of his drink: a Stoly and Dr Pepper that tasted like crap, warm and watered down with melted ice. He'd felt the need for another bracer to get in the gut-spilling mood when they'd sat down at the computers three hours ago. Mike wasn't drinking because he was inside the no booze for eight hours before a flight rule, and Mike never broke the rules—these days, anyway.

Maybe that's why he'd overreacted to Spence's innocent question. "Look, forget it. Don't know why I thought of that. It's not important and wasn't what I wanted to talk about anyway," he said as his voice drifted off as Mike turned around and he got a look at the tense expression on his friend's face.

"What did you want to talk about?" Mike's hard stare locked on Spence.

Spence's hands began to shake and he squeezed them tighter around the empty glass. "It's . . . probably nothing, but I've got a feeling that I can't shake, you know? Maybe if I could get some sleep or get away to the cabin . . ." He set the glass on the desk and wiped his damp hands on his jeans. "Yeah, it's that simple, I need some R&R at the cabin. I'll plan to take the chopper up there next week maybe," he said with an embarrassed shrug and made for the door.

"Bull," Mike barked behind him. Spence stopped and turned around. "You want to know what I think? I think you're in an inverted flat spin with the ground proximity warning screaming, my friend. Look at you—sucking down that prune juice and vodka slop, for chrissakes. The bags under your eyes look like drop tanks. You can't sit still, can't focus. And the way you talk, when you do talk . . . what can I say—it's screwed up."

Mike caught his breath and Spence felt his hands flexing into fists. He splayed his fingers out, turning toward the door. He wasn't going to get into it with the only friend he had left.

"Just hold on," Mike continued behind him. "You came all the way out here to tell me something. Now tell it or get the hell out and let me get some sleep."

"I came for Marty's party," Spence mumbled and

stepped into the hall. "Didn't mean to keep you up. Sorry, Mike." He felt a hand on his shoulder and stopped.

Mike pulled him around and gave him an apologetic grin. "I'm sorry. Come on, tell me what's got you so screwed up."

"Naw, it's too late. Walk me to the bike, I'm afraid of the dark," Spence joked.

"Maybe you should be," Mike answered, looking worried, which stoked Spence's anxiety as he collected his gear from the foyer closet.

Mike snapped off the overhead light, slowly opened the door a crack and looked around before he stepped outside. Once a SEAL, always a SEAL. Spence performed his own quick visual recon before he followed his friend into the darkness.

"Okay, shoot. There's no chance of being spied on here," Mike said, standing in the center of the garden shed that was also a shielded safe room. "What were you thinking, talking about that other business in the house? Anyone could have heard you."

Spence pushed off the closed door, slamming the polished steel with his fists. "You can't even say it now, can you? Why don't we talk about it? Hell, we don't talk about anything before five years ago, let alone the sword that nearly got us all killed. It's like our time with the Teams and flying, working the antique weapons market before you hooked up with Dorel didn't even happen." He popped Mike's shoulder with his finger, frustration mounting. "Well, it did happen. All of it. And you know what—I bet even more went down than I can remember, because I've got this weird black hole in my memory, like a piece of me was cut out. Something just out of range that I know is there but can't see. And I think you know what it is and that Tadatsuna, that one of a kind piece you and Dorel made me destroy, is part of this."

Blind rage lashed out from some undiscovered injury and pounded through Spence's body. He almost unleashed it on his friend. Instead he turned it inward on himself again, driving the feelings back to the black hole within the steel nerves and rigid tendons that his body had become.

Mike blanched and stepped back. "I'd always assumed that you were like me. That you were just acting the part, pretending to forget. But you really don't remember any of it, do you?"

"What the hell are you talking about, of course I remember. You had me searching everywhere for that damned samurai sword. Then Dorel walked into the gun show and tried to sell it to me, met you and everything went to hell from there. You two hook up, off some bad guys, then you make a run for it only to show up a couple of days later and force me to cut the sword up. That was the worst, like cutting my own heart out with that torch. You may not have wanted it anymore, but I sure could have sold that sword to regain my losses, after they tore up my store and nearly killed me—remember that? I sure as hell do every time I look in the mirror. And you did a piss poor job resetting my nose."

Mike looked like he'd been kicked in the crotch and he glanced away. "I'm sorry, Spence. I could never make it up to you for what I put you through. I wish I could have done it differently, made sure you weren't involved—"

"Screw that. It is what it is—or was. Like I said in the house, that's not what I wanted to talk to you about, but I guess it is or I wouldn't have shot my mouth off like that." He shrugged, calming down a little, and extended his hand. "What are friends for if they can't take a bullet for you or get crazy once in a while about a broken nose in the old days?"

Mike took his hand, pulling him into a one-armed bear hug and whispered into his ear, "It's not about the sword or Dorel and me. I think you're remembering, having a bleed through or breach in the deprogramming."

Spence froze then his arm dropped off Mike's back and he pulled away, his mouth open in disbelief. "What the hell are you on?"

"A truth kick. It's bare your soul season and the time is now, looks like."

"Whose truth and whose soul?"

The corners of Mike's mouth turned down into a smirk. "Theirs and ours."

They! Spence nearly staggered. Mike did know who *they* were! "You've heard it, then, the noise, the banging?"

Mike frowned. "No, can't say as I have. Is that what you've got going on? You're getting noise?"

Hope swelled in his chest, making him feel much better. Mike was going to help him. "Yeah, every night for the past couple of weeks just as I get to sleep. Sounds like someone is trying to break in, but there's no one there when I investigate. Someone is screwing with me and I don't know why. So, I was thinking maybe you could help me find these guys . . . use some of the old skills? And to tell you the truth, I feel like I know something that will help me but exactly what it is I can't remember."

"They really cooked you, didn't they?" Mike shook his head in disgust. "Now listen very carefully and for chrissakes don't argue. Just listen and maybe that will open things up. You and I were part of a special black ops unit where we were trained to spy—"

"I know that," Spence spat. "We were attached to Navy Intelligence."

"Yes we were, at first, but then we were trained at an ultra top secret installation to spy on our enemies with a technique called remote viewing." Mike's voice halted and he stared at Spence.

"I swallow my pride to ask for your help and get nothing but crap for my trouble." He pulled open the door. Mike reached past his shoulder and pressed it closed. Spence waited, impatience prickling across his shoulders.

"I never, ever talk crap, you know that. I swear we were trained to transcend time and space, to view persons, places, and things remote in time and space, and to gather intelligence information on them. And that, my friend, is a famous viewer's definition of what we were doing. My take is that we learned to empty our minds and receive information or send our consciousness, sixth sense or ESP, for want of a better term, out in the collective unconscious to gather intelligence without ever leaving the facility."

"You're saying we were mind readers? Get real, Mike. You've been spending too much time communing with the *spirits* in that Zen garden of yours."

Mike ignored his jibe. "We were damned good at it, too. In fact, you were better than me most of the time, until they wanted to move us into some real experimental and, in my opinion, pure evil like dark magic arts and remote assassination. I chose to get out and go through the deprogramming to wipe my memory of the whole program and what we did, but it didn't take. I remembered everything, but kept that to myself. Didn't want them to send *you* after me."

Spence snorted. "Oh, yeah, right. Remote assassination. What's that, hold your breath and wish people dead real hard?"

"You tell me, smart ass. I figure you learned to be a real good remote mechanic in a merciless, scientific and detached kind of way. Just what they wanted, and if they want you, nothing can stop them from getting you. But something happened and they sent you straight to deep deprogramming. Then they were even so kind as to rehabilitate you, teach you a trade, as it were. You became the tech geek security expert you are today—with one tiny problem, that nasty big black hole in your memory. But not to worry, you're busy making big bucks keeping the mega-corporations safe from terrorists and vengeful stockholders or down-sized ex-employees seeking retribution for their raped portfolios."

Mike's voice took on a rhythmic calm tone as if he were talking to a frightened child or freaked out crank addict. "It's true, Spence. You can feel it. Believe. Every word of it. Believe it. Remember."

Spence whirled and stuck his face in Mike's. "That right? Then do it—show me. Do your stuff. Remote view the hell out of something."

"I can't. I promised myself, and Dorel, that I would never do it again. It will open up things that should be left buried. In any case, I'm not going to blow my cover. Believe me, you don't want them to know you can do it and remember what you did."

"Then just tell me who they are, if they really exist, and I'll take it up with them. Ask them if they're trying to drive me crazy with that goddamn noise every night? Remote view that, mind spy, if you can. Prove it. That's all I ask. Just prove it." Spence slumped against the door and rubbed his face with his hands, exhaustion overtaking his mind and body.

After a few moments of silence, Mike admitted, "If I

were still actively viewing like when I was looking for the sword, I could tell you what the noise is and who, if anyone, is targeting you. But I haven't viewed in years and now I can't suspend judgement. I'm prejudiced by my beliefs of good and evil and I'll perceive in the ether what I want or believe. The information I'd view would be tainted or colored by my personal prejudices. It would take me months of retraining with the protocols to overcome this and get back up to speed again. The reality is, I can't prove to you that we were remote viewers or that there is or isn't a *they*. Why or how this is happening to you, I don't know. A counselor might be able to help you kick something loose and help you deal with your repressed memories. Find out why and if your subconscious is creating all this."

"You think I'm crazy," Spence said, his voice muffled by his hand still covering his face.

Mike laughed. "I know you're crazy, but that's not the point. Sorry for the psychobabble, but I think you better get some help before you implode. I've heard about this kind of thing happening with people who've had PTSD—post traumatic stress disorder. They can start to exhibit real problems and physical symptoms, because their conscious mind can't accept the reality of the emerging memories or make sense of them compared to the life they're living."

Spence pulled himself up tall and took a deep breath. "That psychology minor of yours continues to pay off, doesn't it," he said, wise ass smirk and attitude firmly in place. "Problem is, if I go see some shrink with this, what happens if the memories—not saying there are any—start to come out? From what you say, we don't want anyone to know we know, right? If we really know anything real."

Mike shrugged and opened his mouth to answer when Spence's cell phone vibrated against his jeans waistband.

He held up his hand to stop Mike and glanced at the text message before pressing the clear button. "I gotta go. It's the Rotund Bagel Coffeehouse in the U District. There's a programming or wiring problem in the fire sprinkler interface that activates intermittently. The system is faulting again, warning of an imminent wet T-shirt contest for the patrons. They usually have a full house, so it ought to be worth the ride in."

They crossed the yard in silence. Spence pushed the bike to the driveway and sat on it while he fastened his helmet, aware of Mike's intent stare on him. What if he really could read minds? He'd thought Mike and he had no secrets from each other . . . until tonight.

"Don't worry. But you've got to realize that what you've been telling me isn't even on my radar screen. I will get this sorted out one way or another."

"Fair enough," Mike said. "Don't tell anyone else about this. Even if you do talk to a counselor, be careful what you say. Just talk about wanting some help with the sleep problem, and make it up as you go along. If you begin to remember more, keep it to yourself." He leaned close as Spence started the bike. "You're dead wrong, though, about one thing. I did a great job on that slab of meat you call a nose. Looks better than it did before, and that's the truth."

Spence laughed and feinted a punch at Mike's arrow straight nose. "Give Dorel and Marty a kiss for me. Talk to you later." He pointed the bike down the driveway and out on the main road toward Seattle.

Chapter Two

The Rotund Bagel was packed with a disappointingly dry crowd when Spence arrived. The over-caffeinated assistant manager met him at the door and tried to push him through the herd to the control room behind the stage where one of his technicians was hunched over a wiring diagram spread across a table. The open Integrity Security panel behind him showed all green and ready.

"Looks like you've worked another miracle, Jason," Spence said and moved past him to inspect the panel.

The whiz kid jerked his head up. "I don't know, Spence. The system had dialed out to our central system but not to city fire emergency, so we knew it was a Level 2 fault. When I got here it was still audible warning, though the sprinkler circuit breakers hadn't popped. Then about the time I unpacked my tool case, everything went green. I've run a diagnostic, but nothing shows up."

"Could someone smoking in the restrooms make the system give a false reading? I'll go check them out," the assistant manager babbled and left.

Jason threw him an amused glance. "I bet that's his favorite part of the job."

Spence cocked his head to listen. "Did you hear that noise?"

"What?"

"That!" Spence held his hand up at the beeping noise and pointed at the security panel, sprinkler zone lights going from green to red, one by one. "And that!"

Both men stood in front of the panel. "It's a Level 2

again. Probably false," Jason complained and pushed the silence audible fault button.

"I better check anyway and see if we've got a lot of wet, pissed off people out there," Spence said and hurried out of the control room to the hall. He crossed through the small backstage, but was stopped dead by the most haunting and beautiful sound he'd ever heard. As if hypnotized, he was pulled to the stage wings where he saw a dark-haired vision in sparkling white playing some sort of flute center stage.

He wasn't sure when the strange music stopped but it was the thunderous clapping of the audience that pulled him out of his stupor. A very dry audience, he noticed. When he looked back at the stage, the woman had begun to play an acoustic guitar. Her voice was high and a little thin though it had a strange ethereal quality that was pleasant enough and matched her angelic appearance.

"Spence?" Jason jogged his elbow. "Come see, the panel's green again."

He shook his head to clear the surreal detachment overtaking his mind. "Sure. Lead the way."

Jason was right. It had to be a wiring problem. Spence's mind drifted to the woman on the stage. Reluctantly, he pulled his thoughts back to the problem. "Can you track this down with the wiring schematic? I'll check all the sprinkler sensors."

He'd just closed the control room door when the flute music began once again from the stage and he heard Jason's yelp. "We've got a system fault again! I don't think we can take the chance that the system isn't going to dump 1,000 gallons a minute on the place. We better clear the coffeehouse and pull down the entire system for survey and overhaul."

Spence stood in the doorway, watching the blinking red

on the panel that seemed to keep time with the mysterious lilt of the flute. "Wait," he said. "Let's just wait a minute before we take the drastic approach . . ."

Jason snapped his mouth closed and shrugged. "Okay, you're the boss, but I don't think it's wise to delay."

"You're probably right." Spence put his finger to his lips and kept his gaze on the panel while he listened to the almost otherworldly sounds coming from the stage.

The music stopped and one by one the panel's lights changed to steady green.

"I don't believe this!" Jason exclaimed and pushed the test buttons on the panel.

"Me either. And I'm going to go get her," Spence answered and dashed out to the stage wings. The musician was just leaving the stage and he nearly knocked her down.

"Sorry, but could you come with me, please?" he asked and grasped her elbow. She struggled to right herself and hang on to her guitar and flute. When she regained her balance she stared into his eyes as if trying to figure out where they'd met before.

At least that's how he felt, like he knew this tall young woman with faintly olive-toned features, long straight dark hair and eyes as blue as deep water. He could almost see the curves of her slender body through the sheer, crinkled material of her ankle-length white dress. She wore a sprig of tiny white flowers over her ear. With her long-toed bare feet and the faint, pungent smell clinging to her that he was pretty sure was weed, she seemed like a hippie caricature from an Austin Powers movie. He'd always harbored a secret fantasy about an angelic earth mother type, or in this case, a hippie musician chick.

She thrust her guitar and flute at him. "Hold these," she ordered in a sexy voice huskier than the airy high toned one she'd used to sing. "I never wear shoes on stage. It's sacred ground." Slipping her bare feet into a pair of sandals that were soles with a couple of tiny straps, she added, "Uh oh, I'm about to lose my stupid dress."

Sure enough, the sleeveless dress slipped off her bare shoulder and down her arm. He was disappointed when she hiked the dress up. It dipped off the other shoulder, sliding for her elbow, and revealing a flesh-colored tube top thing covering her chest. And so much for his braless hippie chick fantasy.

She grabbed both shoulders of her dress with opposite hands and hauled them toward her neck. "Guess you'll have to carry my stuff for me until I find a huge safety pin or a Dumpster to toss this wretched rag into. So much for the authentic look, eh? That's the last time I borrow a so-called dress from a known felon even if she is my reception-ist's sister's boyfriend's parolee. Now, what was it that you wanted?" she asked and shook her hair back from her face.

He looked at the guitar and flute in his hands, saw her toes peeking from under the hem of her dress, and couldn't think. "Uh, well . . ."

"Rian," she said, still showing brilliantly white teeth. "Rian Farsante, that's my name, and yours is?"

"Jonathan Spencer," he said, confused when she didn't take back her things and continued to stand smiling at him.

"Well, Jonathan Spencer, could you find me a place to change, then something to change into but not necessarily in that order. Hey, we could do the Red Green thing. Got any duct tape?" she added with a grin.

"Uh, no. Fresh out." He was torn. Should he push this weird problem off on some unwary passerby or take her home with him? "Do you have a coat I could go get for you?"

She laughed. "I'm a Seattlite, not a tourist. September is a bit too balmy for my raincoat. I came out tonight fresh as you please in this silly sack. Poor choice, right, Jonathan Spencer?" She shook her head but her blue eyes danced with innocent fun.

"Spence will do." He pointed toward the control room. "Come with me."

"Spence will do what?" she asked behind him as he walked down the hall.

Anything you like. He gave her a smirk as he held the door open for her. She strolled past him into the small control room and stopped behind Jason, who turned and stared. His mouth fell open.

"Dr. Farsante, what are you doing here?" Jason sputtered as if caught somewhere he shouldn't be. The circuit tester he was gripping dropped to the floor and he wiped his hands on his khaki pants.

"Just checking up on you, Jason," she said with a tinkling, fun-filled laugh that made Spence want to laugh too. "You're just the one I need. Spencer here is absolutely useless, couture-impaired for sure. Got a spare frock in that tool kit of yours?"

"N—no," Jason stuttered, looking shell-shocked. "I've got some electrical tape and a T-shirt in my gym bag, though. The shirt is still kinda damp. I came here straight from the club when I got the call. You can use it if you want."

She perched on the edge of the table holding Jason's gear. "I'll take the tape and the shirt. Nearly nude beggars can't be choosy."

Spence watched the woman wind the tape through the dress straps. She wrinkled her nose as she slipped the T-shirt over her head. He laid the instruments on the table and was trying to think of something clever to say when she spoke. "There, all done and not a bad job of it, if I do say so myself," she said. Jason seemed to get into it, too, and offered an idiot grin.

The dress looked ridiculous but didn't detract from her in any way. That she'd actually wear Jason's sweaty shirt was down and dirty and Spence liked it—too much. He found himself edging toward the door. "Where are you going?" she asked. "I thought you needed me for something."

Before Spence could get his tongue to work, Jason asked her, "Was that you playing?" His eyes held a combination of puppy love and fearful awe—just like Spence felt!

"Pretty good, huh? I thought so, too." The strange ethereal expression returned and her voice took on a dreamy quality. "The new music is so—so evocative. It's a joy to play and every time I work with the melodies, they seem to change and grow in complexity. The tones almost magnify or expand to something I've never heard before."

Spence remembered why he'd thought to bring her back to the control room. Her music was somehow related to the sprinkler faults. He cleared his throat and waited to get a word in at the right time, resolving to sound more intelligent than Jason's enthralled "yeah" and "cool".

"Everyone seems to love the music as much as I do, but there's just one little problem when I practice at home. I know it sounds nuts, but when I play particular passages with a very unusual combination of notes on the flute, the appliances turn on. No kidding, the microwave nearly nuked itself to death yesterday before I discovered it." Her dark eyebrows bounced a couple of times over her wide-eyed gaze that she turned on Spence.

"Did you play the same song tonight?" Spence asked,

squinting from her to the panel.

"Yes! Why, did something go wonky in here?" She glanced around with a perplexed expression. "Of course, that's why you're here, Jason," she exclaimed as understanding dawned on her face at Jason's nod.

"Let's just make sure, shall we?" Spence suggested and picked up the flute. "Would you play that last piece again and let's see what happens."

"Sure, why not," she agreed and put the flute to her moistened lips. The haunting sounds reverberated in the small room, sending a wave of tingling sensation through Spence. He had a difficult time focusing on the security panel because the music encouraged erotic and other images in his mind so real that he couldn't swear they weren't.

The panel lit up red and the audible fault howled. Jason jumped to override the system before the sprinklers popped.

"Stop!" Spence made himself yell. She jerked and closed her mouth. They all watched the panel's lights phase back to green and ready.

"Wow!" was all she said and grabbed her guitar off the table. "Jason, next time I see you I'll return the shirt, washed even. Thanks. Jonathan Spencer, it's been interesting." She trotted to the door.

"Wait," Spence ordered. "I want to know what's going on. What's happened here?"

"It must be the frequency generated by the combination of tones," Jason suggested. "That could happen, maybe phantom voltage."

Spence walked to her and focused on her eyes as if willing her to tell him what she knew. "What music is this? Where did it come from?"

She shrugged. "The library—at Alexandria."

"Virginia?" he asked, confused.

"Egypt." She gave him a happy grin. "One of my clients, a musician in this life was a worker in the Library at Alexandria in a former life. He channeled it, I guess you could say."

"What?" Spence gasped and looked at Jason still nodding like an Ichiro bobble head doll. "Your client *channeled* it? What the hell kind of work do you do, and why would Jason call you doctor?"

She took a breath and composed her expression into a more professionally compassionate one. "I've a Ph.D. in psychology, a master's in applied music theory, and a counseling practice on the Eastside, plus I play wherever I can get a gig—coffee houses, weddings, bar mitzvahs, funerals. The usual stuff."

Spence glowered at Jason. "No, no it's not me, I'm not her client," Jason denied, waving his hands defensively in front of himself. "My girlfriend goes to her and I go along to watch."

"Watch what?" Spence asked, cold dread beginning to ripple in his belly.

"The past life regressions. Dr. Farsante hypnotizes Brie to find out why she's having these panic attacks and other stuff," Jason explained with gusto, his nodding kicking up to the palsied level. "It's amazing. Brie and I have been together in many lives before this one."

"Aw, for chrissakes," Spence muttered.

"On the contrary," Farsante interjected. "Her presenting problems do not have an origin in lives during Biblical times."

Spence disgustedly put his hands on his hips and scoffed, "Really? Past lives, huh? Are you telling me that woowoo stuff is accepted therapeutic practice allowed by the State?"

"Yes, actually it is. I'm a licensed psychologist and a certified hypnotherapist. I'm a card-carrying member of several national professional organizations dedicated to past life and more traditional forms of therapy," she answered.

She was passing this psychic hotline stuff off as real, taking advantage of desperate, gullible people who were willing to believe anything phonies like her were putting out there these days. Her flute music couldn't cause the fault in his system. Had to be something else. He could tell by her closed expression that she'd encountered his level of mistrust and skepticism before. It bothered him a little. He wasn't usually so judgmental or closed minded. On the contrary, he counted himself one of the most live and let live guys around. He would have to explain that to her . . . sometime.

"Okay then, *ciao* for now," she answered his thoughts. She stepped out into the hall and in a heartbeat, leaned back inside. "I don't know if this means anything, but it just came to me tell you that the music was used in ancient Egypt to build somehow and to forge metal."

The clang of metal on metal echoed in Spence's head before he hit the floor and surrendered to darkness.

On reflex, Rian tried to catch the fainting man, but with her hands full, she missed and he hit the concrete like a fifty-pound sack of coffee beans. She'd noticed his tense physiology when he'd confronted her as she came off the stage, but his passing out at her feet was as unexpected as his scrambling upright as if he'd intended to give the dirty floor some quick face time.

"Are you okay?" she asked, expecting Jason to help him, but he stayed where he was.

"Yeah." Spencer dusted his clothes with shaking hands

as if brushing off her concern. Keeping his eyes averted, he collected his helmet and left without a further word.

Rian frowned at Jason. "What in the world?"

Jason shrugged. "I don't know. Maybe he's sick or something." He closed the security panel and started packing his tool case.

Sick? Perhaps, but he'd reacted negatively to what she'd told him. "Then someone better check on him," she said and hurried out in the hall. She caught a glimpse of his black leather jacket as he exited the back door. "Wait!" she yelled, reaching the door as it swung shut. She bumped her hip against the bar and pushed the door open, stepping out into the parking lot glistening with rain. Spencer had put on his helmet and was sitting astride a motorcycle next to the building. He didn't look up as she approached, but she felt that he was waiting for her. Rian stopped beside him, the cold rain quickly wetting her skin as she tried to protect her instruments under the oversized T-shirt.

"I told you I was okay," he said in a low, flat voice and continued to scowl toward the dark horizon like some granite tribute to the corporate outlaw biker.

"You're used to fainting, then?" she asked and blinked at the drops falling into her eyes.

"I didn't *faint*," he said gruffly. "I slipped. Water on the floor."

"*Slip* a lot, do you?" She didn't wait for his denial and pointedly gazed at the bright light over the coffeehouse's door that showed a curtain of silvery raindrops. "We wouldn't want you to slip again, what with all this water on the—pavement. Let me drive you home."

"I'm not leaving my bike." He started to turn the key.

"Both of you can ride in the van." She nodded toward a maroon van with the words *Rock Bottom* painted on the side parked fifty feet away.

He followed her gaze and shook his head. "Even if I really needed to, I still don't think you and I are up to hefting a seven hundred pound Harley into the back. Unless you've got a loading ramp on you?"

"I think there is one. The band hauls their gear in it. So, there must be a way to load the heavy stuff. I'm not sure. It's borrowed." She was getting soaked and thinking more about protecting her instruments from the weather than driving this man who didn't want her help, but obviously needed it. Time to try a different tack. "I've got to get my bag and guitar case inside. Can you wait for me so I don't have to do the lone woman in dark parking lot thing? Then we can go our separate but exceptional ways."

He glanced at her with a haggard grin. "Sure. I can always be counted on to help a lady in distress."

"I'll be ever so grateful," she said with a silly batting of her eyelids and tried to open the door. It had locked behind her. She turned around and shrugged. "Hang on, I've got to go in through the front, if they'll let me in like this." Painfully aware of the bedraggled bag lady look she had going, she made a dash around the building and left him sitting in the rain where he probably wouldn't be when she returned.

But he was and that surprised her. She smiled at him as she unlocked the van's back doors and tossed her bag and flute and guitar cases inside. The bike roared to life. Spencer pulled beside her, put his feet down and leaned to look in the back illuminated by the motorcycle's headlight. "Any bad guys in there?"

"Not that I can see," she replied and broke off her visual inspection of him. He seemed steady enough and his eyes looked clear, if a little bloodshot. "We need to find that loading ramp." Rian reached inside and began to paw around a floor that looked like the band's day job was collecting fast food trash.

"Don't bother. I'll wait until the van starts okay, then I'm gone."

Rian blew out a peevish breath. The rain was increasing and she was wet, cold and very weary of his resistance. "Okay, fine. Wait a minute, I want to give you my card," she said and grabbed her shoulder bag, fishing inside for her card case.

Spencer took the card Rian held out without looking at it. He'd probably pitch it away when he was out of her sight, if he waited that long. He stuffed the limp card in his jacket pocket and rolled beside her as she walked to the driver's side and got in. She started the engine and put down the window just as he began to pull away. "Call me!" she yelled.

"What for?" he answered over his shoulder.

For your own good. "Because you know you want to," Rian yelled at his back. He gunned the bike out of the lot and she watched him through the waves of water flowing over the van's cracked windshield and became aware of the soggy seat she'd plunked herself in. Icy drips from above dropped on her head, slid over her face and oozed down her neck. She shivered and looked up, running her hand around the edges of the sunroof. It was leaking right over her seat.

On the drive across Lake Washington on the 520 Bridge to Bellevue, Rian discovered the van's heater wouldn't operate anywhere above whisper tepid. Even cold and in danger of becoming really cranky, she was still better off than Jonathan Spencer was at this moment. With his quiet reserve and penetrating gaze, he was almost an archetype of the silent, wounded warrior. It wasn't his biker regalia that made her think of him as a warrior—it was his tall, spare frame held with military bearing and tightly-reined solemnity. His dark blond hair was made almost stylish by his well-trimmed moustache and goatee, which seemed a grudging concession to keeping up with the times rather than a statement of any latent hipness.

Spencer's rugged, lean face could be considered handsome. When he'd smiled his hazel eyes warmed. His face showed wear and tear, with a nose that sported a bump on the bridge and seemed to lean a bit to one side, as if broken at one time. It wasn't bad looking; instead, the wounded nose made his austere face look more human and less stern.

Rian squeezed the ratty van into her assigned parking slot in the garage beneath the Lake Washington Towers condominiums on Yarrow Bay. She jerked her things out of the back and hurried to the elevator. Glancing around the gated garage's well-lit interior, she shivered when the elevator chimed and the doors slid open. Confirming it was empty, Rian stepped inside and punched in her security code. The doors closed and the elevator ascended.

Once inside her condo, Rian gave the audible command for the computerized management system to reactivate security and set evening conditions. Relaxation warmed her body as her home came alive with soft lighting and the see-through gas fireplace dividing the dining room from the living room ignited behind safety glass. The entertainment system filled the rooms with favorite classical guitar renditions and the framed, large flat panel monitors in each room displayed text headlines scrolling under the subscription fine art.

Rian deposited her instruments in the studio and queried the integrated message center that advised her in its HAL-like digital voice that Rock Bottom wanted the van back and her car was ready. She reviewed her office calendar and messages while she showered. Afterwards, she poured a glass of sparkling cider and settled in front of the fire on the crème-colored silk sofa, deliciously warm in the cozy wrap of her terrycloth spa robe. Rian stared from the fire to the monitor hung above the fireplace where text news and messages marched across the bottom of the monitor's surrealist offering, Joan Miró's *Painting*.

She'd designed the condo's only point of color to be *Painting* with its solid and outlined black shapes with dramatic accents of white and vermilion against a dark background of reds, blues and greens. What she wouldn't give to have the original hanging there instead of this digital copy. Still, the screen's resolution was so excellent, so real that she could almost forget she was exploring pixels instead of the canvas and oil rendered subject matter of Miró's subconscious.

She'd had *Painting* copied and framed, along with other surrealist art, for her office. It was always interesting to observe how patients related to the abstract art. Their reactions, or not, told her much more about them than Rorschach testing did in many cases. But then hers was a very specialized practice serving clients others had given up on. They were resigned to an alternative practitioner, be it massage therapy, acupuncture, aromatherapy, witchdoctor or Dr. Rian Farsante, Transformational Psychologist, practicing last resort past life regression therapy.

Even as a last resort, Spencer won't come to you. You have to follow orders and continue to go to him.

Rian took a bubbly sip of tart-sweet cider, but had trouble swallowing. Spencer was putting on a brave, untroubled facade contrary to the morass of tormented emotions that she was responsible for in large part. Stifling her own empathetic tendencies was becoming more difficult the more she targeted him. And now that she'd met him in the physical, she felt an even stronger connection to him that couldn't be good for either one of them.

Exhausted as he was, Spence didn't sleep after he got home from the Rotund Bagel. He sat in the dark living room, gazing through the rain-spattered windows at the lights twinkling on the shores of Lake Union. Eyelids heavy and beginning to flutter, he followed a faint clanging sound into the dark, feeling his way along the cold, damp walls of a tunnel far underground. The deeper he went, the louder the clanging until he approached a large rock slab blocking the tunnel. It swung open on silent hinges and he felt compelled to enter the light beyond, but fear clamped his chest and his breathing choked off. He wheeled around and staggered back up the tunnel as a shrouded form lunged out with a cry of *Return!*

Spence jerked awake gasping for breath. The coffeepot sputtered and gurgled from the kitchen. He pulled himself up from his chin-on-chest slumped position and stretched, realizing that he'd slept enough to feel pretty good. Maybe he ought to forget going to bed and trick himself into sleep each night in this slouching black leather recliner that Mike had long ago nicknamed Slack Ass. Even back then the name was a fitting description of the patched, broken-down chair that was now the only survivor from the Auburn apartment over Spence's first store.

The coffeepot set to start at 6:30 a.m. was his concession to an alarm clock. If he wasn't impatiently staring at the stainless steel machine, waiting for its noisy brewing of his new favorite Ethiopian dark roast, he was late. He squinted at his watch as he dumped himself out of the recliner and headed for the shower.

Forty-five minutes later Spence flashed his badge at the guard and rolled into the convention center exhibitors' lot. He parked his bike between the two Integrity Security vans that his employees had parked, blocking a loading bay. The exhibition hall was noisy and hustling with the activity of a couple hundred workers and technicians setting up for the Secret Treasures of Egypt show. He had easily won the contract to install the antitheft system, his own design that competitors whispered was possibly pirated military technology.

He didn't have to steal someone else's ideas. Spence credited his training and experiences in the military, his degree in electrical engineering and an admittedly weird imagination with producing some futuristic applications that often surprised even him.

Spence stopped dead, his gut tightening. Mike had said last night that he'd been brainwashed. Retrained. What if—

"Hey, Spence," called his technical lead from within a circular group of display cases.

He shook off the uneasiness and joined the crew standing around the worried-looking lead.

"We've got problems or as you like to spin it, *opportunities*," the lead said as his team members nodded and stared at Spence.

Spence grimaced and said, "Game faces, guys, okay?" He put on his confident smirk for them and anyone else eavesdropping on his business. "Now, Ethan, you tell me what's up and the rest of you find something to do. I'll be with you in a minute if you need me."

The team scrambled back to their individual jobs, acting busy and unconcerned but sneaking nervous glances their way as the wide-eyed lead explained the situation with a frozen smile.

Spence chuckled. "Ethan, you're a hell of a ventrilo-quist. Your lips don't even move."

"This is serious, Spence. We've never had an installation go this wrong. It's like everything is working against us—restricted access to the exhibits we're supposed to wire, equipment failure. Accidents. Dave was knocked on his ass a few minutes ago when the power came up on a verified dead line. If I didn't know better, and right about now I know zip, I'd think someone is sabotaging us."

"Well, I won't say you're wrong. It happened when Integrity was getting started, before you came onboard," Spence replied. "But now we're too big to screw with, the lawyers tell me, and their job is to make sure any idiot who does try would be tied up in court until they're dead or bankrupt." He put a reassuring hand on Ethan's shoulder, taking in the chaos in the exhibition hall. "There's no sabotage, E. Looks like poor planning and a lack of coordination to me. Tell me exactly what you need. I'll take them as action items and work them through the hall's management. We'll get this done," he said with confidence he didn't feel.

The hairs went up on the back of his neck as he left Ethan and made his way through the crates and equipment toward the administrative offices. Someone was shadowing him. He'd sensed it from the time he'd entered the hall.

Chapter Three

Spence stopped at a display case, bent down as if to pick something up and checked for a reflection in the case's glass. No one behind him. He took a deep breath, letting his shoulders drop, and froze. Inside the case lay a single metal bar, about an inch wide by two feet long with a U-shaped hook on one end. There was no informational placard, nothing to identify or explain the bar. He stood and tried to lift the case's lid. It was locked.

It must be part of the exhibit. Not highly valued because the other cases for the priceless artifacts would remain empty until the security system was installed and activated.

There was something familiar about the piece. He leaned closer, pulling a pen light from his pocket and shining it on the bar. Years of experience as an antique arms and sword collector suggested that it looked like the hooked tool swordsmiths once used to straighten a warped or twisted blade.

That's exactly what it was, he'd bet the Harley on it.

He played the small circle of light along the flat side of the bar. The metal was old and hand-forged. Smooth. But rust-free. Strange. There were markings or inscriptions where the smith would hold the tool opposite the hook end. He squinted at the markings.

They were symbols—like the high tech amalgam of Oriental characters, a kind of scientific notation and geometric cuneiform on Dorel's sword—the one she and Mike made him cut up. Ringing hammered his ears and sweat slicked his palms. He had to touch it, hold the tool he knew would fit his hand as if he'd forged it himself.

Spence clawed a shaking hand at the edge of the case but the world slid sideways into darkness at a disincarnate voice's command:

Return to the Forge of Balance and two shall be made whole.

The game was over and the peewee players were loading into the soccer moms' minivans and SUVs when Spence rode into the field's parking lot. He parked the bike several spaces away from the gathering of kids and adults at Dorel's jeep. Spence tried to take off his helmet, but his mitt-bandaged hand was still half-numb and had made driving the Harley a frustrating, time-consuming exercise.

Marty dashed over to Spence's side and unbuckled the chinstrap, then helped Spence lift off the helmet.

"Thanks, M-Man. Hey, I'm really sorry I was too late to see you play, but . . ." Spence waved his hand that would soon wake up and hurt like hell. Should have taken the time to pick up the prescription the ER doc had written for him.

"Don't tell anyone but Dad how it happened," his godson warned, frowning at Spence's injured hand, then smiled up at him. "I made a goal and we're going to Pizza Pup's for our winner's dinner."

"You guys won, huh?" Spence got off the bike and set the helmet on the seat. "Man, I wish I'd been here to see that."

"Me, too." Marty grabbed his left hand, towing him along. "Come with us. You can ride with Mom. I'm going on the Harley with Dad."

"Got it all figured out, don't you?" Spence said with affectionate pride and pulled the boy into a quick hug against his side.

Marty hugged back and gave Spence's hand a squeeze.

"Hey, want me to ask Coach if she's got something for your owie?" He skipped away before Spence could tell him not to ask and buzzed by his dad, pointing back to Spence.

Mike broke away from the adults and came toward him. "What the heck happened to you? Did you lay the bike down?"

Spence snorted. "Don't worry, the bike's fine." He cast a wary glance around and added in a low voice, "I really screwed up, Mike. Today . . . I—I think I really am going crazy."

"Uncle Spence, Coach can help you," exclaimed Marty beside him, pulling at Spence's sleeve.

Spence smiled down at him. "Hang on, M-Man, I'll be with you in a minute. I need to talk to your dad."

"That's okay. All I have is a Midol anyway and judging by the bandage, that hand looks like a Percodan opportunity," a sexy and familiar female voice said behind them.

Spence jerked around and stared into Rian Farsante's laughing eyes. "What are you doing here?"

"Spence, you haven't met our team's substitute coach while Melanie is out on maternity leave. Doc here led us to our big win today. Dr. Rian Farsante, this is Jonathan Spencer, my oldest friend," Mike said. He leaned closer to Rian and stage-whispered, "He's a pretty good guy when he isn't wounded and cranky."

"They already know each other, Dad," Marty said with a smaller version of Mike's encouraging grin.

A couple of beats of silence followed with everyone except Spence smiling at each other. His focus drifted down her long, tan legs to the soccer shoes and no socks, back up to the green, knee-length shorts and jumped to her mouth when she spoke.

"You're right, Marty, we've met." She ruffled Marty's

hair and grabbed his little hand in her long slim one. "I think your mom has herded this bunch of cats into cars. We better go." She winked at Spence and asked if he were coming for celebratory pizza, too. Stricken dumb, Spence nodded as she and Marty raced for Dorel's jeep.

"Gimme the bike keys, Romeo. You better get moving if you want to ride with Dorel," Mike said, holding out his hand.

Spence started to object, but Rian called to them as she got in a cloud white Mercedes convertible. "Dorel doesn't have any more room. One of you can come with me."

Spence dug the keys out of his pocket and tossed them to Mike. "I'll go with her."

Mike laughed. "Really? That's out of nowhere. If you two don't show up at Pup's, I'll just take the bike to the house. Make sure she has you home by curfew, young man."

"Kiss my ass," Spence growled as Rian stopped the two-seater luxury sports car beside them and leaned across the console to open the passenger door for him. He sunk into the charcoal and crème colored leather seat, struggling to look anywhere but at the green team lettering on the yellow T-shirt stretched across her breasts. "Nice ride," he managed and pulled the door closed.

"Thanks. Are you warm enough? I could put the top up."

He frowned. "I'm good—I mean I'm used to the wind riding my bike."

They rode in guarded silence for a couple of miles. Spence shifted in the seat to rest his throbbing hand in his lap.

"There's a drug store in the strip mall next to Pup's if you'd like to get your prescription filled."

His hand sure as hell wasn't numb anymore. Was he so wussed out that a stranger could tell he was hurting? He used to be able to handle pain much better than that, didn't he?

Not now. Not for quite some time.

"Yeah, okay," he agreed and watched the road.

She drove fast and way out in front of the car, like he did. She seemed to anticipate what idiots were going to do and avoid them. Quick reflexes. It was pure pleasure to ride in this overpowered white rocket with her.

"So, did you slip again? You know, water on the floor?" Rian asked and greased the car in and out of slower-moving traffic like a high-speed chase veteran.

"Something like that and thanks for asking."

"I didn't mean to make you uncomfortable. Let's just write it off to professional interest in your wellness and my being an incurable and unrepentant smart-ass." She cut a glance at him and winked.

Spence laughed out loud. Every muscle in his body eased its hard-wired grip on his frame and he leaned back, closing his scratchy eyes. He floated up, sensing his body with her in the white convertible below.

Flying again. Free. Happy.

Never wanting to come down as he flew higher and higher, the blue and white swirled earth shrinking below him. Going home.

Into the darkness of space. An inky specter loomed before him, blocking his flight. As it mutated into a fearful form that beckoned to him, dread weighed him down and he began to sink back to earth. Faster and faster. He smashed back into his body, knocking every bit of oxygen out of his lungs. His eyelids shot open and his mouth formed a noiseless scream.

"Spence! Spence, are you all right?" Rian yelled, darting into a parking lot and stomping the brakes. She slammed the gearshift into park, jumped out of the car and ran around to his side.

He couldn't move. Couldn't breathe. Couldn't do anything but stare in wide-eyed horror at her as she pulled him by his jacketfront out of the car to the pavement. She put her fingers in his mouth, clearing the airway, then began pushing on his chest with both hands. "One-two-three-four-five-six-seven," she counted and blew into his mouth.

Warm air rushed down his throat. His lungs awakened and sucked greedily as Rian returned to pounding on his breastbone.

"Ouch! Stop that!" he gasped, batting at her hands with his bandaged one. Process fault—worse ouch.

Rian stopped and sat back on her heels, shaking her head, her long dark ponytail swishing slowly. "Jonathan Spencer, I wish you'd stop trying to get my attention this way. Keep this up and you're going to be the death of me."

"Not if you get me first," Spence mumbled, holding his burning hand against his chest and feeling like all twenty stitches had broken open. He took a ragged breath and tried to leverage himself up with his undamaged arm. Rian wrapped her arms around him, lifting and supporting his body against hers, and eased him into the car.

An Auburn fire truck blazed into the lot, siren screaming, lights flashing, followed by two police cruisers and an aid truck blaring attention-getting noise. The vehicles drew a tight circle around the Mercedes and emptied public humiliation upon Spence. As the EMTs checked him over, Rian answered questions for and about him as if he were dead.

"Rian, tell them I'm okay," he demanded again and much louder this time.

She stopped talking and gauged him with an expression he now understood as if he could hear her voice in his head. He'd have to agree to this if he was going to avoid an ambulance ride to the Auburn General psych unit. "Tell them you're my doctor and that I'm under your care. I'm okay."

Soccer coach Rian transformed into Dr. Farsante. "While I am not Mr. Spencer's personal care physician, I am a psychologist and Mr. Spencer has entered treatment with me. His present condition could be due to the accident he had earlier today. He believes he experienced a reaction to the local anesthetic wearing off and the subsequent severe pain as he hadn't filled his pain prescription yet. I was driving him to do so when the episode occurred. It seems that someone called 911. We are truly sorry about that."

The EMTs pronounced Spence good to go and were the first to leave the scene, then the fire truck and last, the cops. One cruiser followed Rian and Spence until she parked in front of the drug store at the opposite end of the strip mall, then took a waveoff.

"There they go, thank God," she said, watching the rearview mirror. "Why is it cops always make you feel like you've done or are going to do something wrong? Must be their authority figure-need-to-dominate energy. Give me the prescription and I'll get it. You wait here and rest."

Spence threw open his door with disgusted impatience. "I told you I was okay. You wait." He ambled to the store's double glass doors and bumped one side open with his shoulder, still protectively hugging his wounded hand to his chest. Maybe when he returned she'd be gone, because things had gone bad since he'd met her. He needed his life to get back to normal.

This was his life. Pain. Fear. Going crazy. All this was his normal now. Why in the hell wouldn't she run as fast as she could away from a seriously deranged freak like him? Because you're the kind of wacked out fringe-dweller she works with every day. She had to pay for that pricey Benz somehow and he was a real opportunity.

His hand spiked pain through his body and rolled nausea in his empty stomach. Ten minutes later after paying for the pills and a Dr Pepper, he read the label on the medicine bottle: Take with food.

Spence returned to checkout and grabbed a small bag of peanuts. "Could you help me with these?" he asked the pretty teenager behind the register, giving his bandaged hand a weak wave. She tore open the peanuts bag, popped the top on the can and struggled with the medicine bottle top. Finally, she called the assistant manager, who cheerfully took the bottle back to the pharmacist and returned with it open.

An oddly patient line of people waiting behind him at checkout watched Spence tip one pill onto the counter. The pain was so bad now that he shook out two more and popped all three in his mouth, chasing them with the entire bag of peanuts. He began to chew as he one-handedly recapped the medicine bottle. Still crunching away, he pocketed the bottle and grabbed the Dr Pepper. He saluted everyone with the can and pushed out the doors.

She was still there, waiting for him.

He took a long drink and another, watching her. Rian reached across the car and nudged his door open. He got in beside her without a word. Spence focused on getting rid of the pain. He sensed that she must have understood what he was trying to do, because she didn't look at him again or talk either.

When they arrived at the Pizza Pup, they separated, Rian to one end of the long table of adults and Spence settling between Mike and Dorel at the opposite end. After he confirmed that Marty was doing okay, Spence dully listened to the table conversation with growing detachment and watched the kids running around the place. The pills had kicked in. He was loaded, flying wing low toward a blackout if he didn't get some more food down.

The pizza never came.

Rian followed Dorel home and, after Mike had arrived on the motorcycle, helped them carry Spence to the guestroom. He'd passed out at the pizza party. How many pain pills had he taken? Such bizarre behavior. Good lord, he was a danger to himself, just as she'd been told, though now she was more certain that her mission was exacerbating his condition.

"I can't explain it, Rian," Dorel said and handed her a cup of coffee. "Spence is going through, well, I don't know what's going on with him right now. He is a warm, sensible, intelligent man. Very responsible. We'd trust him with our lives. He's family, so whatever his problems are, they're our problems." She took a thoughtful sip from her own cup. "Let's go sit and talk this out. I feel like you can help and, more importantly, I believe you want to."

Rian nodded and followed her into the comfortable living room, appreciating the tasteful sophistication of the furnishings and art of the Gabrielli home. Asian was an interesting decorating theme, touches of which she'd briefly considered for her own condo. But she was a true tech-modernist and these antiques, though genuine and pricey, just wouldn't work for her.

They sat facing each other on large rectangular ottomans

positioned in front of the fireplace. Rian could hear Mike Gabrielli enjoying the bedtime ritual with his son, a very darling, bright child she was drawn to as if he were her own. She wanted a whole house full of happy, healthy children, like the one she'd been a tiny and briefly well-loved part of so long ago. Having children of her own would add more joy and meaning to her life, a cherished dream polished bright by hope and an abiding trust in the power of love to transform lives.

"Rian, please excuse me for a minute. I want to say goodnight to Marty," Dorel said and left Rian to her thoughts.

The Gabriellis were generous, kind people and devoted to each other. Rian had sensed their special bond from the first time she'd met them. She had no doubt that they were soulmates and had many lives together with their son, the three playing different roles in each life, but always together. And Spence too. He had to be an essential part of their *soul* group, so strong was their emotional attachment to him.

And you? her inner self suggested. What part have you played in their lives before this?

It would be interesting to engage Dorel on the subject of past lives sometime, see if she were open to the idea and perhaps to being regressed. Would she remember a life or lives with Rian? In her own past life regressions neither the Gabriellis nor Spence had appeared. Still, that wasn't conclusive as she believed she'd lived hundreds of lives and had sampled only a small percentage of them in her explorations.

A few minutes later Dorel and Mike returned together. "They're both sleeping like babies," Mike said and sat with his wife on the ottoman.

"Spence is still among the living, breathing and every-thing, right?" Rian gave them an innocent smile and sipped her coffee.

"Yup, though if you want to check for yourself, be my guest. Spence wouldn't mind," Mike said and elbowed his wife who nodded then shook her head. The picture-perfect couple was like sunrise and sunset. Open and energetic Dorel's green eyes and red hair were a striking counterpoint to conservative and quiet Mike's dark hair and blue eyes.

"I was telling Rian that Spence isn't usually this . . . umm, tired. He's going through a rough patch right now," Dorel said with concern, holding Mike's gaze that changed from adoring to vigilant the instant she finished.

He threw a reassuring glance at Rian and clasped Dorel's hands in his, directing his cautious-sounding comment to her. "Spence is fine, you know that. Don't worry about him. He'd be upset that you're thinking he's not okay, wouldn't want to worry you, would he?"

Dorel blinked. "Oh. Of course not."

Rian laid her hand atop the couple's locked hands. "Spence is the luckiest man in the world to have your love and respect. Bless you both for caring so much about him, but please know that however well-intentioned your protec-tion is, it's not going to help him in this case. I don't believe that I'm compromising doctor-patient confidentiality if I share with you that he has agreed to enter counseling with me. Whatever you can tell me that will help me help him makes my job so much easier and his complete healing more certain."

A silent agreement passed between Mike and Dorel and they turned their determined gazes on her. "Rian, we don't know you very well, so you'll understand our caution," Mike said, slipping his hand out from under hers.

Dorel gave Rian's abandoned hand a squeeze before she withdrew her own. "We do know that you are great with kids and love them. We also know that you spent years training to be a health care professional, so you have to care very much about people to make those sacrifices. I said before that I thought you wanted to help Spence. I believe that, and if Mike agrees, I'll help you all I can." She gave her husband a questioning look and he nodded.

Rian's relief changed to fascination as the extraordinary and private life of the man down the hall and dead to the world was exposed through the lens of those who loved and feared for him most. Though they had talked way into the night, when Rian left the Gabriellis she knew there were still many vital secrets that they thought they had withheld about Spence. That was expected, for they had trust issues, though they didn't suspect what they had told her she would use to manage his behavior and induce him to unearth the repressed memories imprisoned in his subconscious that were so important to her mission.

She'd navigated Spence's inner landscape long enough that she should be able to sideline his emotions, keep them separate from her own. But it was becoming more difficult to keep her emotional distance. His pain was her pain. Why should he suffer when she knew she could treat him, help him without harming him?

Nevertheless she had her orders. Though if she stayed within the mission perimeters and produced results, they would *have* to allow her to treat him, wouldn't they?

There were more lookers than buyers at this month's arms collectors show, a sure sign of the dicey economy in Seattle these days.

From behind his usual table, Spence rubbed cleaner on a

broadsword's blade with a polishing cloth and watched the assembled vendors size up the parade of the collectors shuffling up one aisle and down the next. Most were looking for bargains they wouldn't buy but later wish they had. Several marched along with their own long guns slung over their shoulders and sprouting homemade for sale signs in the barrels.

People eyed the contents of Spence's table with open interest and appreciation, and many stopped to talk but few were serious buyers. Seeing him trying to polish swords one-handed, a couple of long-time collectors pointed to his bandaged hand and asked if he'd cut himself in his sharp dealings. Har. Har.

The gun show was the one place that Spence could relax and enjoy the friendly give and take between buyers and vendors, but not for the last month or two. Maybe it was because he hadn't seen anything worth buying or made a sale in months, though he wasn't interested in selling. The swords from his collection displayed on his table were simply to draw the attention of those who might have an old cavalry or samurai sword collecting dust in the attic. Not that Spence would even make an offer unless it was a fine and rare piece—like Dorel's sword.

Killing that sword was still a raw wound every time he thought about it, more so everyday.

Somewhere deep in his heart the belief he would find that sword kept him coming to the weekend gun show once a month, hoping it would somehow appear on his table like it had before. Mike and Dorel had said that the one of a kind, priceless Japanese samurai sword had *disappeared*. He wouldn't push them on it, but what the hell did *disappeared* mean? If it meant that someone had stolen it, they would want to sell it. Not that they could get anywhere near the millions it had been worth when it was whole, but even parts, the handle with its unusual goddesses and the blade pieces with its strange marking still had huge value to a collector.

He couldn't help thinking that if they'd just given him the sword as he'd asked, he could have somehow fixed it, made it whole again, a vain wish because he knew very little about re-forging such a blade. Gut feelings told him he could have done it, and he'd even dreamed about re-forging it for a while after the sword disappeared.

The hairs on the back of his neck began to prickle. He put down the polishing cloth, rolled his tense shoulders and scratched his neck. Then he saw her. The tightness in his shoulders spread to his belly and further as he watched her thread her way through the crowd, targeting him like a Sea Hawk gun ship making an extraction. Her glossy dark hair hung straight and long over her shoulders. She wore a black denim jacket open on belly button-skimming white sweater riding high above hip-hugging black jeans. She looked six feet tall in her high platform sandals.

Her smooth and pure beauty made an innocent yet sexy picture like those underwear angel models.

Rian stopped at his table and pulled off her sunglasses. "Don't you have something to say to me?"

Say? Looking at her, he could hardly breathe. When he did inhale, he caught a delicious whiff of her that kick-started his favorite fantasy—hot, sweaty sex on the display table while the crowd cheered. He hit the mental stop button before Rian made sure he was one ball shorter with the dullest blade on the table.

Spence coughed into his fist and forced himself to lean back in the metal folding chair, resting his bandaged hand over his lap. "Hey, what's up, Doc?"

Rian clasped her hands together low in front of her, car key dangling crotch level as her body rocked with laughter. "You know, Jonathan Spencer, I don't have to chase down clients. Yet I drive thirty miles through the fourth worst traffic in the nation to get you. Why do you think I did that?"

"Uh, you wanted to see me?" He sure hoped so and nodded at the gunsmith on the opposite side of the aisle who flashed a thumbs-up as he eyeballed Rian's ass. Spence noticed that she was stopping traffic for fifty feet in any direction. Not good. Things could get ugly and she wasn't even aware of her effect on these hornballs. He stood and pulled his table back out of line, opening a space to walk through. "Would you like to come in and sit down?"

She'd stopped laughing and dropped her hands to her sides. "First, tell me why you haven't called to make an appointment with me. We had an agreement."

"Whatever," he said. "Come sit over there." He pointed to the steel locker he transported show goods in. "You'll be safe." When she sat down, he pulled his chair close to her, his back to the crowded aisle.

Rian fixed him with a studying gaze. "Spence, was I in danger?"

"What do you mean?" He turned sideways so he could keep an eye on the testosterone troop behind him. *Move along, you horny bastards. She's not your kind of woman.*

"You said I'd be safe here. What makes you think I wasn't safe out there?"

Spence faced her, scooting his chair back a little. Crossing his right ankle over his left knee, he bumped her. "Sorry." She smiled, the corners of her blue eyes crinkling with humor. He could almost taste the sweetness of her perfume. "I was just making conversation."

She crossed her legs, her pink lips forming a lazy smile as her eyes went soft and bedroom sexy. "Oh, okay then, let's converse."

He couldn't keep himself from grinning like an idiot at her, amazed that his muscles unkinked as an easy warmth flowed across his shoulders.

"You and I haven't had much of an opportunity to get acquainted. Is now good for you?" she asked, a tinge of business in her melodic voice.

Spence barely stopped himself from blurting *hell no*. "I don't think this is really the best place to—talk about . . . things." He frowned and jerked a nod toward the aisle. She followed his gesture.

"Right. I see what you mean. Those beautiful swords get a lot of attention and must be very special for so many people to be so interested. They are yours?"

"Yeah, all mine, just a couple of pieces from a larger collection." Weird that he wanted to impress her. "Antique swords."

"Very nice," she said, sounding like she meant it and nodding as her gaze played over the display, then she winked at him and pulled a palm computer out of her jacket pocket. "Let's see what we can do . . . how's Monday at 2:30?"

He narrowed his eyes with the tenseness creeping up his spine. "How's Monday for what?"

"Our appointment."

Screw that. Did she need business this bad? "I can't." He got up, moved the table and rearranged the swords.

She was beside him in an instant with a touch on his arm that spread heat from that small point of contact. "I want to help you and I know I can, if you'll give me a chance, Spence."

Chapter Four

Every time she said his name his belly warmed like it'd been hit with a double shot of Napoleon brandy. Spence crossed his arms over his chest. "Look, Doc, I don't believe in all that past life crap. I only believe in now. Right now. Good, bad or mediocre, now is all I've got. Dredging up a lot of childhood memories or supposed past lives isn't going to make a damn bit of difference in what I'm dealing with. Now, if you've got some proven, quick fix or even good drugs you can give me, then I'm in. But not for that woo-woo psychic stuff. Don't waste my time with crap like that." He stared at her hard.

Rian didn't blink. She took a breath and crossed her arms under her breasts, her expression gentle and sympathetic.

"Do you think you could let yourself trust that I can help you feel better, and that's the most important thing, not what kind of process or therapy that you may have misconceptions or fears about? We're not going to do anything that you'll be uncomfortable with."

He didn't respond. Why she was working so hard at making this sale?

"Would it help you feel better and more trusting of yourself if we got to know each other a bit first in a nonprofessional way? I confess that I know more about you than you do me."

He squinted suspiciously. "How's that?"

"Mike and Dorel are concerned about you and we're hoping that you'll allow me to help you."

What were they doing talking about him behind his back? How could they confide in an outsider? They'd broken the code. His expression must have betrayed his thoughts because Rian's eyes widened and she waved a hand.

"No, Spence, don't misunderstand. They didn't tell me any confidences or betray your trust. They shared with me what they thought might be helpful and you wouldn't mind their sharing."

He calmed down a little, but he was still pissed and wary. Whatever their reasoning, it wasn't right for them to discuss him with anyone. He wouldn't do that to them, wouldn't break the code.

"You still feel upset, and that's okay. I understand. They said you wouldn't like this. I admit I wouldn't take no for answer and, since they care so much about you, they wanted to help."

"Why do you care? I don't get this. You're tracking me. Hell, I'm not that interesting, I assure you."

She slapped her hand over her eyes, shaking her head. "Oh, this is just great. The person I'm trying to impress thinks I'm some sort of freaked out stalker."

Her obvious distress got to him and he kicked the atti-tude down a notch. "Look, whatever they told you, my problem is not being able to sleep as well as I'd like. I'm getting used to it so it's no big thing. If it gets too bad I'll get my doctor to write a prescription for sleeping pills."

Rian peeked through her fingers at him, then dropped her hand. "Spence, you might want to consider that your fainting episodes could be something more serious mani-festing."

"It's nothing, some sort of blood pressure thing—you know, getting up too fast and feeling faint. Nothing to worry about." Now who was working hard to sell who? He broke eye contact with her and focused on smoothing the rumpling tape on his bandage.

"Spence, would it be worth something to you if I could show you a way to feel better, to get the rest and sleep you need without pills and prescriptions?"

"Look, I'm doing okay. I'll get this worked out."

"So, you're performing at the top of your game and your life isn't being adversely affected." She touched his hand.

He dropped it to his side. "I'm okay."

"What about when you hurt your hand? Were you doing okay then, handling everything just fine? Can you remember the last time you felt really good? Had energy? Relaxed even?"

Her concern for him, impersonal and altruistic as it was, affected him. He wanted more of her attention, but he couldn't allow it. "Let's just forget this—"

Rian lunged by him and clamped her hands over the scabbarded blade of his most valuable Tensho-style *katana* on a black display stand. Snaked between bodies clogging the aisle, a disembodied arm locked on the samurai sword's woven handle jerked Rian across the tabletop.

Shining blades scattered. "Watch it!" Spence yelled in the glittering wake and threw himself over her, pounding the big fist on the sword's handle with his left hand while trying to pull her back with his right arm vise-gripped around her waist. The thieving hand let go and disappeared back into the crowd that erupted with yelps and scuffling as they dodged and grabbed for the fallen swords.

Spence's dealer friends leapt over their tables and joined the fray, rescuing swords and retrieving a couple claimed as finders-keepers opportunities. Spence lifted Rian off the table to her feet, the sword still gripped in her white-knuckled hands.

Fear made him yell in her shock-pale face. "Are you hurt?"

Dazed, Rian shook her head and shoved the sword at him. Her mouth worked a moment before sound came out. "I—I'm insane!"

"Yeah," Spence said with real admiration. "But are you physically hurt?"

"Just take this." When he did, she stepped back and tried to pull her sweater's bottom over the red scratches on her belly. She shook her hair back, her wide-eyed expression bewildered. "I'm going away now."

"You stay put," Spence ordered and wrapped his arm around her shoulders that seemed small and trembling. "Anyone I.D. that guy?" Spence directed at the mob stalled on the opposite side of the table.

Security showed in force and started peppering the thinning crowd with questions, soon leaving Spence and Rian to grill. There weren't any other suspects as available or easy to look at as Rian, so they zeroed in on her. Spence didn't like it.

"We don't know any more than Rian saw the guy reaching for the sword. No one saw his face that's willing to say so, anyway. I haven't lost anything, thanks to Rian and these guys," he said, nodding toward his vendor friends who'd retreated to their stalls.

Spence pulled a folding chair up to the table for Rian. She filled out the incident report forms for him under the leering eyes of the remaining Security doofus, while Spence packed the swords into the steel box. The *katana* Rian had risked her life for was the only piece not bearing smudges and minor scratches.

What made her put herself at extreme risk for a thing

that wasn't even hers? He could almost believe she'd have used it against the thief, too, like an avenging angel. That fantasy faded a little when she, delicate and pale as her white sweater, stood with a wobble and handed the forms to the Security officer.

After he left she lifted the bottom of her sweater off the red streaks on her stomach and frowned at Spence. "You sure know how to show a girl a good time."

"That's what they all say." Spence closed the lid on the rolling storage case, tipped it on end and popped out the handle. "Let's get out of here. Warrior princesses first," he said, motioning her through the gap in the row of tables and followed, dollying the case in front of him.

When they reached the parking lot Rian helped Spence unlock the Integrity Security van and load the case in the back. They hadn't discussed it, but Spence knew it would be useless to try to argue her out of helping him or point out that he'd unloaded fine without her. Spence closed the lift gate and they stood looking at each other.

"Can I drop you at your car or maybe the Emergency Room where you can get your belly patched?" he joked.

"So you can build points on your frequent patient card?" Rian smirked.

"Good one." Spence got in the driver's seat. "Come on, I'll buy you a cup of coffee. It's the least I can do since you saved me close to twenty grand today."

Rian pushed his door closed and leaned on it while he ran down the window. "Are you saying you owe me one, then?" she purred.

Uh oh. He smoothed his fingers over his moustache and goatee. "No. Well, maybe. But coffee's all that's on the table right now."

"Or how about this, and relax, it's something I think you

might enjoy. There's this barbecue I'm supposed to be at right now. Come with me. We can bond."

"Bond? Why?" Spence started the engine, his blood thrumming in his temples.

"Because I want to and you owe me. No pressure, I promise, just nice people, good food and great music."

"I'm not much of a party guy—"

"Me either, but having friends has certain responsibilities. Relationship maintenance, you know. That means you sometimes go to dinners or parties that you'd rather skip than attend, but you go and they come to yours. Societal balance maintained. The American way of life preserved."

"Wow, who'd have known?" The more he was around her, the more she got under his skin, and maybe even in a good way. It was hard to tell when she was pushing him for treatment, though.

"Tell you what, you can follow me, that way you'll have your car and can leave anytime you want." She raised her eyebrow. "What do you say?"

"Yeah, okay, but I can't stay long."

"We'll see. I bet you're the last one to leave," she said with a smile lighting her pretty face. "I'm parked in the next row. Their house is a couple of miles from here, but stay close as it's tricky to find."

As she walked ahead, he leaned out the window and yelled, "I thought you drove all the way down here just to see me, but I was on the way, huh?"

"You were on the way to what?" she called over her shoulder and disappeared between cars.

Don't want to go there again, he resolved and turned the corner.

Rian waited until after they'd eaten to bring up the subject of Spence's bandaged hand that was now dirty gray and appeared to need changing. The man didn't seem to take very good care of himself and that had to change.

"When does the bandage come off?" she asked and waved back at the people motioning for her to join them.

Spence cleared his throat. "I wondered when you'd get around to asking about that."

"I'll be right back." Rian piled his empty paper plate on hers then carried the trash into the kitchen. She positioned herself so Spence could see her talking to the other guests and kept him waiting while she did so. She could feel his impatience radiating at her and after a couple more minutes returned to him.

"Sorry, I got waylaid," she said, sitting by him on the sofa, her thigh touching his and pushing the boundaries of his personal space. He didn't move away but she sensed his tension. She scooted and said sorry.

"No problem," he said, his shoulders dropping a bit.

She matched his posture, positioned her hands in her lap like his were and watched him relax further. Good. "Do you play an instrument?" she asked, confusing his expectation of her asking about his hand again.

He shook his head. "No, I'm just a listener and not that much these days. Noise kind of gets to me."

"I know what you mean. It can get very loud in these jam sessions."

He watched the musicians taking out their instruments. "Loud isn't the problem. When there's background noise I sometimes have trouble understanding what I hear. It's no big deal," he added.

Not happy sharing about himself. Rian nodded, keeping her gaze on the group rather than on Spence, and waited for him to continue. He didn't. After a lengthy silence that she thought was uncomfortable for him, she excused herself and joined the jam session forming in the dining room.

Spence's *I'm not much of a party guy* was an understatement, Rian decided as she tuned her guitar. When they'd first arrived, Rian made sure that she eased him into the situation with as few introductions within the group as possible. As it was, he hadn't moved from his defensive position on the sofa against the wall.

"Who's the hottie and does he play?" Adie asked Rian. She drew a violin bow over a cake of rosin and inspected Spence. "Though with that Lord of Darkness chinny fur, he looks like a refugee from a boy band. Maybe he sings?"

"Maybe he does sing." Rian met Spence's gaze. A little thrill flashed through her as his stern mouth eased into an intimate smile that quirked at the corner.

"Wow, great smile, and all for you it seems," Adie said with disappointment and tucked her violin under her chin. "Okay, gang, let's do *Dirty Ole Town*. Who wants to take the vocal?" She stared at Spence, causing everyone to stare at him.

Before he bolted, Rian spoke up. "Rob is the Irish music master. I love the way he does that song. Can you do it, Rob, please?" She gave the keyboard player an encouraging smile and he counted the musicians in then broke into a nasal country-twanged tenor that was perfect for the Irish politico-pub dirge.

Rian strummed chords and sang harmony, while keeping an eye on Spence. Her intended bond with him was strengthening. She sensed his mood and anticipated his behavior, all necessary if their counseling sessions were to achieve what he needed before she had to bring him in.

She'd worked to establish rapport and put him at ease, conditioning him by mirroring and matching his mannerisms and speech pattern so that he wasn't aware of her copying him. He was only conscious of liking her attention and feeling that he had something in common with her, more so each time she used his name. His physiology—relaxing muscles around his eyes, color flushing on his neck and loosening of his defensive posture—showed that he was responding well to the behavioral management techniques. While Spence didn't seem to get into the music, tapping a foot or humming along, he wasn't yawning and bored either. His focus was on her, watching, listening and that's what she wanted.

"Enough of the Guinness and shamrock crap," said the mandolin player after they'd jammed through several Irish songs. "Rian, break out the flute. Let's hear that new Egyptian stuff."

Rian saw a wary look cross Spence's face as he sat up tall and tense. He'd formed a negative association to the Egyptian music. She wouldn't risk their rapport by playing the music that made him anxious. "Sorry, not tonight. I'll be playing flute at the open mic at the Antique in Tacoma next week. Who's going?"

Spence looked more than ready to leave. While everyone else re-tuned and grabbed another beer, Rian slipped her guitar into its case at Spence's feet, then made her quiet good-byes to the hosts. Outside in the clear, cool evening, she thanked him for coming with her.

"Sure," he said with a shrug and took the guitar case from her. "Does this fit in the trunk?" He frowned at the sleek sports car.

"Not with the top down. I just strap it in the seat." She got in the car and he set the case on the seat. "Thanks for coming with me, Spence. It's hard to be around a bunch of musicians if you're not one. Even if you didn't get into the music, hope you enjoyed the food. Can you find your way out of here?" she asked, starting the engine.

"Yeah." He glanced toward his vehicle. "Got time for that cup of coffee I owe you?"

Excellent. He wanted more time with her and she wanted to, but being too available wasn't wise. Better to leave him reaching for more. "I wish, but I can't. Though we can set our appointment now if you like."

He thought about it and nodded. "Yeah, okay, I'll try to make it."

"Great! Monday at 2:30, remember. See you then." Rian drove away, thrilled to have made such progress with Spence. He had to keep the appointment. She'd overcome a huge percentage of his resistance and he would respond very well to treatment, she was certain. However, there was an attraction on her part that she hadn't counted on. That could be problematic during treatment and after if she weren't careful.

Spence beat himself up all the way home. Why in the hell had he said he'd see her? She should have learned from her other head cases that saying you would and doing it weren't the same things. It couldn't be that important to her, yet she'd backed him into a corner where he owed her. Now he'd have to go even though the ice churning his insides warned him not to. It wasn't safe or smart to spill his guts to anyone, let alone someone like her. She'd push him on what happened to his hand and make him tell her all about his latest freak zone episode that he hadn't even told Mike and Dorel about when they'd asked the morning after the pizza party. Marty didn't ask how it happened because he just *knew* the details like he always did, but he did advise him to tell Mike. And he better do it.

Spence thumbed Mike's number on his cell phone. "Hey, you're still up. Thought I'd drop by if that's okay." Mike said it was and agreed that they needed to talk.

He hung up. The strain in Mike's voice meant they were going to get into some things that Spence would much rather let lay, but maybe that's just what needed to happen, even if it killed him.

When Spence arrived at the Gabriellis' rural compound, Mike met him at the front door and ushered him directly to the garden shed safe room. Once inside he sat in a rolling desk chair while Mike paced the room, working himself up to speaking his mind.

Mike stopped and whirled on him, running his hand through his hair. "It's been almost six years since I've felt like this. I used to wonder if they had us under surveillance, but I'd put it out of my mind. Why should they watch me? You, sure, but why me? I don't get it."

Mike wasn't making a lot of sense but Spence let him talk, fatigue overtaking him. The room was warm and humid, womb like. He was almost asleep, floating in and out of a soft focus awareness like standing in front of several huge TV screens playing different programs.

". . . but I've learned to pay attention to what he says, like you do. You and Dorel have always accepted Marty's— insights. Every time he'd come up with weird stuff or know those things, I'd go into denial, even though deep down I knew better."

Spence's eyelids fluttered and he shook his head against the seductive image of a faceless female figure backlighted by a bright violet-tinged glow. She reached for him. He was pulled toward her, wanted to go to her again where he belonged.

A voice, a feeling he couldn't quite remember called to

him. "Spence! Come back!"

Spence's eyes flashed open and he jerked back from Mike yelling in his face. "Spence, come back!"

"What the hell are you doing?" he asked, groggy.

Mike glared at him. "You back?"

"Back from where?" Spence leaned away from Mike as far as he could, his head pounding with a high pitched whine in his ears like a faulting system.

"You were gone, man. I could sense your astral energy body hovering above us like a ghost then it was out of here like a shot. I called you back."

Spence sidled to a stand, wiping his wet palms on his pants. "No way. I was dozing. Dreaming, I guess."

Mike stepped back, giving him some space. "Dreaming about what?"

The dream had evaporated, left him with a vague uneasiness that made him shudder. "I don't know. Light, I think. Someone . . . or something. A voice, but that was you yelling at me. Why *come back* and from where?"

"That's what they tell viewers—remote viewers who send their consciousness out to gather intelligence, beyond the now and into other times and other places. When a viewer gets out there in the ether sometimes they can disassociate. They can feel a loss of connection with their bodies or the present time because they're so focused on the target. The monitor will initiate the exit protocol and order the viewer to return. I sensed you were gone and called you back. You responded just like you were trained. That should convince you that what I've said about our being trained as remote viewers is true."

Spence shook his head in denial. "Come on, Mike. I woke up because you screamed at me with that Dumpster breath of yours."

Mike chuckled. "Smart ass. You're still in an altered state, my friend, and hypersensitive to perceptual stimuli. If you can smell my breath, I bet you've got ringing in your ears or maybe you're hearing your own blood thumping along in your arteries?"

Spence allowed a single nod and slumped back in the chair, stunned. Mike pulled a chair up close and began to fill in the black hole in his memory.

"I'm not sure exactly how they first determined we were possible recruits for the remote viewing program. Might have been from our Navy Intelligence psych profiles. Do you remember when we were pulled out of SEALs Ops for the special intelligence briefing?"

Spence struggled to find the memory.

"We took EEGs, remember?" Mike searched Spence's eyes like he could find the memory there himself.

Yes! A washed-out picture flashed in his mind's eye of sitting in some kind of lab with electrodes stuck to his head. He nodded.

Mike grinned, excited. "Now we're getting somewhere! Anyway, that wasn't just a regular electroencephalograph machine. They could measure our brainwaves and they were looking for a certain frequency range, a broad bandwidth. The rat lab guys' research showed that there were certain brainwaves or frequencies where the subconscious is accessible, which is considered to be the creative state where psychics, intuitives and clairvoyants function. These Black Ops guys were looking for intelligence people whose brains operated in broad frequency bandwidths. Then they trained us to access whatever state of mind that we needed to bring back information blocked from ordinary perception by distance, shielding or time. Remember?"

Spence wanted to say that he did remember, but to make

the leap from a spotty memory of a lab to being recruited and trained as a remote viewer was a jump too long. "Go on," he said, "maybe something will key up."

"We were both in the range, and we both also had intuitive flashes or episodes that we were stupid enough to tell people about. Remember how interested the psychologists were in our dreams and such? Well, somewhere they put it all together and we were targeted for recruitment. SEALs Special Ops was just the beginning. They were watching us way before then when we graduated flight school—"

"Who the hell are *they* that you keep talking about?" Spence demanded. "Navy Intelligence? CIA? NSA?"

"No, not those guys. Private sector government contract, Datascape Systems International."

Spence reeled back. "Datascape? You've got to be kidding. They're my biggest account. Integrity has been doing business with them since the beginning. Hell, they've got the integrated multimedia for the convention center's Egyptian show that we're doing security for . . ." His thoughts shot back to the hooked tool in the glass case he'd broken trying to get his hands on it. The back of his neck began to prickle and he covered his mouth, smoothing his hand down his moustache, over his chin to his throat. "Damn."

"It's a bitch, ain't it," Mike growled and began pacing anew. "They've got us again. Or worse, they've never let us go."

"Mike, this is some kind of screwed up coincidence that we're reading way too much into. Datascape is a huge multinational corporation and into a lot of secret stuff that we can't even imagine, but it's hard for me to believe they were training psychic spies—"

"Not was—are. Datascape isn't just training remote viewers, they're using them, hiring their viewers' services out to anyone, for any purpose, who can pay the fee. Question is are they involved somehow in what's going on with you and why?" Mike glanced at Spence's hand. "I think you better tell me what happened with that."

He didn't want to tell him and his hand throbbed agreement. "It's not important. Just cut myself is all."

"Where?"

"The other day. At work."

"Where at work?" Mike narrowed his eyes. "Something happened at the convention center, didn't it?"

Spence shrugged, his stomach tightening, ready for the punch. "Yeah, I slipped and fell against a display case. It broke, cut my hand."

Mike smirked. "I guess it did. You wouldn't have punched the case, would you?"

"No. It wasn't asking me a lot of stupid questions. It was an accident." He got up and headed for the door.

"What was in it?"

Spence rounded on him. "None of your business. In fact, I'm real goddamn tired of being grilled by you all the time. Just leave me the hell alone." He jerked the door open and started to step into the darkness of the yard, but Mike's deadly serious tone stopped him.

"Marty thinks they're trying to bring you back in. Something to do with my sword."

Chapter Five

Spence stepped back in, closed the door and rested his forehead against the smooth metal, his back to Mike. From the depths of the black hole in his memory a great churning began, deep and distant. Unreachable, but not for long. Cognizance was coming. Full knowing. Truth that would be too difficult to bear and would take them down, but he would deny it as long as he could. "We don't want Marty in this," he murmured.

"I know that," Mike snapped, "but you can see that whatever is happening is about to go high order detonation. And if Datascape is trying to bring you in, I don't know that there is anything we can do to stop them."

Spence turned to Mike sitting on the chair, his face in his hands. "Why would they want me? I don't know anything or remember. I'm no psychic spy or any use to them that way."

"They may have found the sword or know where it is. You're the sword expert, remember?"

"Yeah, but you know more about that particular item than I do—all that research you did. It's history?"

Mike rubbed his eyes and shook his head. "You've always been a pretty good epigrapher and able to interpret symbols and inscriptions. You decoded some of those on the blade, didn't you? Or maybe it's just enough that you know the sword exists. I don't know. Marty will drop something like this on me, and then start talking about Josh's birthday party next week. It's like stream of consciousness with him and he says whatever comes in. He'll have to learn to control it."

"If what you say is true about this remote viewing psychic stuff, why would you want to teach him to use it better? I've always thought he was smart, genius even, not psychic. That kind of thinking isn't good for any of us. We can't let him say these things, can't encourage him any more."

"We can't stop him, Spence. He is who he is. We've got to teach him to protect himself. Because what I'm thinking, and you're not going to like this either, is that maybe Datascape is interested in him—"

"Shut the hell up! Don't even think it. That crap is pure conspiracy fiction. Even after all the down and dirty you and I got into, I refuse to believe that our government would use children."

Mike snorted. "Just listen to yourself. What a load. You're parroting what they programmed in you with the best technology and drugs that the U.S. taxpayers can provide, my man."

"If you believe that why are we standing here? Why haven't you spirited Marty away to somewhere safe?"

"I've been trying to tell you that there's no hiding from a Datascape viewer. Unless you're broadcasting an interrupt frequency. Most viewers believe that can't be done, but I'm telling you it can. The Soviets were trying to develop a shielding generator, but we didn't think there was a functional one yet."

"Well hell, if you can't protect yourself from a mind reader, why bother with this safe room that was designed to shield electronic surveillance?"

"They don't just use viewers and psychics. Datascape has a whole cadre of specialists like you, theoreticians and engineers. They're into witchcraft, black arts, reverse-engineered UFO technology, anything that would give them an edge—"

"An edge for what? Making a profit? Keeping people employed and the economy going? Mike, I know Datascape," Spence interjected, trying to keep himself calm. "I've met top management, designed the system for their home office in Denver and the branch offices. They're just people with families, mortgages and worried about their retirement plans like we are."

"Sure, it feels like they're just like us. We are. That's they way they designed it."

Spence dropped his shoulders and blew out a disgusted breath. "You say you used to do this psychic spying? But not any more, right?" At Mike's reluctant nod, he added, "If you could do the psychic spy thing on Datascape, I believe you'd find that they don't give a crap about you and that I'm just a subcontractor. Nothing more."

"If I were to try to view inside Datascape with any accuracy, they'd know I'm targeting them."

"How?"

"A viewer can sense other viewers' energy bodies like ghosts. The people they've got targeting us will know."

"Then following that theory, don't they know right now? Wouldn't they be listening to us now?" He made a sweeping motion with his hand. "Are you getting anything? Anyone spying on us?"

Mike rocketed to his feet with a grim expression that didn't do much to disguise his fury. "Listen, I've told you before, if I go *online* again my energy signature will draw them right to my door quicker than anything else and put Dorel and Marty in mortal danger. I know they've got people watching me, have been since I left the program. It's the smart thing to do. But they don't expend the manpower to target me twenty-four seven. They've probably assigned a viewer to me who takes samplings once or twice a day. I'm trusting like hell that they aren't doing it right now, but I am beginning to believe that they've got lots of people on you. That *is* dangerous for you *and* my family. I've got to think, got to figure out what to do . . ." He started pacing, rubbing his palms together and focusing a frown on the concrete floor.

Spence felt bad that Mike was so pissed at him. He'd always trusted Mike, but people changed, their priorities in life shifted. Dorel and Marty were his top priority now, and rightly so. He may not believe what Mike was saying, but he'd work with Mike to protect his family from whatever he thought was a threat. "Hey, if it helps any, I'm going to go see Rian on Monday. Maybe she can help me."

Mike stopped. "Good! That's good. They'll be viewing your session with her for sure. Make sure you *remember* all sorts of weird stuff about your childhood. That will keep them occupied, convince them that the deprogramming isn't breaching . . . maybe. At least it'll buy us some time."

"Time for what?"

"To teach you to remote view again so that you can lead this situation and help me protect us."

"Aw, hell, Mike!" At his dark look, Spence added, "Okay, okay. Whatever you need to do, I'm in like always. You can trust that."

Spence left Mike at the front door and drove back to Seattle, barely able to keep his eyes open. When he got home he hit the sack and woke up hours later in the dark. He set up the coffeemaker and went back to bed, not waking again until the pot's gurgling. He was surprised and more than a little worried to discover that he'd slept all the way through Sunday.

★ ★ ★ ★ ★

On Monday at exactly 2:30 p.m., Rian's receptionist Clarissa ushered Spence into her office. Even before he walked in, she'd perceived his energy. Oh, he *so* does not want to be here, poor guy. Better get right to it so he doesn't have an opportunity to act on his avoidance inclination.

"Spence, you can just go ahead and make yourself comfortable in that chair there. Can I offer you some water?"

"Got a Dr Pepper?" He cut a nervous glance at the black leather recliner that faced a copy of Miró's *Painting* hung on the wall behind her desk.

She smiled. "No, sorry. Just bottled water."

"No thanks." He sat down and let himself settle into the cozy leather.

Rian picked up a folder from her desk and took her chair opposite the recliner's left side. She pressed the button on the tiny digital recorder on the table between them. "I record every counseling session for reference. The recordings as well as all your patient information are kept strictly confidential, so you can feel safe to express yourself freely. In fact, the freer you feel, the easier we can get to the origin of what's bothering you and let it go."

Spence shrugged and gave a curt nod.

She matched his posture and tapped her left forefinger on the arm of her chair as he was. "Before your session I'd like to talk a little about what I do and the process I use, maybe answer some of the questions about hypnosis that you have on your mind."

"I know I can't be hypnotized, if that's what you mean. And people who think they're hypnotized are just imagining it." His nervous finger tapping increased a beat or two.

Rian began to slow the rhythm of her own tapping. "It's

possible, though that hasn't been my experience or that of the hundreds of patients I've treated," she offered, keeping her voice soft and reasonable. She handed him a clipboard. "Here's a pen and a piece of paper for you to write down any questions you think of as we go along so we can clear them up later."

He set the clipboard in his lap and returned to tapping on the recliner's arm with a cadence now matching hers. "That's right," she said in a half-whisper, looking down at her intake sheet. She stopped tapping and he unconsciously followed her lead. His shoulders dropped, his facial color shifted nicely and the muscles around his eyes slackened a bit, all signs that she'd paced him into rapport and a level of relaxation where they could begin to work.

"Let me clear up some common misconceptions about hypnosis. I know that you are a process-oriented man and like to understand how things work. You want to understand how hypnosis works. To know that, it's important to understand how the mind works—the conscious mind where we spend most of our waking time and the subconscious or the inner mind."

Spence listened as Rian explained the analytical, rational and the willpower parts of the conscious mind, but he leaned forward when she began to describe the subconscious as the storehouse of memory and learning. "The subconscious mind is extremely powerful. It can transform you into anything you'd like to be: wealthy, famous, sexy, athletic and well-built, clever, joyful, or sad if you choose. It's the real you. The majority of our mental functioning is below our conscious awareness and has huge impact on everything we think, do and feel. The subconscious has several functions, one of which is controlling the body's mechanisms. I like to think of the subconscious as both the operating system and the hard drive of the brain, if you will. One part of the brain regulates the autonomic nervous system, controlling every organ and gland, but research has shown that the subconscious controls many such mechanisms and is probably able to control chemical and electrical reactions as well. Isn't that interesting?"

Spence nodded and smoothed his hand over his mouth to his chin.

She could see he was thinking. Keeping her voice soft and rhythmic yet inflected with interested tones, she continued the pre-talk, the important initial element of the hypnotic induction. "Our subconscious minds record every perception our senses register. Most of us don't consciously recall more than a small percentage of things that happen to us, but the subconscious records everything in the greatest detail. A lot of what we consciously forget, such as sad or frightening events and emotions, still affect us in many and sometimes very debilitating ways.

"Using hypnosis, we can access the memories that are negatively affecting us. In regression hypnosis, we can travel back in time it seems and relive specific childhood events such as your first birthday, or your birth or perhaps even before that. It's so much more than simple recall, it's like you are there and it's happening in real time. You can see, you can smell, taste and hear very clearly. We may not recall everything at a conscious level, but it's all there. We never really forget anything."

"What if I don't want to remember?" he asked, holding her gaze with a slight frown. "Are you going to make me tell you anyway?"

"No. Doesn't work that way. Not I, nor any hypnotherapist, can cause you to do anything you don't want to do, make you reveal secrets or act contrary to your moral code or best interests. A very important part of the subconscious mind is the protective mind that protects against danger, real or imagined and is always alert to guard you, keep you safe. It's always aware and functioning even when the conscious mind is knocked out or anaesthetized. Protective of you as it is, it can also cause illness and even self-destructive behavior."

"Why would it do that?" he asked and leaned away, gripping the chair's arm with his white-knuckled left hand.

She leaned back a little, too, lightly resting her left hand on her chair's arm. "There's one more part of the conscious mind that I haven't told you about yet. It's called the critical factor and its job is to keep us safe from what we believe from experience or have been taught will harm us. It sends us signals like *I can't, I won't* or *I haven't been able to before, so I can't now.* And this function is necessary when it reminds you that, say, it wouldn't be wise to toss a plugged-in toaster into the bathtub with you."

Spence chuckled and nodded. "Yeah, I can see how that'd be problematic."

Rian chuckled too. "Electrifyingly so." She waited a moment then continued. "The critical factor needs to be overcome when it cripples you with negative habit patterns, when sound wariness becomes incapacitating fear. Functioning ideally, your critical factor monitors impulses, filters out the harmful, and helps you set realistic goals. But because the critical factor reacts to the protective subconscious, the critical factor does not always function ideally.

"So, using hypnosis, which is a state of intense focused concentration, we can access the subconscious, the intuitive inner mind. I use a variety of techniques to help you bypass your conscious mind's critical factor and take it off line, if you will. Then while that is idle, a helpful suggestion or two can easily be incorporated by your inner mind. Do you have any questions?" She saw he'd written nothing on the sheet, but he had been taking in everything she'd said.

"What kind of suggestions would you give my mind, if you can get me under?"

"You don't need me to get into a beautiful deep state of hypnosis. And you don't need me to give you suggestions of positive change in any area of your life. You can do all that yourself. But you don't know how, isn't that right?"

Spence gave her a confused frown, but he nodded agreement.

"Spence, I have many therapeutic processes at my disposal, but I choose to use hypnosis because it's effective and not harmful in any way. In hypnosis all of your senses are many times better than they are right now. I'm going to teach you how to achieve a beautiful state of hypnosis and experience physical relaxation and mental alertness. It's the easiest thing in the world to do because all hypnosis is self-hypnosis. That's right, it's a completely consensual state. You must allow things to happen. You can stop them from happening by simply thinking that you don't want them to happen. There's no clucking like a chicken or singing like Elvis here—unless you want to, of course," she added with a wink and smile.

"What if I go so deep I don't wake up? That is, if I go under at all."

"Hypnosis isn't sleep, Spence. Even if I left the room while you were in a hypnotic state and didn't return for a time, you would either return to full consciousness or catch a little nap and wake up refreshed. And remember, if I were to ask you for information about something that was none of my business, you would tell me it wasn't my business— probably more readily than when you weren't in trance.

Hypnosis isn't a truth serum. If you want to lie about what you're experiencing in trance, you can easily do so if you choose. Before you go further into trance, don't go now, but soon, do you have any more questions?"

The confused expression appeared again and he shook his head.

"Fine, that's fine. I'm going to help you get into a beautiful deep state of hypnosis where we can discover the origin of your difficulty in sleeping. Is that right?"

"Yeah," he murmured. "I guess so."

"That's right. Now with your permission I'm going to stand in front of you and ask you to look up while pressing down with your left hand on top of my hand. Is it okay that I touch you?"

He nodded.

"Fine, that's fine. Could you sit forward, please, with your feet flat on the floor." She stood in front of him, holding her right hand above his forehead.

"Spence, go ahead and look up at my hand. That's right. Now press down on my hand. Good, that's right. Press down. Down. Keep looking up. That's right." She swept her hand down from his eyebrows. "Close. Close your eyes. That's right. Keep pressing on my hand. Heavier." With a last sweep of her hand downward, his eyelids fluttered and she jerked her hand out from under his with a loud, "Sleep now!"

Spence's eyelids slammed closed and he fell forward. She caught him, placing him back in the chair and went behind him, still holding his head by the sides of his neck.

"Very good. That's right. Nice and relaxed now. Keeping your breathing very deep and regular." She put his head on the headrest and came around in front of him. "Very good, Spence. You're in a beautiful state of relaxation and I'm going to help you go much deeper. I'm going to lay the recliner back so that you are nice and comfortable, then I'm going to tap you on the forehead. Each time I tap you, you go much deeper into hypnosis."

After several deepening techniques to which he responded very well, she wasn't surprised that he was such an excellent subject. He could reach the deepest levels easily. "Spence, I'm going to count from five to one and when I reach the count of one, I want you to find yourself in a wonderful, happy memory of your teenage years." She counted him down, then prompted, "Okay, now Spence, you are there at the happy time. Bring it all into clear focus, that's right. Very good. Just let it become clear. Now tell me what you are experiencing."

Tears formed at the corners of his closed eyes and a huge smile played across his mouth. "Um," he cleared his throat. "He's gone. I'm so happy."

"Who's gone?" Rian asked, writing on her notepad. She relied on her written session notes more than the recordings, which were more for legal protection.

"Dad. He's left her again. Maybe this time he'll stay away for good."

"How old are you?"

"Fourteen. It's my birthday. Cool." His smile widened. "Mom is taking me to the air show anyway. She won't let him screw this up for me."

"Who goes with you? Do you have fun?"

"The best. Just Mom and me. The best," he whispered, still smiling.

"Go ahead and enjoy that memory, Spence. Be there with it, take it all in. That's right."

She caught up her notes for a few moments, then added, "All right now, Spence. Let's just let that happy memory fade, but keep those happy feelings with you because you can remember them anytime you need to feel happier. I'm going to count from five to one and when I reach the count of one I want you to go back to an early childhood memory. You can make it a happy one if you wish or you can choose a memory that may help you understand why you're having problems sleeping now. Five. Nice and relaxed, breathing easily and regularly, maintaining your deep state of hypnosis. Four . . ." She continued to count down to one.

"Now, you are there. An early childhood memory. Just bring it into clear focus. Let everything become very clear."

Spence's face contorted with the sob that escaped his closed lips. He squinted his closed eyes tighter, rolling his head from side to side, and growled deep and feral.

"Spence, it's just a memory. It can't harm you. Maintain your deep state, breathing easy and regularly. Tell me, where are you?" she asked, watching him.

"Don't know."

"Allow everything to become clear, bring all into focus. That's right. Now look down at your feet. Do you have on footwear or are you barefoot?" she asked, grounding him in the memory.

After a few moments, he answered, "No feet, can't see."

"Fine. That's fine. What do you hear?" Rian prompted.

"Voices. Angry. Can't sleep."

"Whose voices do you hear? You know who is angry, who is it?"

"Dad. Yelling at her. Can't sleep."

His breathing had stabilized and he'd stopped thrashing in the recliner. "That's right. Very good," she said, reinforcing his calmness. "Staying nice and relaxed now. How old are you?"

"He's eight months."

Spence's use of the third person showed he was in a very deep state and disassociated from the event. "Okay, Spence, you're eight months old and listening to your dad yelling at your mother, is that right?"

Spence sighed and nodded, lying still in the chair.

"Are you in the same room?"

"No. My crib. Can't sleep."

As always happened, Rian felt herself connect psychically with her hypnotized patient. The connection was more than empathetic. It was as if they were on the same wavelength. She began to anticipate Spence's next response. "Why can't you sleep, Spence?"

"Too much noise. I'm afraid of the noise. Afraid of what I can't see but hear."

"What can't you see?" she pressed. "You can know what you can't see. Know it now."

"He's hurting her. She lets him so he won't hurt me," Spence said in a tiny little voice. "If I sleep, if I don't keep watch, he will hurt her too much."

"Spence, can you as a baby keep your father from arguing with or hurting your mother if he wants to?"

"No."

"Is there anything you as a baby can do in this situation?"

He shook his head, but then added, "Yes. I go to her when she sleeps and remind her that she is loved."

A thrill shivered through Rian. "How do you do that, Spence?"

"I talk to her on the soul level. Strengthen her with my love. Like I always do when I'm her guide." His voice had changed from childlike to wise.

"Oh, you're her guide? What is a *guide* exactly?"

He smiled, eyelids fluttering as if in REM sleep. "Come

now, Doctor, you have heard of such as we many times.
You know what we are."

Rian bit her lip to stifle a wild giggle. Contact with the
other side always unnerved as much as inspired awe in her.
"Yes, I know, but I do love to hear it. May I ask you a question?"

"You may ask and I may not answer."

Excitement rising, she asked, "Is this situation the origin
of Spence's current difficulties?"

"Yes. And no, as you are well aware."

"Is there more that I can do to help him?"

"You know what is right and that what you have been
doing is not," the guide said. "You must allow the love of
the past to transform the present for both of you."

Rian shivered. "I don't understand."

"You have not trusted wisely and are not yourself worthy
of the love you seek," was the answer she didn't want to
hear. Despite Rian's repeated questions the guide remained
silent.

She gazed at Spence who now seemed to be resting. He
knew! Somewhere is his subconscious, in the Universal
Mind connection of all souls he knew what she had been
doing to him. The guide had suggested that they had a past
life connection to each other. It was possible, because she'd
learned long ago to view each person who came into her
life, even for the briefest moment, as someone she'd known
in a past life who may be acting a new part now.

Though she hadn't experienced a past life regression
where she'd known Spence, they had an undeniably strong
connection. She'd been trying to rationalize her growing
feelings for him as empathy or compassion, but the guide
mentioned *love*. She had to keep that possibility in mind as
she worked with Spence, even if she were to treat him with

more kindness and attention to his comfort. And to do that she must focus on helping instead of manipulating him. His subconscious had brought up the memory of being an infant who couldn't sleep because he feared for his mother as the source of his sleep problem today. She'd exacerbated that dysfunction with her nightly out of body travels to prepare him for re-entry to the program. It was her duty to remove the harm she had caused. And a good start would be to help him heal that emotional wound from so long ago.

"Spence, I want you to access that memory of being eight months old again. Bring it clearly into focus. This time, experience the memory as if it were a video, a movie playing on the screen in your mind. You see yourself as a baby. You love your mother and your mother loves you. Focus on that love. Your only responsibility as a baby is to grow strong in your mother's love and you did. Let any fears or worries about that time in your life sparkle away. Perhaps you can hear a tinkling sound as those negative emotions sparkle away. That's right. Let it go. Preserve the love you learned from the situation. There's always something to learn in any situation that can help you and others. Can you do that, Spence?"

He nodded with a small smile. "Yes."

"Fine. That's fine. Very good. Just let the fear and the worry go, understanding that you can now sleep well and undisturbed as your body requires. You can relax and sleep. Noises will not bother you. You will sleep soundly and at the right time, when you need to, you will awaken relaxed and refreshed, feeling wonderful." She gave him instructions to remember everything, except for the guide's specific words to her, that had transpired during the session and that each time he was hypnotized he would go deeper and quicker, then counted him up to conscious awareness.

Spence opened his eyes half way and stretched, becoming aware of a carnation-like scent that reminded him of his mother. A wave of loving nostalgia hit him and he blinked back tears, but for the first time since her death, he wasn't sad remembering her. He glanced at Rian who met his gaze. "Wow."

"Don't take this the wrong way, but you couldn't be hypnotized, huh?" she asked. "You were so gone, from the moment you sat in the hypnosis chair. Come on, admit it. It's good to accept that you were wrong. Besides I love to hear how good it was. And it was great, wasn't it?"

Spence grinned and pushed the footrest down as he sat up. "Yeah, I feel good. But I'm not sure I was hypnotized. I think I was making the whole thing up."

"That's what being hypnotized feels like. You're aware of being you and aware of the being in the memory. Now you know what to expect. You did so great. What a wonderful subject you are. Next time you'll drop into state very quickly and we can get to it. Snickity snick."

"Mom used to say that." He shook the memory from his head and tried to focus. "Am I going to remember this? I feel kind of woozy or detached."

"Oh yes, you'll remember everything and more. You were only able to verbalize a very small amount of what you were experiencing in hypnosis. It's like a holographic memory. As time goes on you'll be remembering more and also making connections from that memory to your now. It's amazing the way it works. Tonight you'll sleep like a baby."

"Instead of like the dead? When I got home on Saturday night I pretty much slept straight through to this morning."

She looked thoughtful then smiled at him as she stood up. "Guess you needed the rest. Now your sleep patterns will normalize, you'll see. I expect a good report when I see you next week," she said with a glance at her watch. "Let me walk you out. You can set up the next appointment with Clarissa."

In spite of feeling punchy, he realized he was being dismissed and followed her to the door.

"If you're still feeling a little floaty or a bit disoriented, you can sit in the waiting room until the sensation clears if you like. Sorry, I have another patient due any moment. Do drink lots of water and try to take it easy for the next couple of days. You've done a lot of good work here today and your body will need to clear toxins and adjust to the changes that have been made." She stuck out her hand and he gave it a weak pump. "Thanks for keeping your appointment, Spence. It means so much to all of us."

Spence wandered out to the elevator and focused on the floor numbers flashing by as it descended to the parking garage. When the doors opened he wasn't sure where he was, but managed to make his way to the bike and climb in the saddle. How long he sat staring at nothing he wasn't sure, then pulled on his helmet and rode out of the garage. The next thing he knew, he was twenty miles away and stopping the bike in Mike's circular driveway.

Chapter Six

Spence realized where he was with a start and turned the bike around. The front door opened and Marty barreled out the door toward him.

"Uncle Spence! You came. I called you and you came just like I wanted," the little redhead bubbled and gave him a hug around the waist.

"Hey, M-Man." Spence got off the bike and pulled his cell phone out of his pocket. No messages. "Did you call the house, Marty?"

"Nope, I imagined a string from your heart to my heart. I sent you a message on it like a telephone." He grabbed Spence's hand and tugged. "Come on and play Game Box with me. I've got a new *Everlasting Warriors* game. It's fun. We can do fights with magic swords."

"Is your dad home?" Spence let Marty drag him into the house. The Airedale was on him in a flash, licking and pawing.

"Off, Katana," Marty ordered and the dog dropped to a sit on Spence's foot. "Dad's in his office working. Come play with me when you're done," he said to Spence and skipped off to his bedroom.

Katana leapt up and trotted ahead of Spence to Mike's closed door, then stood and put his front paws on it. "Katana, get off the door. Go see your mother," Mike's voice said from inside.

"It's me," Spence announced, sidestepping the dog and pushing the door open.

Mike, dressed in his TransAsia captain's uniform, sat

back from the computer. "Hey, just the guy I wanted to see. What's going on?"

"Nothing much." Spence opened the French doors and took a quick look outside at the empty garden, then closed them. "You coming or going?"

"Going." He pulled back his white shirtsleeve and looked at his watch. "I have to leave in about fifteen minutes. Our pull chocks time is 6:45 for Singapore. Can you clear your calendar Friday after next? That 747-400 is coming out of service in Miami and we need to ferry it to the modifications center in San Antonio."

"Yeah, okay. Are you going to have JET Aviation Services take care of all the paperwork and get the airplane ready to go?"

"Doing that now." Mike hit the enter key and confirmed the arrangements online with the international aviation services company. "We're good to go."

"Sounds fun. Speaking of, I just had my appointment with Dr. Rian."

"Yeah? How was it?" Mike began keying again.

"Okay, I guess. Nothing really happened. I think I was making it up." He knew he hadn't made it up. What he experienced was too real.

"They say it always feels like that no matter how many times you're hypnotized. What did she do?"

"Talked to me about my childhood and I came up with a couple of memories. Then I told her I was my mother's guide and she asked me some questions." Spence heard Mike stop typing and suck in a loud breath. He didn't turn around, didn't want to see that look on Mike's face.

"What kind of questions?" Mike asked quietly.

"How she could help me."

"What did you—I mean what did the *guide* say?"

"I'm not sure. Something about love, I think. Isn't that what guides are supposed to talk about?" He sat down in the chair next to the desk. "What the heck was I talking about guides for, anyway? I don't believe in that kind of thing."

Mike frowned at him. "Are you worried about it?"

"No. I feel pretty good now that I'm awake. I didn't plan on coming out here, but here I am. Marty says he called me on the heart line and I showed like I was supposed to." He bounced his eyebrows up and traced his hand in an imaginary line out of his heart in a Roman salute. "You know, I didn't need to go see her. I've slept great the last couple of nights. No noise. No weirdness."

"That's great. But it was okay to see her too, right? I mean she isn't hard to look at and seems easy to talk to."

"Thing is, she did most of the talking and then the hypnosis for the lack of sleep thing."

"Are you going to see her again?"

Spence rubbed his eyes. "I'm supposed to next week. But if I'm sleeping okay, and I am, what's the point?"

Mike put his elbows on the desk and tented his fingers. "You and I know that the sleep disorder isn't the problem, just a symptom of something bigger. Something worse."

"You'll have to convince me, Mike. Everything seems pretty decent right now."

Mike shrugged. "Tell you what, let's just give it a couple of days and see how you're doing. If things are still good, then fine, but if you pass out again or hear noises that aren't there or break into display cases with your bare hands, then we've got to get this handled."

"Did you talk to one of my guys at the convention center?" Anger simmering just below the surface, Spence opened his clenched fists, letting off pressure.

"Marty told me. Described the whole thing. Said there was an old tool in the case that belonged to you a long time ago and that you wanted it. Please tell me that wasn't how it went down."

Mike's anxious expression was a mirror for Spence. "Oh, hell . . ." He covered his mouth with his hand, letting it slide to his throat.

"Great. Just great. What were you thinking?" Mike started jamming papers in his pilot's case.

"Should be pretty obvious I wasn't thinking. I thought someone was following me. When I stopped to check there was this hooked tool lying in a glass display case. Mike, I think it was used to straighten warped swords. And that isn't the reason I freaked. On the handle of the thing were inscriptions and markings just like those on Dorel's sword, I'd swear to it."

Mike snapped his case closed. "So you decided to do a smash and grab in front of a hundred witnesses? Makes sense. Did you get the thing?"

Spence shook his head. "I don't think so because I don't have it and I didn't get arrested. People told me I fell on the case and it broke. I don't know, because I don't remember anything from the time I saw the markings on the tool until I woke up in the ambulance on my way to Harbor View."

Mike slipped on his uniform coat, pulling his shirtsleeves to show a quarter inch of white at the cuffs. "Are you sure you're going to be in shape to fly? When do you get the stitches out?"

"This Friday. I've changed the bandage myself today. It looks worse than it is. I'm good to go." He moved to the door and started to open it, but Mike stopped him.

"That would be a welcome change, because I think things are worse than they look. I'll be back on Thursday morning. If anything happens that you have even a nanosecond's thought about, and I mean anything, you call me. Don't go dicking around with that antique .45 of yours at weird noises or otherwise incur the interest of types who don't get you like we do, okay? Keep your appointment with the doc. In fact, if you're so good at sleeping now, why don't you just go to bed early tonight and stay there until I get back?"

"Bite me." Spence opened the door and Mike walked through, stopping in the foyer.

"You first. Just take care of yourself, okay?"

"Spence! I didn't know you were here," Dorel said and gave him a kiss on the cheek, then turned to Mike, straightening the gold wings on his jacket. "Take care of yourself, best pilot in the world."

He kissed her then called Marty, who ran down the hall and jumped in his dad's arms. Mike swung him around. "Your mom's got the controls till I get back. Don't give her any trouble, okay? Now give me a kiss." Marty giggled and smacked a wet one on Mike's left eye. Mike kissed him back and set him down, wiping his eye with his coat sleeve and picking up his pilot's case. Spence followed the family outside.

Cars were pulling into the driveway as Mike got in his SUV and drove away. "I better go," Spence said to Dorel. "Looks like you've got company."

"Just the soccer team boosters. We're working on a fundraiser. Please stay. There's some pretty good food in it for you," Dorel said with a coercing smile. "Besides, you can play with Marty, keep him out of our hair."

"Sure. Sounds fun."

A look of genuine pleasure flashed on Dorel's face and she winked at Spence, then called to one of the arriving guests behind him. "Hi! I didn't think you were going to make it. I'm so glad you came. Spence, you remember Rian Farsante, Marty's soccer coach, don't you?"

Spence's mouth went dry and mind blank as he turned and met Rian's turquoise eyes twinkling with fun. She looked hot in the black power suit she'd worn at the office earlier, but the form-fitting jacket was unbuttoned and open on a deep v-neck translucent white blouse that showed lacy edges of her bra.

"So, we meet again," she said, her voice low and sexy in his ears. "It's like déjà vu all over again."

She wanted him. All evening she'd made sure he knew it by the way she looked deep into his eyes when she talked to him and seemed to know what he was thinking or going to say next. Every time she said his name it was like a deep kiss. Rian had spent most of dinner talking and laughing with people on her end of the long table. At the other end, Spence kept Marty occupied and tried to help Dorel take care of her guests. When Rian did send an inclusive comment his way or sneak a glance at him, he knew she wanted him as much as he did her. He hadn't realized how well they fit together, how much they had in common, and how alike they were until the hour and a half alone with her today.

Her soft, feminine voice had stroked and aroused him like a tongue feathering caresses over his skin, making him feel things he wasn't sure he'd ever felt before. That a beautiful woman cared so much for him that she pursued him, was amazing enough, but that he could care for her was a whole new experience with incredible possibilities, and consequences. From the moment he met her, every move of her head, blink of her eye, her smile was an echo of another long ago.

Spence shook off the mystical train of thought and focused on what Marty was chirping away about. ". . . when Momma was Michiko she gave me the sword to keep for her. *Everlasting Warriors* is sorta like that except there's these magic swords." The little boy took a swallow of juice and wiped his mouth on his arm. "Uncle Spence, do you like Coach Rian?"

The question caught him off guard because he was still trying to wrap his brain around *when Momma was Michiko she gave me the sword.* "Huh? Here, use your napkin. Yeah, Rian's okay. What sword?"

Marty swiped at his mouth with the linen napkin. "Coach likes you too, but she's not so happy about that," he said, watching Rian talking animatedly with a friend of Dorel's. "But you can like her. You're supposed to."

Spence stared at Marty, wondering if he'd ever get used the kid's always truthful and often scary insights. "What do you mean I'm supposed to like her?"

Marty met his gaze and blinked. "You know, like you agreed before you came here to help Dad."

"Before . . . when? Before I met your dad in the Navy?"

He shook his head. "I'm finished, Momma. Can Uncle Spence and me go play now?" he asked Dorel as she set a tray of sliced cake on the table beside him.

"Sure, sweetie, go ahead, but Spence can't play. He has to help me serve the cake." She shoved the tray across the tablecloth. "You can start at that end. I bet Rian would like some dessert." She wrinkled her nose and crossed her eyes at him.

"Jerk," he teased and stood with the tray.

"Don't waste your charm, what little there is, on me. Spread it around where it will do you some good—we can only hope." She sent a meaningful glance in Rian's direction, then followed Marty out of the dining room and went to the kitchen.

When Rian took the plate Spence offered her, her fingers brushed his and he knew she felt the massive zing, too. He returned to his place, but she kept glancing at him, sometimes with a smile or a playful lift of her eyebrow.

The meeting went on long after Marty was bedded down. Dorel stifled yawns that Spence empathized with. He caught himself nodding off several times, but Rian aimed a question or a comment at the right time and brought him back. The group made leaving noises and after a few more tabled decisions and prolonged good-byes, they trooped out the door.

Rian stayed a few more minutes, chatting with Dorel and Spence, then said goodnight to both of them and started to leave.

"Spence, why don't you walk Rian out? She's parked on the darker side of the garage," Doral suggested. Spence grabbed his gear out of the foyer closet and gave Dorel a peck on the forehead, then charged after Rian.

She was standing half in the dark beside her Benz, waiting for him. Spence dropped his gear by his bike and strode quickly to her. He grabbed her by the wrists and pushed her backwards, pinning her arms above her head against the garage wall and ground his lips on hers. Her lips parted at his tongue's assault. She moaned and made a weak try at freeing her arms. He loosened his grip just enough for her to escape if she wanted to, but she didn't. She got into it and he could feel the heat from her as she pressed against him. Spence dropped his hands to her shoulders and slid them to her breasts, dipping into the vee, skimming his fingertips over her velvety skin.

"Please, Spence, we can't do this," she protested against

his mouth, dropping her arms to her sides. "You've got to stop."

He couldn't stop. She'd waited for him. Wanted him and now he had her. He pulled her shirt out the waist of her skirt and ran his hands over smooth skin and lace, laying hot kisses down her throat.

"I can't do this," she growled and pushed him away with both hands on his chest.

He stumbled backwards and clamped his hand over his mouth when he saw her. She stood stone still, the garage light illuminating half of her expressionless face that was like a death mask with its grayish skin tones and cold, staring eyes. "I—I'm sorry. I thought you . . ."

"Wanted it?" She held his gaze as she pulled her jacket closed and smoothed the strands of hair back into her ponytail.

"Yeah," he admitted then regretted his honesty. She looked like she was going to kick his ass and he was going to have to let her.

"First, I'm not into wallbangers in the dark with patients. Second, I don't do patients. I'm not that kind of therapist. And third, you are my patient. I am your therapist. It is unethical and illegal for us to engage in any sort sexual relationship while you are in my professional care. And last, you are my patient. No matter how much I'm attracted to you or perchance come to loath you, my attorney, the laws of this state and my malpractice insurance provider will not allow me to bang you or kill you while I am treating you. Do you understand?"

"What if I wasn't your patient? Would you want to go out?" He thought he'd give it a shot, but was ready to dodge the sure to be incoming kick in the crotch just in case.

She buttoned her jacket and smoothed it over her hips. "As your therapist it is my judgement that you need my professional help far more than you need to get laid—those two not being the same thing as you have now discovered." She got in her convertible, started the engine and looked up at him. "Well, what's it going to be? Therapy with an opportunity to feel better and quickly become a former patient with a possible healthy relationship on the horizon or take the former patient option now that includes not a chance in hell of ever getting me in the dark alone again."

"See you next week," he answered and stepped back so she couldn't run over his toes unless she tried real hard.

"Good choice. You win and thank you for playing, Jonathan Spencer. And a good night to you." She backed out to the driveway and screeched away from the house.

Spence climbed on the Harley and watched the Benz's taillights grow fainter. He turned the key and the engine barked a low, throaty roar that vibrated through the bike's body to his still sensitive crotch. He gunned the throttle a couple of times for the pure sensual joy of it. Then he remembered that Marty was sleeping, and idled down the long driveway, feeling more alive than he had in a long time.

Rian keyed in her security code on the pad outside her condo's front door. A message that she'd never seen before flashed on the pad's tiny screen: Visitor granted access.

What in the world could that mean? She let the door swing inward and leaned in, scanning the foyer and what she could see of the living room. From that position, she commanded the system to turn on all lighting.

"Audible review of all system messages."

"One system message logged at 10:32 p.m. Visitor access

104

granted," the Hal-like voice intoned.

Rian backed into the hallway. "State number of occupants in the house now."

"One."

"Identify the occupant," she ordered, her shaking hand reaching to pull the door closed.

"Unknown."

"911 now!" she yelled and slammed the door, but it bounced off the jamb and hung open.

"Unable to establish data link," the system informed her as a man stepped out of the hall into the foyer. Fear screamed *run,* but she scrambled backwards, dropping her briefcase and handbag, and brought her hands up defensively, balancing on the balls of her feet.

"Calm down, Rian. I must say I'm surprised you didn't know I was here."

His voice registered through her panic and she recognized him, dropping her hands slightly. "How did you get past the system?"

"Binary sweet talk, though perhaps you should have a security specialist you trust look at it," he smirked and beckoned her. "Come inside and close the door. Your neighbors are no doubt peeking at you through their peepholes, not that they'd get involved."

Rian glanced up and down the hall, then gathered her things and stepped boldly into her condo. "Set at home conditions." The music came up and several lights went off. At least the wretched system hadn't been entirely compromised, but she would never trust it again.

Ian Stoddard sat in Rian's favorite white leather wingback chair and picked up a Baccarat crystal tumbler on the side table. "To you, my dear." He took a long drink, emptying the glass. "Excellent scotch. I do believe I'll have another. Will you join me?" A smile quirked the corner of his thin lips. His high cheekbones and thin face with a long straight nose underscored by a well-groomed dark beard would make him look wolfish if not for his soft brown eyes.

Rian set her things on the sofa. She took the opened bottle off the top of the liquor cabinet where he'd left it to make a gray ring on the hand-rubbed finish. Pouring him a neat double, she asked, "What are you doing here, Ian?"

"Waiting for you. You haven't reported in for five days. Why?"

She carried the bottle back to the cabinet and put it inside, closing the door. Maybe he'd get the intended message. He knew he shouldn't drink so much. "There isn't anything to report yet."

"Then you're moving too slow. Certain circumstances have come to our attention and we believe that he is more of a threat—to himself and others—than we first thought."

He was scrutinizing her. She strained to keep her physiology and thoughts under control. "I don't agree. He isn't violent or suicidal. He is confused, however, which is affecting his health and functioning. And no wonder under the current strategy, which in my opinion must become less intrusive and return to monitoring now that he is in treatment and motivated."

"We have information that if he goes rogue, and that seems imminent, he's a threat to national security. We want you to step things up."

"Nonsense!" she snapped. "The deprogramming is still intact. He remembers nothing."

Ian set his glass down and leaned forward, his elbows on his knees with his steepled fingers tapping his closed mouth, which conveyed the subliminal order for her to seal her own lips. "Rian, you can trust that this case has top level attention and priority allocation of resources. That's why we assigned our best operative to it—you. You're a scientist. You don't allow your emotions to get in your way. You follow the game plan to the letter. Always. Every time. We respect and appreciate your skills as well as your insights and opinions. You are a consummate professional because you always listen to those with more experience or information than you might have at the time."

"Don't work me, Ian. Just tell me why this has become so huge all of the sudden and why you aren't listening to me, your so-called best operative working in-skin level on this case?"

He let his hands fall to his knees and sat back with a resigned exhale. "Can't do it, Rian. I wasn't blowing smoke when I said the highest levels were interested in this. These are the orders I've got. Now just do it, please? In addition to the anchors in place in his subconscious—metallic sounds, children in danger, swords—there's one more when fired that triggers a certain response we're looking for."

She knew before he said it. "Me."

Ian nodded. "Not you specifically, of course, because you were just coming into the program when he was exiting. His childhood had very much conditioned him to respect and protect women because of his close relationship with his mother, but he doesn't really trust anyone, which you know from his psych profile."

"The protector complex," she added and sat on the edge of the marble coffee table, facing Ian. "He doesn't trust anyone to care for themselves and has an unrealistic belief that he alone is responsible for their protection."

Ian waggled his empty glass at her. "Get me another one, would you, my dear? Where was I? Oh yes, this new anchor. During deprogramming he was conditioned to repress his emotions, which suppressed his ability to remote view as well. We don't want him doing that until we can get him back in and guide him. But if the competitor gets him first, they won't be at all concerned with protecting his health, mental or otherwise."

She refreshed his drink, setting the bottle on the table next to him. "But we don't know if he can bring his skills online again and we trained him. Any other organization wouldn't know how or what to activate, would they?"

Ian's eyes narrowed at her over the rim of his glass. "Perhaps, but we have information that there is a threat to his life and others that I can't discuss because I don't have a need to know—just as you don't. Understand?"

She thought about Spence's episode at the Egyptian trade show that she'd had nothing to do with. Perhaps someone else was remote influencing him, besides herself. "Are there other viewers in Datascape working this?"

"No. Just you. As I said, he's been anchored and conditioned to respond with trust to particular triggers. Most of them you've already been firing, but developing conditions require that you become more . . . directive."

"But he's coming for treatment and responding well," she objected.

"His doing well in treatment hasn't ever been the objective in this reclamation. That must be undertaken inside. If, as a psychologist, you have a problem with this, we'll have to replace you on this case."

"Wow, Ian. That's a first. You've never questioned my loyalty or my application of the process before. Why now?"

"Don't overthink this. Just accept that things have changed. We've got to have him, one way or another, by next week." He picked up the bottle, hovering it over his empty glass, then set it down and grabbed a look at his watch. "I must go." He stood and brushed the wrinkles from his charcoal Brooks Brothers suit. "Do as you must, but by this time next week, if he isn't receptive and compliant, the reclamation team takes it out of your hands. That's how serious this is, Rian."

Her stomach clenched and a chill shinnied down her spine. Why? There was nothing in Spence's file or in the remote viewing she'd done of him to warrant this kind of attention. They'd initially told her that he was being targeted by rogue elements who might be able to breach his deprogramming, and would be very messy about it, jeopardizing Spence, the company and national security. "We've already endangered his fragile mental health. I need time to repair the damage and build an infrastructure that generates trust."

Ian ambled to the door. "He responds to a certain kind of woman. You've portrayed that for him. If you want to continue your work with him now and on the inside, you get him open now, then he will be manageable and you can avoid the team's intervention."

"You're suggesting his base chakra be activated now? That will certainly initiate a chain reaction up the energy centers, but given his current confused state it could blow him wide open. All his memories and abilities will explode into his conscious mind. That's not what I would call manageable. It's dangerous, for him and us."

"Don't mistake this for a suggestion. It's a directive. Remember, keep your shielding fortified and changing or the rogues will be able to trace your energy sig and target you. Of course that means we can't reach you either, but I expect you to report in every day on this nevertheless. Just send a coded fax to me or I'll have to get on a plane and come visit you again, though I always enjoy seeing my favorite protégée," he said with a warm smile.

Rian opened the door for him. "I love seeing you too, Ian, anytime. However, I have to tell you this visit hasn't been terribly wonderful. I'm worried that we're going to do harm here."

He gave her an affectionate hug. "I know, my dear. Sometimes this business is just that, business, and rather grim at that." Ian released her and stepped into the hallway. "Trust me, Rian. All will proceed as it should if we adhere to the process as we always have. That is our protection, and his, too. Spence was once as important to me as you are now. I want the best for all my operatives, regardless if they're active or not. Deprogramming him was best for him at the time and sending you to bring him back in is the best we can do for him again." He patted her shoulder. "And we'll continue to do everything possible to help and protect him, because he's one of us, and we take care of our own."

Hearing her dearest Ian's impassioned reassurance was all she needed to let her concern fade. "All right, I'll do it your way."

"Not *my* way, Rian. It's the process. Only the process," he said with a wry smile and headed for the elevator.

"Night," she called as the doors closed and went back inside her condo, the door locking automatically behind her. Tomorrow she would accelerate the process as ordered and keep telling herself it was the right thing to do.

Chapter Seven

"Spence, there's a woman here to see you," his office assistant Sharon said over the intercom.

The back of his neck started to tingle as a picture of Rian Farsante playing her flute in her hippie getup flashed into his mind. "Who is it?" He heard Rian and said, "Send her in."

His office door opened and Rian, dressed in a long gauzy white skirt and matching over-blouse cinched with a wide black belt sporting a large turquoise and silver buckle, walked in with a paper cup carrier holding two lattes. "Here's the cup of coffee you owe me. That will be $2.50, please."

He dug into his slacks' pocket for his wallet and pulled out a five. "I figured on buying both," he said, grinning, and took one of the cups, tucking the money into the carrier. "If you've got time, I'll show you the best place in town to drink coffee or anything else." He gestured to the bank of windows overlooking Lake Union.

She shook back her dark hair over one shoulder, revealing a long silver beaded earring that threw sparks from the sun streaming into the room, and took a sip. "I think I'd sit at this table all day and stare out the window. It's so beautiful and peaceful . . ." she said and floated into one of the chrome and leather chairs. "I love watching the sea planes take off. They're like birds with huge feet staggering into the air."

"The landings are more interesting," he said, taking a chair on the opposite side of the table. "Getting those birds down in one piece is a little more complicated, especially water landings."

The sparkling clear September day outside the windows had no interest for him at all. Everything beautiful and pure was right here inside, and he couldn't keep himself from staring at her. She tipped her head back and closed her eyes against the brightness, sunning herself with a small contented smile on her sweet lips. "Ummm, this is nice," she murmured.

There was that wonderful Rian smell again. Understated like a whisper but sexy and inviting. Even though he didn't speak and disturb her, Spence's thoughts were anything but calm. Images of a sleek nude woman dancing to the seductive Egyptian music that she played on a flute flashed like a montage on the screen in his head. Her back to him, she undulated away from him, placing her bare feet this way and that. Graceful. Fluid. Step. Step to the rhythm. He followed her, captivated by the music, wishing the woman would turn her face to him as the dangling earring glittered and twinkled in the sunlight.

". . . see you because I want to talk with you about moving up your appointment," he heard her say. Spence shook his head and massaged the frown away with his fingertips. She stared at him. "Did you hear me?"

"Yeah, sure." What the hell had she said? It was as if he'd been somewhere else with her. The woman in his daydream, or whatever that was, was right here, fully clothed and so was he, which was a disappointing wakeup.

"Great. If you could spare a couple of hours, we could get a lot done here in this beautiful, warm spot. Or we can go back to my office and do it. Whichever works for you."

Confusion rolling in like a fogbank, he set the coffee

down and stood. "I—I'm not sure. I mean, maybe here isn't a good idea."

She stayed where she was, her smile beguiling. "You can tell your OA not to disturb us and lock the door, if you want to do it, and you do, right?"

Hell yes, he wanted to do it. Wanted to do her right here, right now. Spence walked to the outer office and instructed his surprised OA not to disturb them, then returned and locked his office door. When he turned around Rian was moving stacks of papers off the sofa.

"This looks comfy. Shall I use it or do you want to?" she asked with a twinkle in her eyes then broke into a laugh. "Go ahead and get comfortable, Spence. I'll sit in the chair."

Spence hesitated. This was moving too fast. He wasn't sure what was going on or what to expect. Couldn't even be sure of where he was. He glanced around the familiar seeming room, but couldn't connect with anything. Not even with hands that appeared to be his own held in front of him, which he examined with a detachment that suggested an echo of some distant thought or sound.

"Spence?" lilted across the space between them.

He followed the sound and lay down, waiting for her to come to him.

"Spence, just allow your eyes to close. That's right. Settle into the sofa. Feel it firmly yet comfortably supporting your back, your hips and your legs as you relax and just sink. Down. Down. Deeper and deeper into relaxation," she whispered, enticing, seducing him.

He felt his limbs getting heavy, sinking into the sofa. Her enchanting silken tones encouraged him to go back, way back in time. He drifted along, snatches of images, sounds and sensations swirling around him.

"Where are you? Bring everything into focus. Clearly into focus."

As if he were looking through a focusing camera lens . . . *he sat in a smoke-filled Ready Room on the 04 level, scribbling on a pilot's clipboard while the Carrier Air Group Commander briefed the pilots on the mission. An elbow hit his ribs. He turned to the khaki-clad Navy officer with curly blond hair beside him who murmured, "You're it, Romeo! You owe me five bucks."*

"Shut up, Ev," he hissed out of the side of his mouth, keeping his eyes on the CAG.

"Where are you?" Rian asked from far away.

Spence wanted to hear what the Carrier Air Group Commander was saying. After she asked him again, he said, "Carrier."

"You're on a carrier. What are you doing?"

"We're in the Ready Room getting ready for a mission."

"What year is it? Just the first thought that comes."

" '45. August. The Japs have surrendered."

"You can know your name. Tell me your name," Spence heard Rian say.

"Paul. Or Romeo, maybe. Ev calls me Romeo."

"Is that your name?"

He listened to the CAG then thought a minute. "Um, no. Rom—romeo. Romero. My name is Paul Romero. Lieutenant."

"What do you do, Lieutenant?"

He pulled his leather helmet on and climbed into the cockpit of a Dauntless Dive Bomber. Ev boosted a portable radio in first, then settled into the gunner's seat behind him. The Yellow Shirt airplane handler signaled him to crank his engine. The engine pulled through about nine blades and then sputtered to life with a cloud of gray oil smoke.

"If there are others in the past scene with you, do you

114

recognize them as someone in Spence's life now?"

Tears stung behind his eyelids and he dabbed at the corners of his eyes with the back of his bandaged hand. "Yeah, Ev," he said with a happy smile. "God, it's great to see him."

"Is Ev someone you recognize from Spence's life today?"

"Sure. Marty, of course. Mike's boy," he disclosed, wanting her to shut up so he could talk with Ev.

"Come on, Romeo, I don't know what my sister sees in you, but kiss her good-bye and let's get this overweight pig in the air," Ev said over the intercom while the radioman was hooking them up.

He pulled the snapshot out of his shirt pocket and put her beloved picture to his lips.

"You're going to wear a hole in that thing. I don't want to fly with you when you do, because all your luck will leak out," Ev complained.

"You OSS guys are all CS." Paul tucked the photo back in his shirt, watching the boatswain's mate signal break set. The carrier was turned into the wind with thirty-five knots of wind coming directly into the face of the airplane. The Yellow Shirt stood legs spread off the right wing, holding his arm high, rotating it, signaling him to bring the engine up to take-off power. After a few seconds of the airplane vibrating and jerking with the prop's pull, the Yellow Shirt opened his left hand. Paul released the brakes. The Yellow Shirt leaned into the wind, knelt and pointed down the deck.

"Do you and Ev fly together?" Rian's voice interrupted.

"Yeah, sometimes. I've run insertions before," Spence answered, bracing himself as the airplane hurtled down the deck, off the end and settling a moment toward the water as it increased airspeed and developed lift.

"Where are you flying today?" Rian asked.

"China." In an instant Spence experienced the entire memory as a massive holographic download.

Ev, sitting with his back to the pilot's seat, pulled the canopy open. Paul rolled the airplane inverted at 2000 feet above the insertion point. Ev released his harness and dropped free of the inverted airplane, the radio attached to him on an umbilical, and popped his chute. Paul dropped the airplane down to low level to mask the insertion point, then turned for home. Anti-aircraft fire shot up all around him with strings of tracers zipping past the airplane. He flew low and fast trying to evade through the treetops, then out over the sea, so close to the water the plane was leaving a wake. He never saw the patrol boat fire its 37mm anti-aircraft gun. The round hit the center of the radial engine just below the prop hub, breaking the lower engine mounts and buckling the engine underneath the airplane. The SBD pitched up into a full stall. "Oh God!"

"What is it, Lieutenant?"

"I've been hit. We're going in. Got to see Meredith. Want her to be the last thing I see. I've got her picture in my hands as I fight the airplane. It's going wing over into the water." Spence's heart raced and his breathing came in panicking gasps.

"Just hover above the scene. That's right. It's only a memory. Observe it as if you're watching an interesting movie. Keeping your breathing easy and regular. Holding on to your deep state of relaxation, feeling safe, secure and relaxed. Observing like a reporter," Rian said in a rhythmic, almost emotionless voice.

Spence took a deep breath and pulled himself above the scene as she suggested and reported, "The crash takes off the canopy. Breaks my legs. Oh God, I'm drowning in this son of a bitch. Meredith!"

"Calm. Relaxed. Let yourself hover above the scene.

That's right. Now, do you recognize Meredith as someone in Spence's life today?"

It was her eyes. He'd known from the moment he'd seen the photo. Recognized her immediately even though they looked so different, then and now. He couldn't let himself tell her. "No."

"Are you ready to make the transition?"

His breathing calmed as a floating sensation replaced the pain. Spence nodded.

"That's right. Leave that life, that body behind. Free from pain. Free from fear. As you float into the light you can look back and know what that life was about. There were lessons to learn. Allow all the negative emotions and energy from that lifetime to just twinkle away as you ascend into the light. That's right, let all the negative energy go. Freeing you. Opening you to the positive learning of that life. Only positive learning is carried into the light. Let everything else go. Allow the emotions, let the feelings come, beginning to bubble up gently like a fine champagne, full of taste and delicious enjoyment. Freeing you from the prison of your past unhappiness. That's right. If you are met in the light, allow yourself to bask in the eternal love and heal the soul wounds. I will be silent for a few moments so that you can do that."

Rian struggled to calm herself. Her psychic connection with Spence had strengthened to the point that she saw in her mind's eye what he did in trance before he even spoke. He'd told her only a small portion of what he experienced in the regression. But she'd felt his joy meeting Ev again and his excitement at the mission briefing, could even smell the fuel on the carrier deck as he prepared to launch. When he kissed the precious photo, Rian wept at the love tingling over her skin and flowing into her heart.

She had long ago been trained to use photos in her remote viewing, but had never experienced anything as intense and true as this. As a trainee wired to a machine that registered the bioelectric current generated by all living things, she learned to perceive the energy that her skin was recording when someone viewed a photograph of her and later targeted her psychically. She hadn't needed to ask Spence if he recognized Meredith from someone in his life today, but wanted to know if he would admit it. He didn't. And that didn't matter because Spence's memory had opened her to her past life of love and loss as Meredith Everly, younger sister of Martin Everly and fiancée of his best friend, Paul Romero.

Rian longed to be alone to process this life and reconcile the memories, but she had to complete the session with Spence, formerly Paul, the man Meredith would never see again. She loved Paul so much that she couldn't think of life without him. A Navy nurse serving in the South Pacific, she'd grabbed a ride on a plane being ferried back to the States after the war. It crashed, killing all aboard. As Meredith rose into the light, Paul was waiting for her. She was embraced by the arms of eternal love again.

Rian swallowed tears and cleared her throat, the ache in her heart palpable. Would she ever feel or give that pure love again? She gazed through tears at the man she'd once loved more than life itself. "Spence, it's time to come back. I'm going to count from one to five." She counted him up, giving him suggestions to remember more and more of his past life as Paul Romero, to open to his emotions and to incorporate the positive learning from that life in his today.

Spence blinked open his eyes and swiped at the wetness on his cheeks. He stretched and sat up, swinging his feet to the floor. He wouldn't meet her gaze, looking at his hands in his lap.

"Would you like a drink of water? Remember, you must keep hydrated when doing work of this . . ." Her voice drifted off as he leveled a sharp squint on her, his mouth a thin line of anger.

"What the hell was that? Why did you make me see that?" he growled, looking like he was about to beat the hell out of someone.

Stunned at the force of his fury, she sat back, her muscles tightening with fight or flight hormones pumping through her body. "Spence, it doesn't work like that. These are memories from your subconscious. I am very careful not to suggest or lead—"

"That crap can't be real or from my subconscious. You're the hypnotist. You made me see it." He rocketed to his feet, scowling down at her. "Why are you screwing with me like this?"

"I'm not," she assured, holding his gaze. "You know what you felt. Trust your feelings. That's the important thing in this—your emotions. Releasing the blocked energy of the negative emotions that keep you from feeling well and living the life you want. Whether you can prove there was a pilot named Paul Romero who died in the war isn't important. You might think of your experience as symbols and metaphors of your subconscious which have meaning for you. Consider what it all means and how that meaning can help you in your life today. That's the objective of this work—to let go of what isn't working so that you feel and perform better."

"I—he loved *you*," Spence murmured, his eyes glittering with sadness.

"I know."

Spence was agitated, deep and unrelenting. After Rian left he sat shaking on the sofa, his nerves on the edge of meltdown. She'd tried to talk to him afterwards and gave him some crap about the great advances they'd made today and how he was going to feel much better.

He didn't. The top of his head was about to blow off. He was using all his strength to keep it on and cram the agonizing feelings back down into the black hole. He gritted his teeth against the pain threatening to crush his skull from the inside and dragged himself to his desk, searching for the pills he then realized were upstairs in the medicine cabinet.

Staggering to the outer office and unable to answer Sharon when she spoke, he stumbled into the elevator. The chime sounding as the door slid open to the living room was like a hammer on the steel of his brain and he almost passed out. Clawing his way up the stairs, he made it to the bathroom's doorway before he crumpled to the hardwood floor as heat boiled up from the base of his spine and exploded out the top of his head in a roaring collage of color and sensation.

Time stopped for Paul as he gazed at Meredith's picture even as his wounded airplane wing-overed toward the water. Something had torn a hole in the photo right through her heart, and he now realized through his own chest. Like Ev said, his luck was leaking out—spreading red across his shirt. The Dauntless cart-wheeled across the light chop in the Sea of Japan, slicing into the cold water. Hovering a moment on the surface as the cockpit flooded, the bomber made its last dive toward the bottom.

Spence came to, sputtering for air. His lungs stalled in his chest and his heart cavitated, unable to pump against the paralyzing pain of loss. He rolled to his side, curling into a fetal position and willed himself to breathe as he tried to remember anything real and true.

"Uncle Spence, come play with me," he heard Marty's little voice whisper and opened his eyes, sucking ragged breath. He flopped onto his back and made himself breathe deeply. His cell phone vibrated against his waist and he groped for it.

"Yeah, hello?" he panted into the tiny phone and struggled to sit up.

"Hey, Spence, what's going on? You sound weird," Mike Gabrielli's voice came through loud and clear. "Did I interrupt something real good?"

"Yeah, and it wasn't so good." Spence rested his throbbing head in his bandaged hand and wondered how much to tell Mike. A silent warning wove its way through the banging in his head: *say nothing*. "What's up? You still in Singapore?"

"Yes. I just got a call from our attorney. The airline wants to close on this Miami airplane sooner. They're proposing a discount for early closing. They're hurting for cash."

Spence tried to focus. "Uh, is Avion's take-back team finished with the airplane audit review?"

"It's going really well and they anticipate being done by the weekend. We could do a formal review on Monday to close Tuesday. If that's going well, we'll have our attorney preposition the money on Monday. Will you be ready to commercial out to Miami on Sunday?"

Spence's mind began to run their leasing company's checklist of airplane acquisition procedures. "Yeah, I'll get everything squared away on my end." A flashback to the broken SBD flooding and dragging him to the bottom freeze-framed on the life-size screen in his mind. He heard himself gasp.

"Spence? You okay?" Mike asked, concern riding his voice.

"Yeah, yeah, I'm good. Hey, stay with me, Mike. Let's make sure JET puts an over water survival kit on that airplane, okay?"

There was a moment of silence, then Mike answered, "We don't have to have one to ferry to San Antonio—"

"You do if I'm going to fly over more than a thimble full of water," Spence objected, feeling a chill snake into his belly.

"Since when? That's a ten thousand dollar expense we don't need."

Mike's surprise jarred Spence out of the past, but he couldn't shake the illogical compulsion to make sure the kit was loaded on that airplane. "So, charge it to me. I don't want to talk about it right now."

"Okay, you got it. See you Thursday," Mike said and hung up.

Spence hauled himself to his feet, leaning on the doorjamb. Rian said he would feel better. Just when was that supposed to happen? He tossed his phone on the counter then dug through the medicine chest. Finding the pill bottle, he flipped off the unfastened cap and swept it into the trash. He stared down the tube in his trembling hand at the two remaining blue tablets.

The blue intensified and blurred . . .

Meredith's sea blue eyes twinkled as she laughed at him. "Paul! Take the picture, will you? The sand's too hot. My feet are burning."

"Hold it! Perfect!" He pushed the button on her little Kodak and wound the film forward, watching her dash to the water's edge, splashing ankle-deep in the surf. Her filmy white and black polka dot dress clung to her wet legs as she gam-

boled in the incoming waves.

"Come on, Paul. It's wonderful. You'll feel great, trust me."
Meredith threw him a kiss. He set the camera on their shoes sit-
ting side by side on the white sand and ran after her. He caught
her slim body around the shoulders and turned her to face him.
Rian looked love up at him and whispered, "You're
feeling better, Spence. Trust me."

Spence shuddered and his eyelids fluttered at the image
in the mirror. He wanted to smash his head into the haggard face that wasn't his. He dumped both pills in his
mouth, chasing them with a handful of tap water. The pills
stuck in his throat. He choked and coughed them into the
sink, watching the tablets spiral down the drain.

He was still sitting on the edge of the tub, head in hands,
when he heard the elevator chime and the door slide open.

"Spence?" Sharon called. "Are you here?"

"Yeah, just a minute," he answered and smoothed his
hand over his moustache. He stood, tucked his shirt in and
brushed his khakis off then went downstairs, adjusting his
expression to one that wouldn't make her freak.

"The Datascape people are here for your three o'clock.
Hey, have you done something to your hand again? Better
let me look at it."

He looked with surprise at the pinkish stain on the bandage. "I'll take care of it. Tell them I'll be right there."

Sharon shrugged and left, shaking her head. Spence hurried upstairs and unwound the bandage into the bathroom
sink. The two-inch diagonal slice across the heel of his hand
was red and zigzagged with stitches, but not bleeding. He
taped a gauze square over the wound and gingerly flexed his
fingers. Still tender, but healing despite the misuse. As he
stepped into the elevator he realized that the crushing head-
ache was gone and that he did feel much better.

Throughout the hour long meeting with the Datascape marketing team, Spence's thoughts drifted to Meredith as more memory fragments sifted into his consciousness from somewhere. Soon, Rian's face superimposed itself over Meredith's in each fleeting glimpse of the past life they'd shared.

"Spence, good to see that you're doing okay after that nasty accident at the convention center," Nick Brooks said as the four Datascape management heavies gathered their papers at the end of the meeting. "What the heck happened?"

He let his hand fall to his side as he stood. "I slipped or tripped on a cable. Fell into a case. Probably one of your guys left it there on purpose, trying to make me look bad. It worked," he joked and moved with the other three toward the door. They each shook Spence's offered left hand and left. Nick lagged behind.

"The show's promoters and Datascape want me to give you their best wishes greased with a little forgiveness incentive. Between you and me, I think they're scared you're going to sue the hell out of them. Don't know what this is, but they thought you'd like it," he said, handing Spence a chamois-wrapped, two feet long parcel.

Spence stood staring at the heavy package in his open hands long after Nick left. He didn't have to open it. He knew what it was—the hooked tool he'd tried to break out of its glass case. They knew he'd tried to steal it. How? And why did they give it to him now? It was valuable, ancient, older than anyone thought, and not what they believed it was. What the metal tool really was, he wasn't sure, but he had once known, if not used it.

He shook that stupid thought out of his head. The only thing familiar about the hooked tool was the inscribing on the long shaft. He started to unwrap the piece, excited to inspect the markings up close, but stopped. Dorel should see this. Would she remember if they were the same as those that were on her sword? Spence laid the package on the conference table and dialed the Gabrielli home number.

Dorel answered and laughed at his cryptic explanation of why he wanted to come to the house. "Don't be silly. You know you can come out anytime you want. Besides, Marty said he's been calling you and that you were coming this afternoon."

Spence told her he'd bring teriyaki takeout for dinner. An hour later he parked the Integrity van in the Gabrielli driveway. Marty opened the front door. The dog busted past him in a black and tan streak to jump on Spence who held the bag of food above his head. "Get off, Katana!"

The dog dropped his big front paws off Spence's chest and backed off a step or two, plopping his butt down on Marty's feet. Dorel grabbed the dog's collar and hauled him up, giving him a push toward the house. "Come on in, Spence."

As they took the food out of the bags in the kitchen, Spence and Dorel discussed business and the airline's intention to close on the sale of the airplane early. An aeronautical engineer, Dorel directed all the freighter conversion engineering modifications of the former airliners their company purchased and leased to cargo carriers. She agreed the bonus was worth having to change arrangements and reschedule their acquisition of the airplane.

"Marty, would you please set out the napkins and place mats?" she asked the little boy hovering at Spence's elbow, trying to tug him away to his room to play. Dorel related to Spence that they'd have to pay storage fees to park the 747 until the mod center could get the airplane in the line in its pre-assigned order. "And Mike says you now want to rent an over water survival kit or you won't fly." She took two filled plates to the table, leaving Spence's for him and calling over her shoulder, "While we eat maybe you'll tell me why." Dorel set Marty's plate before him and sat down.

"Uncle Spence doesn't wanna get drowned again, Momma," Marty explained and lifted a clump of steamed rice with his chopsticks to his mouth, chewing. "I love rice."

Dorel frowned at Marty then looked at Spence. "What do you mean, Marty?"

"When he was big before he crashed his airplane in the water." He took a drink of milk and pooched his white-rimmed lips at his mother. "See, I have a mushstash like Uncle Spence."

Spence was crashing in a full-blown flashback when Dorel put her hand on his shoulder, drawing him into the present. "Spence, are you okay?"

He managed to nod, hanging onto right now by fixing his eyes on the little boy beside him, but the child's face was overlayed by another's. "Ev . . . ?"

"Momma, you need to tell him it's okay. He can believe it now," Marty said to her then winked with both eyes at Spence and continued to stuff rice into his mouth.

Dorel's face reddened and she sat back, laying her chopsticks on the side of her plate. Spence tried to swallow but his throat was dry. He stared at Marty then raised his eyes to meet Dorel's gaze. "Believe what?"

Chapter Eight

"Long ago, at the end of the war my grandfather, who Marty is named after, was on a secret mission for the military," Dorel explained. "He was dropped into northern China by his best friend, a Navy pilot named—"

"Romeo," Marty interjected with a giggle and sneaked a piece of chicken to Katana sitting between Spence and him.

"—Paul Romero who was engaged to my grandfather's sister Meredith. Paul was shot down over the China Sea after he'd delivered my grandfather to the drop point. The sad thing is that Meredith didn't learn of Paul's death before she was killed in a plane being ferried back to Honolulu where she and Paul planned to marry . . ." Dorel's voice dwindled. An expression of shocked awareness claimed her features as she scrutinized Spence. He tried to control himself, but his face betrayed him. "Oh my God, it's you!"

Spence shook his head. "No. You're wrong. Not me. She's done this. Not me," he yelled over the roaring in his ears and grabbed the table's edge, anchoring himself in his seat.

Marty put his warm little hand on Spence's clammy one clamped on the table. "You have to remember now. It's time. I need your help again because they're coming to get us." He slid off the chair. "I'm going to go play *Everlasting Warriors* now. You can play too when you're ready 'cause the sword is so cool."

Spence and Dorel watched Marty skip out of the room then turned to each other in bewildered silence. "You first," he said.

Dorel took a deep breath. "I told you once that I believe Marty is the reincarnation of my grandfather Martin Everly. You didn't believe it then, but am I mistaken to think that you might be more open to the idea now? What's happened?"

"It's got to be some sort of weird hallucination or maybe a kind of brainwashing. It started during a session I had today with Rian. She regressed me and I saw the whole thing like I was there. The crash, Ev—"

"Ev?"

"Yeah, your grandfather, I guess. Only I called him Ev. He nicknamed me Romeo when he and I were competing for Navy nurses in Honolulu. I was more of a player than he was, until I met his sister . . ." Spence stopped. Where the hell did that come from? Did he just make up what seemed as real as his own hand still clutching the table's edge?

"You experienced all this in a past life regression? With Rian today?" Dorel asked with a frown.

"Yeah. Crazy, huh?" He made himself release the table and sit back.

"No. Tell me more."

Spence laid it all out in as much detail as he could remember because she was so open and interested. And understanding. With the telling he could almost believe it was real, too, especially when he told Dorel about her Aunt Meredith. He didn't reveal that Rian was . . . what? Meredith in a past life? No one would believe that.

Rian does, reverberated through him. He shifted in his chair. "I don't know what to make of the whole deal other than I'm crazy."

Dorel wiped her eyes with her napkin and sniffed. "How can you even question the veracity of such a wonderful experience, Spence? Look what it's given you and us—a soul connection. We've always known that you must have been with us in lives past, even though we haven't seen you."

He groaned. "You and Mike believe this? You've done this past life regression stuff, too?"

"No . . ." She raked her top lip with her teeth and sighed. "How to explain this? Remember when I brought my grandfather's sword to your table at the gun show? You introduced me to Michael and from that moment we reconnected. I began to have visions or spontaneous regressions where I was a Japanese woman in China at the end of World War II. Michael was my husband in that life and was killed. I took the sword to Martin Everly and told him to save it for his granddaughter. Me, Dorel." She frowned and wrinkled her nose. "I know this is convoluted, but stick with me."

Spence shrugged. "Yeah, go ahead."

"When my grandfather died I received the sword as a legacy, but I didn't have any money so tried to sell it to you. But Michael had already targeted me and my sword at the gun show and showed up. That's when all the trouble began."

"Oh yeah," he said and rubbed his nose. "What do you mean by *targeted you?*"

"With remote viewing. He found me and was also able to perceive when Inada's men were coming for us. The problem was the sword wasn't just an antique, Spence. It seemed to have powers of some sort over Michael. At least he, and Inada, thought so. Michael and I had many lives together with that sword. We were bound to the sword in some sort of eternal trust where Michael was the Defender wielding the sword and I was the Guardian of it. At the end of each life I somehow knew what my next incarnation was to be. I made sure the sword would pass to myself to guard for Michael when we'd meet in the next life.

"But in this life I fought the eternal trust. After the trust nearly got us killed several times as well as you, I persuaded Michael to give up the power. That's when we asked you to cut up the sword, because as long as it was whole and could be used, it would have power over him. So I guess the very roundabout answer to your question of do we believe in past lives, the answer is yes."

The back of his neck tingled and itched and he felt like someone was watching them. He glanced over his shoulder toward the living room but saw no one. "Speaking of the sword, I've got something to show you." He went to the foyer and grabbed the wrapped parcel off the table. When he returned to the dining room Dorel was beginning to stack the dishes.

Spence unwrapped the tool and it rolled out on the table. Dorel stopped, set the plate down she was scraping and tucked her red hair behind her ears. "What's that?"

"I think it's a tool to straighten a warped sword after forging. Take a look at this." He traced his fingers over the inscribing on the smooth metal.

She bent over the tool, her hands behind her back as if she were afraid to touch it. "What does it say?"

"I haven't had the time to work it out yet." He wrapped his left hand around the lower end of the shaft. Fire shot up his arm like a thousand volts. The screen in his head went hyperdrive with images and sounds that melded into a swirling miasma. Clanging of metal on metal pierced the cacophony and close-focused a single image in his mind's eye. A bald man, naked from the waist, glistening with sweat as his well-muscled arm touched the hooked tool to a long strip of metal creating an explosion of white sparks.

A disembodied voice he'd heard in his dreams boomed:

Return to the Forge of Balance
Swords clash and blood mixes
Minds meld and both become whole
Eternal power shall be reforged

Spence dropped the hooked tool burning the image into his mind. It banged off the table's edge and fell on the floor. Dorel moved to pick it up, but he stopped her. "You don't want to touch that."

"Why?"

He rubbed his burning eyes. "This is messed up, but I think I heard what those symbols mean." And he told her.

"That's sort of the way we heard, well, what we thought was the sword speaking to us. But what this is or means, I don't know. I'll tell you I don't like this one bit. Not at all," she said and wrapped her arms around herself, backing away to the other end of the table.

"What happened to the sword after I cut it up?" Mike wouldn't answer, but maybe, after what had just happened, she would tell him.

"It disappeared."

"Did someone steal it?" He moved toward her, but she kept moving away from him, her eyes huge and frightened.

She shook her head. "Spence, I can't tell you. Michael and I promised each other we'd never tell—"

"Guardian took him home after Daddy came back," Marty's little voice trilled behind Spence.

"Go back to your room, Marty. Do it!" Dorel shrilled and snatched the stack of plates as she shooed the boy through the kitchen.

Spence followed, listening to Marty protest all the way to his room. "He's got to know, Momma. It's time. They're coming. He's got to know!"

He met Dorel in the hall. "I've got to know what?"

She pulled Marty's door closed, brushed by him to the foyer and stood waiting in the middle of the living room where he caught up with her. "I don't understand how Marty does it, but as you know he's had this *ability* since he was born. But he's also a five-year-old child. So sometimes it's difficult to tell the difference between his child's imagination or something else. In this case, it's very clear to me that it's not kids' stuff. He says you've got to know, and I'm going to tell you. Sit down and try to listen with an open mind."

When he sat on the sofa, she paced a moment, then began. "After you cut up the sword, Michael put the pieces in the scabbard and laid it in the back of the drawer there in the bookcase with his others and everything was wonderful. Then one night when we came home Inada was waiting for us. He killed Michael and made me give him the sword—"

"You mean he wounded Mike." Spence leaned forward, trying to make sense of her jumbled story.

"No! He killed him. Michael was dead, I tell you. After Inada left I went to find his body, but it was gone. I thought Inada had stolen it."

"Inada took the sword and Michael's body?"

"No, neither. Inada just left as if he was compelled by . . . a higher power. At dawn I saw Michael on the deck. He was absolutely unharmed and he told me that he had indeed died. Gone to the other side but was given the choice to come back. He did and changed . . . everything. The past. The present. At that moment the sword appeared to us whole, in one piece, then disappeared in a flash of light with that voice saying it wasn't ours to destroy and it would pass to another." She gazed into his eyes. "Please, believe me, Spence. That's what happened. We promised each other that we wouldn't talk about it to anyone and neither of us would invite visions or remote view or even read our horoscopes. We just didn't want to start all that up again, you know? Then comes Marty, remembering everything from his former lives and with incredible prescient ability and here we go again," she said, holding her head.

Spence sat back, his mind tumbling the bits and pieces of memories, events, Mike and Dorel's revelations, Marty's warnings and Rian's actions, knocking off the jagged, ill-fitting edges and forming a smoother, almost polished whole concept that must have shown on his face.

"Gentlemen, we have cognition," Dorel proclaimed, gauging him. "You may still have doubts and really hate the idea of all this, but I think you believe or at least understand now, don't you?"

He nodded slowly. "Yeah, maybe. What I don't get is where the sword went when it *vanished,* which had to be some kind of mass hallucination. But projected by whom?"

"Oh, it was no hallucination," she countered. "When Michael and I broke the trust, we thought we destroyed our connection to the sword. Did you hear Marty say the Guardian took it home? There must be another poor couple bound by the trust," she said with a shiver.

"He's just a little kid and getting it mixed up with that game he's been trying to get me to play with him—"

"*Everlasting Warriors?* Spence, that game is about a magical sword that gives warriors vast powers. Do you see any parallels here? It may seem that Marty mixes things up, but if you listen to him."

"I know." His gut tightened and the back of his neck began to tingle. "Where'd he get the game?"

"It's a beta copy from that marketing research company that came to Marty's playgroup a couple of years ago. We checked them out and allowed them to send the kids all kinds of toys that we parents have the option of returning if we don't approve or let the kids play with and evaluate. In return, the kids keep the toys they like and the company donates to our chosen charities in our playgroup's name."

"That company wouldn't also sponsor the soccer team, too, would it?" He didn't know why this was important, but a connection of some sort was taking shape, casting a tepid light into the black hole in his memory.

Dorel's forehead creased with a frown. "Yes, but so do a lot of other businesses. I'm afraid our little team is a good bit more well-heeled than other teams in the south county league. Most of the parents own their own businesses and put their money behind their kids," she said, crossing her arms. "Why?"

"Don't know. Just wondered. There seem to be a lot of coincidences lately." He gestured to the hooked tool on the floor. "I tried to rip that off a couple of days ago. I don't even remember the details or when I cut my hand or why I wanted it, other than the markings seemed to be the same as those on your sword. Then this afternoon the people I tried to steal it from gave it to me. And what's more it came through my biggest account that Mike says we used to work for as some sort of psychic spies, but I guess you know about that?"

She didn't look like she did. "We don't talk about that time in his life because it's connected with things that we don't want to open ourselves up to again."

"Understandable." He got up and walked to the tool on the floor. Taking the chamois off the table, he used it to pick up the tool and rewrapped it, rolling it on his thigh. There were no sensations. No noise. No pictures. Just the weight of the metal piece in his hands. "I'm going to go say good-bye to Marty." Dorel nodded and returned to the kitchen. He walked down the hall to the boy's bedroom.

"Hey, M-Man," he greeted from the doorway. "Want to see what I got today?"

Marty turned in his chair in front of the computer monitor and grinned at him. "You got it back?"

Spence smiled wryly. "Do you know what this is?" He held out the wrapped package.

Marty nodded and returned to playing the computer game. Spence stepped into the room, ducking around the fleet of model airplanes suspended from the ceiling and stepping over toys and books to the computer center spanning the entire wall. He stood behind the chair and watched over Marty's head. Grunts and groans accompanied clanging steel as the armor-clad warriors fought across the screen. "Which one are you?"

Marty moved the mouse and punched keys at the same time, making the figure slash and deftly parry his opponent's advances. "The Defender. His *katana* is like Momma's, huh?"

Spence leaned over Marty, squinting at the samurai sword on the screen. His knees buckled. He grabbed the chair's back to steady himself. "Stop! Marty, stop the action. I want to see that sword."

"You can see it better in the armory," the boy said and switched screens.

The view changed to a dimly lit cavern with lit torches stuck into holes in the stone walls. In the center of the cavern was a large rectangular brick box. On top of the box lay a sword in a carved spiral scabbard.

"Can you zoom in on the sword?" Spence asked.

Marty zoomed the view and Spence clearly saw Dorel's sword or a precise copy from the black lacquer spiral scabbard to the plain rectangular gray hilt with a red silk cord running though a small hole to the woven handle. "Can you take the scabbard off?"

The boy punched in a new screen. The samurai sword's naked blade gleamed in the meager light, but the markings on the steel were clear enough. Spence clawed the wrap off the tool, careful not to hold it in his bare hand and held the inscription side close to the monitor.

The markings on both were the same. Spence wheezed. This time his rubbery knees gave way and he fell on his butt, letting the tool go.

Marty laughed. "This is a fun game!" He climbed off his chair and picked up the hooked tool, wrapping the chamois around it. "Here's your key, Uncle Spence. Better guard it from the evil warriors."

Spence ignored it and rolled to his feet. "M-Man, in the game is there a glossary or something to tell you what those markings mean?" He pointed to the sword on the screen.

The boy shook his head. "But I know." He set the package on the desk and got back in his chair, clicking to the fighting scene again.

Spence waited the few seconds he could for him to answer, then urged, "Can you tell me?"

Marty paused the game and looked up at Spence tolerantly. "You know. When you held the key and heard the voice, remember?"

Hell, he could barely remember his own name. "Why do you keep calling the hooked tool a key? Isn't it for straightening warped swords?"

Marty grinned. "Uh huh. And getting things, too."

Frustrated, Spence bent and hit the back key to the armory screen and the sword. "Do the markings on the tool and the sword say the same thing? Or maybe the tool is some sort of key to the inscription on the sword?"

Marty yawned, rubbed his eyes and frowned petulantly at Spence. "I'm tired of this game. You don't play right, 'cause you won't listen."

Spence took a deep breath and backed off. "Okay, M-Man, I'm sorry. Can I see the box the game came in?"

"Very good, Uncle Spence." Marty flashed him a thumbs-up and pulled a box off the hutch's shelf. "But it doesn't tell you how to win the game. You have to remember."

"All I want to know is who made the game and how they got an exact replica of the sword." He turned the empty box in his hands, searching the small print for the developer's name and website.

Mary giggled. "That's good, too, but you won't find them that way."

Spence wanted to pitch the box across the room. "Oh yeah? Why not?"

"I already told you," Marty complained, then rocking his little red head, recited in a bored sing-song voice, "Because they found you first."

"Okay, they found me. So, what do *they* want?" Could the boy know? Oh yes. Marty had the power.

"You. You gotta go see Coach again. Besides, you want to," Marty said with a sly smile. "And she wants to see you."

"Marty, what does my seeing Rian have to do with these guys that you say are coming after me?" He picked up the tool and waited for an answer while Marty stared into space.

"They can hide what they're doing. When Daddy teaches you again, you can hide from them. Rian will help." Marty yawned again and scrubbed his little hand through his curly red hair.

137

Spence caught him up in the crook of his arm and blew raspberry kisses against his neck while Marty giggled and ducked his head. "I'm headed home. Anything I should watch out for on the way?" he asked and set the boy down.

Marty followed him down the hall. "Traffic's okay. Tell Coach hi from me." Dorel joined them in the foyer.

"I won't see her, M-Man. I'm going home," Spence said, and kissed Dorel's cheek. "Don't worry. We'll get this all straightened out when Mike gets home."

She nodded, but looked worried. Spence wondered if he should leave them alone with Mike out of town.

"Go on, Uncle Spence. We'll be okay," Marty said and gave him a little kid-sized push on his lower back.

"Bye, guys. Call me straight up if you need me. I'll be checking on you." Spence tossed the wrapped tool into the back of the van and climbed in the driver's seat, waving out the window as he drove away.

Rian eased out of her meditation position on the yoga mat. She stretched her arms over her head and brought them down with her palms meeting at her breast, then came up on her knees and blew out the single candle on the twelve-inch high table in front of her. Her body had spent the last three hours in this serene, if a bit austere, cedar floored meditation room at home, while she cast the energy of her consciousness out into the ether, targeting Spence.

Not only was she able to trace his energy and follow him to the Gabrielli home in the hours before, she was able to discern his feelings, listen to the conversation, even smell the Japanese food he shared with Dorel and Marty. At one point she was certain that Spence was aware of her energy, but she fortified her thought form shield, and he was left thinking he'd only imagined that someone was watching him.

No one had ever been able to breach her shield, and any target or viewer saw or felt only what she wanted them to.

Datascape had taught her that nothing—people, emotions, concepts or things—could be shielded by time or space from a remote viewer, though the company worked to develop functional and reliable electromagnetic energy shield technology. Until then, Datascape viewers learned to conduct their lives as if they were being videotaped twenty-four seven. They chronically monitored their thoughts, focusing on a favorite benign memory or reciting the times tables if their minds strayed into classified territory. That passive technique had bored Rian to death. Her keen musician's mind was too creative and active. She modified and expanded upon an old dowser's trick she learned from the mother of her foster parents. The old woman was an Eastern Washington ranch wife who made extra money water witching and was known as something of a *bruja* or witch herself. Elena continued to grandmother her long after she'd been moved to other foster care.

"Thought forms, Ana. Pure illusion, but people see or hear 'em just the same. You're creating a mental image that people can perceive then you can control 'em," Elena had said the first time she went dowsing with her.

As they walked across the harrowed field, Elena held her L-shaped dowsing rods out in front of her squat, chubby body, chatting along, instructing the young girl on arcane secrets of her trade. "You can just make a good, strong picture in your mind, ya know, whatever you want. And peoples will see it if you aim it at 'em. I could create good water right here, about twenty feet deep, coming in at twenty gallons a minute—a thought well? Another dowser could come here and pick it up with his rods. He'd know how deep and how much water, just like I'd made in my thought. 'Course there wouldn't really be any water if he drilled. I'm not that good, but that thought form of the water would stay there forever until I removed it. Because, you see, Ana, it's just energy. Thought is energy and can become a real thing, but you can make a thought form so good, no person or animal can tell the difference if you're sending them a thought picture. If it's strong enough, they'll believe it until you remove it."

From that crystalline moment, nine-year-old orphan and runaway Ana Sanchez took that simple process of make believe and began to create a new life.

Fresh from her workout and lingering soak in a scented bath, Rian strategically dabbed on perfume instead of underwear and dressed in black silk pants, a soft cashmere crème sweater, and stiletto-heeled black mules. She gazed in the long mirror to verify that the wardrobe part of the seduction suite was well-orchestrated, but the reflection struck a discord within her psyche. What she saw was Meredith—the smiling blonde woman with pale skin gazing back at her with Rian's own turquoise blue eyes was in love with the man Rian was going to reawaken tonight.

The moment Spence opened completely to his past, he would be lost to both of them again.

Rian drove out of the condo's garage at 8:45 p.m. and arrived at Spence's offices twenty minutes later, stopping in front of the closed gate to the parking lot. An Integrity Security van pulled in behind her, its headlights illuminating the inside of her Benz. Shielding her eyes against the glare from the rearview mirror as the gate swung open, she pulled inside, allowing the van to pass her.

A steel door at one end of the building rolled up and the van drove inside. Rian followed and waited as Spence got out and walked back to her car with a sexy smirk on his mouth. He opened her door without a word. Rian rose out of her seat, the hard steel between them, and held his penetrating gaze that ignited a sensual warmth at the base of her spine. She paced her breathing with his, mentally sending him a soft-focus picture of a couple making love on a moonlit beach that pulled her in before she could stop herself. Consciousness blurred to duality and she became the memory, seeing through the eyes of Meredith and feeling Paul's loving touch upon her wet skin.

Spence's face flushed and he stood taller, his broad shoulders squaring. He took her hand and led her to the elevator, never breaking eye contact until the doors opened on his apartment.

Rian, already in the stimulated state that she wanted Spence in, focused on him, letting herself be motivated by his arousal as she began to undress him. He rushed to take off her sweater. She stopped him, not so gently holding his hands to his sides and shook her head. She didn't touch him again until she'd dropped his clothes piece by piece on the floor. He stood naked, his lean athletic body cut and hard. She snaked her arms around his waist, slid her soft cashmere covered chest down his body but stepped out of his embrace, skimming around to his broad back and running her hands over his tight butt. He groaned but stood rigid, straining for control.

"That's right," she whispered against the smooth skin of his back and quickly pulled off her clothes. She stepped down out of her slides and realized how tall he really was as her arms went around him again, her bare breasts much lower on his back. His hands came back and clamped on her bottom, hauling her tight against him. She ground against him and he swiveled to face her, raising her arms to his neck and lifting her off the floor. She wrapped her legs around his waist and he pumped into her as his tongue dove into her mouth.

The sex was silent and without endearments or any of the tenderness that Paul and Meredith had shown each other that night on the Hawaiian beach, but Rian climaxed anyway and again when Spence came with a growling shudder.

She put her feet on the floor, supporting him with her arms around his waist as his physical strength drained away in a great whoosh of breath. Rian sensed the change in the energy field surrounding him. The root energy center between his legs blasted open, unleashing a chain reaction that rolled up the remaining six chakras and out the top of his head like a mushroom cloud. His aura expanded with the explosion. She felt it blow right through her and keep on going in vast waves across time and space, reconnecting with the Source.

Chapter Nine

Sucking in a breath and stiffening against her, Spence looked down at her, cupping her face with his hands, turning it up to him. There it was in his eyes, recognition. Unrestrained power was taking shape that would soon turn cold and destructive if he weren't well-bonded with her and guided very carefully now.

Rian stood on her tiptoes and placed a gentle kiss on the hardening line of his lips. They didn't yield and his hands dropped off her face. She gave him a sated, sexy smile and moved away from him. She slipped her feet into her shoes, bending from the waist as she reached for her clothes on the floor. He grabbed her from behind, pushing her toward the sofa, then pulled her backside into his crotch and whispered in her ear as he bent her over, "You said you didn't do patients."

"I don't. This is my way of telling you that you're not my patient any more," she murmured, leaning on her hands as they sank into the cushions, and spreading her legs as he clamped his hands on her hips and entered her.

Afterwards, he carried her upstairs to his bed, crawled in beside her and fell into a restless sleep. Rian lay in the dark, staring up at the ceiling as she continued to telepathically broadcast agreeable screen memories of Spence's work at Datascape to him so that he would be accepting of returning. She had to remote influence him as much as possible now before he regained his memories and came online. After that, if he was as good as she'd been told, no one would be able to get to him. Until then, he was vulnerable,

143

still suggestible and she also wove into the mental tapestry suggestions that he needed their help and would feel better, happier each time he heard or thought about Datascape or her. And perhaps more selfish, Rian sent her beautiful memories of Paul and Meredith, their tender, passionate and selfless lovemaking becoming the replacement recollection of the heartless copulation that had happened between Spence and her tonight.

Exhausted, Rian finally allowed herself the luxury of sleep, resting in the arms of the man she loved and lost a long time ago, and was about to again.

The sound woke him up. It wasn't the usual metal clanging, but familiar, one he heard every time he came home. The elevator! He bolted out of bed and froze. A naked woman crouched behind the girder at the top of the stairs to his loft, looking down over the side.

Rian! "What—" he said and started toward her.

"Shhhh!" She put her palm up to stop him. "There's someone downstairs," she whispered.

Spence motioned her away from the railing. She crawled toward him as he grabbed a pair of shorts and his .45 out of the drawer. The sons of bitches had gotten smart and given up trying to break in through the fire escape, but how had they got past the security system. Damn! He'd been so hot for Rian, he must have forgotten to close the rollup door in the shop after they drove in. He pulled on the shorts and jacked the slide. Stepping over Rian, he told her to call 911. He held the gun in tight to his chest and hit the light switch on the girder with his shoulder.

The downstairs blazed with light. Three figures in tactical gear dove for cover, one rolling under the metal staircase to the loft and the other two into the kitchen area below the loft's overhang.

"Hey down there. I'm armed and the cops are on the way. If you want to stay alive, get out of here."

Three figures separated from the shadows like wraiths and converged on the darkened elevator, slipping inside the open door that closed with a chime. Spence took the stairs two at a time to the bottom, sweeping the room with his gun. He sidled into the kitchen, kicking open the pantry door. Seeing that it was empty, he crabbed to the living room and the bank of security monitors, bringing the shop's camera online to see the three figures running across the shop and out the door. Spence selected the yard view and watched them go over the fence like they had wings and disappear. Strange. He hit replay on the control panel and watched the escape again, pausing when the men got to the fence and zooming in.

They wore full tactical gear with masks, but had no weapons, not even side arms.

He blew out the breath he must have been holding during his sweep and uncocked the hammer on the .45.

"Are they gone?" Rian asked right behind him, making him jump.

He whirled on her. "Get some clothes on. The cops will be here any minute."

She moved the sofa and picked up her pants, stepping into them and pulling them up her long legs. "I didn't call the police."

"You kidding me?" He slapped his hand over his mouth and stared at her while she calmly finished dressing. She stepped into her heels and gathered her long hair behind her neck, releasing the shimmering cascade down her back.

She headed for the elevator and pressed the call button. "Do you need to do something to let me out of the garage?"

"Yeah, I'll close the shop door like I should have if I hadn't been thinking with my dick." He grabbed his pants off the floor and put them on, sticking the .45 in his waistband at the small of his back. "Okay, let's go."

The elevator arrived and Spence tightened the unscrewed light bulb in the ceiling fixture before Rian got in. They descended to Spence's office, crossed through the complex and opened the door to the darkened shop. He turned on the lights and, confirming that the shop was secure, stepped inside. Rian strolled to her car like she was walking in the mall and opened the door. Her purse was still on the seat and the keys in the ignition. She didn't seem to notice the paradox and got in.

"Guess they didn't need a Benz, huh? Better check your wallet."

She smiled and dug into the bag, pulling out a red wallet. "Apparently all here."

Despite her composure, she was concerned, almost scared. It radiated from her like a static discharge. "Are you okay?"

Surprise flickered in Rian's eyes. "Yes, of course. And you, Spence, you're well, right? Alert. In control."

"Yeah, soon as I change my shorts," he joked, but he did feel alert and in control as she said—like the old days when he was Ian's best viewer. He frowned at that thought, noticing that Rian watched him with narrowed eyes. "Hey, I know you want to go."

"Even though you're not my patient now, I'd still like to see you," she said with a shy smile. "I have appointments until early afternoon. I'm coaching the game tomorrow, so if you're coming to watch Marty maybe we can get together before or after if you'd like?"

Rian was a beautiful, sexy woman with a weird fetish for

screwed up loners. Hell yes, he wanted to get together with her again. "Sure." She told him she was looking forward to it and drove away. He waited until she'd crossed through the gate and it swung closed before he rolled down the door, locking it securely. Opening the door to the office complex, he traced his steps to the elevator and his loft.

He sat up the rest of the night, monitoring the sweeping security cameras, and watching the tape of the intruders over and over again.

There was something bogus about the whole operation.

On the drive home, Rian fought to control her turbulent, unfocused thoughts that someone could hone in on if they were targeting her. And they were, if the attack tonight meant what she thought it did. The rogue viewers had been able to get to Spence because she'd forgotten to shield him properly, just as he'd left the door open for them in the shop. Stupid. Careless. And unlike her.

Rian focused on setting a thought form of herself and Spence, absorbed in the music, with 50,000 raucous concert fans at the Tacoma Dome. It would take any viewer many hours of trial and error to sort their energy out of the crowd's, then try to blueprint them, only to discover too late that he was working with ghosts. In the meantime, she could remote view the rogues or contact Ian who would assign an in-house team to the rogues, if they were indeed rogues. That thought had been hovering at the edge of her consciousness. Something wasn't right. Would rogue viewers intent on kidnapping Spence have shot him with knockout drugs or taken more drastic measures? These had given up too easily—as if they were just there for effect.

The shielding thought form in place, Rian sent Ian a coded fax as soon as she got home. Five minutes later the phone rang while she was in the shower. Ian breaking his rule of no telephone communication? She turned off the water and shrugged into her robe, instructing the communications system to take the call.

"Rian, you don't send me that kind of thing at 2:00 a.m. then make me talk to a machine dammit," Ian's voice demanded in every room.

"Transfer to office and secure." She left the master suite and picked up the phone in her office. "Good morning to you, too."

"What happened?" he blustered.

"On the phone?" she asked, leaning back in her chair.

He told her to be circumspect in choice of words and she succinctly laid it all out for him, keeping a part of her mind directed to perceiving the subtext of his responses. Ian knew something. Perhaps he was testing her.

"That wasn't the reclamation, was it?" she probed.

"Of course not. I told you that wouldn't happen unless you couldn't deliver."

"Any ideas, then?"

"The competition, of course," Ian countered. "With this new development, we're going to have to accelerate things even further. And to that end I take it things went well tonight? We're looking at a contract?"

She took a deep breath. "Yes. However, the deal may be a little unstable and still requires time and careful handling."

"Time we don't have and handling is up to you. I think we need to send in some contract specialists to protect our interests."

What the hell? He wasn't threatening her this time. Sending the reclamation team now was what he intended to do. "That is not necessary. The dotted line will be signed by the weekend, Monday at the latest. Any other input will only complicate things."

"You have until Sunday night. That's when the transfer will occur regardless. Don't concern yourself. We consummate this deal as expected and I'm not unhappy. Goodnight, my dear," he said and hung up.

Rian stared at the dead phone in her hand. Why had her mentor and best friend in the world just let her know that she was well and truly screwed?

The next morning, a last minute cancellation allowed her time to focus on Spence. She took three deep breaths and went out of body on the last exhale through her crown chakra at the top of her head. Her spirit, propelled by her intention, found Spence in the convention center meeting with four men of similar energy. Though they presented friendly and open demeanors, she detected that they were united against Spence and subliminally broadcasting a subversive frequency that opposed his.

As they talked, Spence kept smoothing his hand over his mouth and down his throat and turning to keep them on his right side as they toured the Egyptian exhibit. Good. He may not understand why he felt uncomfortable or what he was doing, but he was defending himself as he was trained. Spence stopped and rubbed the back of his neck, glancing over his shoulder.

He sensed her energy!

Rian was elated and uneasy at the same time. Spence was at his most vulnerable as his fragmented psychic skills came online, making him ultra sensitive to remote influence, just as these men were trying to do now. And if he didn't remember how to protect himself, he would react based on some pre-programmed trigger that would feel like his own thought.

Who were these men? She moved her invisible energy form among them and approached the one with the strongest energy. Rian read the I.D. badge clipped to his shirt pocket: Daniel Freeman, Account Manager, Datascape Trade Show Productions.

Spence had been under direct management and surveillance since his deprogramming via Datascape's substantial continuing investment in his company. And these ordinary looking technobusiness geeks were much more than they appeared to be. A pre-reclamation survey team, perhaps?

They could be pre-prepping him for the intake that would pop before the Sunday deadline Ian had imposed on her. She had to strengthen Spence's connection with her, get full control of him before they determined he was too dangerous and snatched him.

Rian flashed back into her body and took a deep breath, centering her astral body within her physical one. She brought up Spence's patient file on the computer, then dialed the cell phone number she saw there. He answered on the first ring.

She calmed and warmed her voice to steamy. "Hi, it's Rian. What are you wearing?"

He laughed and lowered his voice, "More than I was. What about you?"

"Oh, very little of this and absolutely none of that. Want to have some fun?" Rian sent him a picture of herself last night, nude except for her four-inch stiletto mules. She heard his sharp intake of breath when he got it. He asked her to hang on and told the men he had to take the call.

He came back on the phone. "Fun? Yeah, but I've got to work."

"I bet you have a couple of minutes for some phone sex, don't you?"

"Uh, depends on what I have to do with the phone in a public place."

Rian laughed. "All you have to do is hold it to your ear—phone, that is. Are you someplace where you won't be disturbed and ready to play, Jonathan Spencer?"

"Go for it." The excitement in his voice stimulated her.

"I want you to think about last night with me. Bring the scene fully to mind. See what you saw. Hear what you heard. Feel what you felt. That's right," she whispered. "Really get into it. Are you?"

"Uh huh." His breathing had picked up and her own matched his.

"Now, fully in the moment, enjoying yourself. When you feel it the most, when it's the best, almost ready to come, is it?"

"Yes," he breathed into her ear.

"Spence, touch the top of your left wrist with your right index finger. That's right. Release." Waiting a moment, she quickly changed subjects. "I am going to see you before the game?" She heard only rapid breathing on his end, then he cleared his throat.

"Uh . . . yeah. I think so."

"Very good. I can come now and get you."

"Yeah . . . I mean no. No, I've got to finish here. I'll see you."

She smiled and suggested, "My office at 2:30." He agreed. "Now, Spence, are you still by yourself?"

"Yeah . . ."

"Press just once on the back of your left wrist in the same spot as before. Go ahead. Release." Holding her breath, she waited as he fired her conditioned tactile anchor that rolled waves of uncontrollable raw sensation peaking through him.

151

"Ohhhh. Something just came up. I gotta go," he muttered and hung up.

At 2:30 exactly her receptionist showed Spence into the office. Rian pointed him to the recliner. "How was your day?" She slipped off her jacket, hung it in the closet and started unbuttoning her blouse.

He fidgeted and smoothed his fingers over his moustache, eyeing her. "Good. It was good. Yours?"

Rian made innocent small talk while performing a calculated striptease, piece by piece, down to her black bra and thong, until Spence couldn't manage any more than monosyllables. She shimmied her coach's shirt over her head and pulled on her green shorts and long socks, then grabbed her shoes and bag. "If you'll drive, I can finish in the car. We're late."

The drive to Auburn in rush hour traffic gave them plenty of opportunity to talk. Rian tried to draw him out, but Spence wouldn't engage. He seemed to be ruminating about something and that worried her because she couldn't get a clear read on it. She decided to try the direct approach. "Something bothering you?"

He glanced in the rearview mirror and at both side mirrors. "No."

"You seem nervous?"

"Is that your professional opinion?" he asked, attitude asserting itself as he scowled at the mirror again.

"No. Just an observation." She formed a picture of Meredith's smiling face and projected it to him.

He threw her an angry glance. "Why are you screwing with me?"

A chill of alarm rang through her. She attempted to latch on to the predominant emotional energy whirling around him. Anger. Confusion. Fear. "Why are you afraid that I am?"

"I don't get this. Nothing about you and me makes sense."

"Does our attraction have to make sense?" she murmured and put her hand on his thigh.

"Yeah, you know. I think it does. Call me an ungrateful son of a bitch for looking a gift screw in the mouth, but one minute you're the tight ass therapist that doesn't do patients. The next you're bonking my balls off at my house, not to mention talking me off over the phone and stripping like a pro in your office. What the hell is going on, Rian? I don't even know you, but you're sure making me perform like a trained seal," he said with a disgusted shake of his head.

Rian took her hand off his leg, feeling her way through this mental minefield that could blow them both to hell. "Spence, do you really think I can make you do anything you don't want to do?"

"Dammit! There you go again, Doctor. Stop answering my questions with a question. That drives me crazy," he huffed.

"Drives you crazy?" she joked, giving him a cross-eyed smile. He glanced sideways at her and his angry scowl dissolved.

"Yeah, crazy. Like you." He dropped his tense shoulders and blew out a breath. "Come on, Rian, what is this?"

It was time to tell him what she didn't want to admit to herself. She loved him. But would he love her when he realized what she was and what she'd been doing to him, even if she'd believed it was for his own good? "I believe we were lovers in a past life. And I want that again. With you."

His hands tightened on the steering wheel and the muscles along his strong jawline flexed for a moment before he said, "Go on."

"It started with your regression to your past life as Paul Romero. How can I explain this? When my patients go into trance, I go, too, in a way, because we've established a sort of reciprocal psychic bond. And it isn't just me. Many hypnotherapists experience this bond with their clients. I saw Paul from Meredith's eyes and experienced their profound love for each other . . ." Rian swallowed and wiped away the gathering tears with her fingertips.

She looked out her window at the traffic flowing with them toward Auburn. "You can't tell me you didn't feel it, too. That I was Paul's Meredith, who loved you more than anything in this world." Turning toward him, she said, "I wanted that again, Spence, and thought if I could interest you physically you might—"

"Learn to love you," he said without emotion.

"Something like that. Pretty needy, isn't it?"

Spence drove the Benz into the field's parking lot and parked well away from the other cars. He shut off the engine and turned to her, his arm on the back of her seat. "I've never been the sex object of a really screwed up but beautiful woman before. So I don't know what the game plan is. Things are pretty intense for me right now and I'm just trying to get through it. Making love with you is great, but you've got expectations. I don't. If we can leave it at that, we can give whatever this is a shot."

"Okay." She wished he'd take her into his arms and tell her what she wanted to hear. Instead she stuck out her hand. "Here's to giving it a shot."

He took her hand, searching her eyes. "And maybe someday you'll tell me what's going on."

"Trust me, I already have."

After the game Spence helped Rian gather up the equipment. Dorel, who usually backed her up, had dropped off Marty on her way to a doctor's appointment. Spence kept an eye on his godson running around with the other kids, while parents passed out snacks and drinks. There would be no winner dinner this evening. They'd lost big despite Rian's active and encouraging coaching.

"Who's that Marty's talking to?" Rian jerked her head toward the restrooms where Marty and a teammate were looking at something a man in a ball cap and gray sweatsuit had in his hands.

Spence dropped the ball bag and jogged the twenty-five yards down the field towards them. The man put his arm around Marty's shoulders and led him quickly around the building, leaving the other kid behind with what he'd given him.

"Hey you! Come back! Marty!" Spence broke into a full run around the side of the building as the man picked up Marty and ran toward the parking lot where a van was waiting with its sliding door open.

Panicked, Spence sprinted across the sidewalk, making a grab for Marty. Out of nowhere, Rian flew at the kidnapper with a body block that staggered him. Spence ripped Marty out of the guy's hold as he stumbled, recovered and scrambled into the van. The door slammed closed as the van screeched out of the lot.

Rian picked herself up off the asphalt and limped over to Spence. "Marty, are you okay?" She brushed his curly hair back off his pale face with a trembling hand and gave Spence a fearful glance. He shifted Marty to his hip and put his arm around her, hugging them both against the deep, visceral fear drilling his body.

Marty put his little hand on Rian's cheek. "Don't be sad, Meredith. They don't want him yet. They want me."

Neither they nor the other witnesses were able to supply the police with much information about the kidnapper's description or the van. Though Marty did remember that the man had called him by name when he showed him the little model airplane. Spence tried to tell them that the man had to know something about the family to use such effective bait, but the police seemed to think that was a lucky guess as well as his knowing Marty's name that he could have heard from the kids.

Spence pushed it. Why would the guy go to so much trouble? he asked. Random, he was told, but that was crap. He continued to try to persuade and downright argue the police into using their goddamn heads.

By the time Dorel got there, Rian was busy psycho sweet-talking the cops into not hauling Spence's ass to jail, then she had to calm Dorel down. Marty was the only one not upset and shouting by the time the cops left. Rian took charge, putting Dorel in her car with Marty and Spence and following them home in her Benz.

"Rian, could you talk to Marty, please? Help him talk out his fear. Don't you think he needs to do that?" Dorel asked after she'd gotten Marty fed, bathed and playing in his room.

Spence disagreed. "He's a little kid. Yeah, it was scary, but he'll forget about it. He's not that upset. Just ask him."

Dorel huffed and gave him an annoyed look. "We're talking about Marty here, Spence. He thinks about things very deeply and doesn't forget anything."

"Yeah . . . but. Okay, you're right." He glanced at Rian sitting on the sofa, her clasped hands clamped between her bare knees, looking like a little kid herself, and a scared one at that.

"Dorel, you should have seen Rian. She threw a block at

that guy that would have taken Godzilla down. Where did you learn that?" he asked Rian and caught an image of her in black sparring with another white-clad trainee in a martial arts dojo.

"I've studied martial arts for years." She stood and asked, "Shall I go see Marty now?"

Chapter Ten

Dorel nodded and took her to Marty's room. Spence followed them down the hall and ducked into the bathroom, shutting the door. He washed his hands and was drying them when he heard Marty's voice coming from the floor vent beneath the towel rack. Sitting on the edge of the tub, he cocked his head closer to listen.

"You called me Meredith back at the field, do you remember that?" Rian asked.

"Yup. Do you like my airplanes?"

"Yes, I do. Was the airplane the man showed you like one of those?"

"Uh huh. The SBD. That one over there. You remember," Marty said.

"Sort of. Is that your favorite?"

"No, I like the Corsair, but Paul flies the Dauntless, that's why I gotta like it. Daddy flies a Triple Seven."

Rian laughed. "Yes, I know. Are you going to be a pilot, too?"

"I hope so," Marty answered. "Daddy and Romeo, I mean Uncle Spence are getting another plane when Daddy gets home."

"That's good. Would you like to talk about the man today, Marty?"

"I guess I gotta because Momma wants me to. It will make her feel better."

"That's nice of you to think of your mother. Why don't you just go ahead and tell me what you and Jared were doing when the man talked to you."

"Ian sent him to get me."

"What?" Spence felt the shock in her voice.

"Ian knows you were my sister and Romeo's girlfriend. That's why he picked you." Ian? Spence knew that name. He shuddered, struggling with a remembrance that was just out of reach.

"Marty, is Ian trying to take you?" Rian asked with a strange edge to her voice.

"I'm sleepy." He yawned. "Don't let them get me or Uncle Spence, Mere. They're mean."

"I won't let anyone hurt you, Marty."

"Uncle Spence either," he murmured sleepily.

"Uncle Spence, either. And you can help yourself stay safe, too. You can feel inside when people are good or mean, can't you?"

"Uh huh, in my tummy."

"Then trust those feelings and don't let anyone near you that doesn't feel right in your tummy. Yell very loud and run away. Today you didn't do that. Why?"

Spence strained to hear Marty's soft reply. "I wanted you to see them so that you and Uncle Spence could stop them."

"Why do they want to take you away?" Marty didn't answer and Rian repeated the question.

"You know." Another huge yawn. "Uncle Spence, can you sleep over with me?"

Spence jerked back. He walked to Marty's room and knocked on the door. "You called me, M-Man?"

Rian opened the door. "He wants you to sleep with him tonight. I think it might be a good idea. Night, Marty. You're a very brave boy."

"Bye, Coach," Marty said with another yawn as Spence ducked and sat down on the end of the bottom bunk.

"Are you staying, Spence?"

"Yeah, camping out with M-Man. I'll swing by to-morrow and pick up the car at the office."

Her smile was melancholy as she said goodnight and closed the door. Spence pulled the stuffed animals off the top bunk, listening to Dorel show Rian out and set the alarm. Dorel came back to the bedroom and tucked both in and wished them happy sleep. Spence didn't think that any of them had much chance of that the way his mind was churning up images and thoughts. Theirs probably would be, too.

He stretched out as much as he could on the bunk and closed his eyes, relaxing to Marty's regular little breaths coming from the bed below. Kids were amazing—able to sleep after an experience like that.

"Romeo! Wake up. I've got things to tell you."

"Go away, Ev. I'm trying to get some sleep," he said and *rolled over.*

"You are asleep, jackass. Look!"

He opened his eyes and looked—down from the corner of the room where he was floating with Ev. His body lay on the bunk above Marty's who was curled up asleep with his favorite bear. *"What the—"*

"Yeah, yeah, how could this be happening, oh my, oh my," Ev jibed. *"Now, listen up. Things are about to go high order."* He blew out an exasperated breath. *"Will you pay attention? I forgot how no one listens to a little kid no matter how smart he is. God, that's frustrating."*

"You aren't a little kid." He was Ev, looking the same as he did that day he'd dropped him over China.

"You know I'm Marty this time, Spence. Now cut the flack. Let's make this more interesting—for me, anyway. Let's play truth and a load of crap, okay?"

Spence nodded, his ghost-like body bobbing with the movement.

"Everything Dorel told you is true—the sword, the past lives, everything."

Spence opened his mouth but no sound came out.

"You don't have to talk, just think it. And you're wrong. What she told you is true and a lot more. Next question, what Mike said about Datascape is a load of crap?" Before Spence could think an answer, Ev interjected, "Nope. All true. They're bringing you back in, my friend. You haven't had a breach in your deprogramming—they've busted you wide open on purpose because they want you for a special job, something sharp, now broken. Hint. Hint. Jeez, when you decide to get stupid, you do it up good. Here's what I want you to do. See that glittering stream above you?" Ev tipped his head up, pointing.

Spence followed his gaze and saw a broad stream of sparkling stars flowing in the infinite black velvet of deep space.

"Nothing teaches better than experience. You just think yourself up into that and hang on. You're in for a hell of a ride, hotshot."

Spence launched like a missile into the shining stream, changing from particle to source wave. One with infinite wisdom flowing seamlessly into eternity. And as the whole, he was light, color, sound, pure plasma from which he came and never separated. Within that creative energy of infinite spectrum, he had only to focus and he was the thought. His lives, disincarnate and in body, were a hologram of action and reaction, glowing with brightness. But there were darker areas, too, reflecting little light. Becoming aware of them, he joined with them, again experiencing a gestalt of past and future. He recoiled and fell back to Earth.

He jerked awake and hopped down to the floor, peering into Marty's bunk. The little boy was sleeping, his arm around a tattered, well-loved bear. Spence crept out of the room and almost tripped over Katana lying in the hall outside. He gave the big dog a pat on the head and continued to the living room, leaving him behind to guard Marty.

Staring out into the moonlit back yard, Spence's cosmic reconnection actualized itself into a moment of singular clarity and acceptance of what he really was. A psychic spy. A trained mental assassin who had suffered a nervous breakdown and been released from active service. But the company continued to control him, and Mike, with economics, providing and facilitating financial prosperity that kept them complacent and malleable. Now they wanted him back and had sent their best to reclaim him.

"Rian!" he spat into the silent darkness as betrayal-born hatred boiled in his gut.

Mike dragged in about 11:00 a.m. He sat at the dining table, fighting to contain his fury as Spence and Dorel recounted Marty's kidnapping attempt yesterday, while the boy played in his room. Mike glared at Spence. "What the hell have you brought to my door?"

"Wait a minute, Michael, Spence saved Marty," Dorel said, grabbing Spence's hand across the table in a show of support. "Don't you dare blame him for your not being there!"

"Hold on, guys," Spence said, giving her hand a squeeze. "It's not our fault. These guys were after me and just using Marty to draw me out."

Mike glared at him. "How the hell do you know?"

Before Spence could answer, Marty piped up from the doorway. "You're wrong, Uncle Spence. They're gonna get you after me." He crawled up in his dad's lap and leaned to Dorel. She brushed a red curl off his forehead and gave him a kiss. "I called Roshi, Momma. He's coming to get me."

Dorel went pale. "Wh—what are you talking about, baby?" she stammered.

Marty turned to his dad and Spence, his child's voice inflected with a serious, adult tone. "I lived with the Buddhists at the Sangha. The Roshi was my teacher and friend. I'll be safe with them."

"Don't be silly, son. You're safe here with me. I'm here now to take care of you." Mike gave Marty a hug and gave Dorel a rueful glance.

Marty pushed out of his father's arms. "I have to go with Roshi. Momma, tell him to let me go."

Dorel frowned, her eyes glittering with tears. "Marty, I can't."

"Let him go," Spence enjoined, drawing invisible symbols on the table's polished wood with his fingertip. "It's the best place for him."

"Since when do you get to say what's best for my son?" Mike snarled, jabbing a finger in Spence's direction.

He continued to draw on the table, clearly seeing in his mind's eye the symbols he traced. "Since I was his best friend and loved his sister a long time ago. And since you made me Marty's godfather. Dorel knows the Roshi. She met him when he brought her the sword."

Mike sank back into his chair, his eyes wide with awful comprehension. "Oh my God, you're open."

Spence nodded. "I can't put it together yet. Pretty much a jumble of memories, impressions, flashes of stuff. But I think Marty's right. He'll be safe at the Sangha."

"No! That's crazy," Dorel cried. "You said that whoever they are wanted you, not Marty. If that's true, you've got to go, Spence. You're putting Marty in danger by staying here."

The doorbell chimed and Katana charged into the foyer, barking. "Roshi!" Marty cried and ran to the door before anyone could stop him, and pulled it open.

An old, bald, orange-robed Buddhist monk stood in the entry, smiling like the Dalai Lama down at Marty. "Greetings, old friend. Good to see you once again."

Dorel reached the door and gave a little yelp, snatching Marty back behind her. "What are you doing here?" she demanded of the monk.

Spence reached across Dorel and extended his hand. A spiral of warmth swirled up his arm when the Roshi took it in both of his. "Greetings, friend of Martin," he said, waiting while they stared at him. Mike told the monk to come in and Marty grabbed his hand, leading him into the living room.

"Do you like my house, Roshi?" Marty asked.

"Yes, it is positioned well to the rising sun and mountain. It is good," the monk replied, beaming at the view of Mt. Rainier through the French doors. "As you remember, the Sangha is well positioned, too. You will enjoy your time there."

"Mr. Roshi, there's been some mistake. Marty can't go with you. I'm so sorry that you made the trip all the way over here for nothing," Dorel said, abject fear riding her features hard.

Marty turned to Spence. " 'Member what I said last night about nobody listens to little kids, Uncle Spence? Make them listen. I have to go with Roshi."

A huge chunk of the infinite now fell into his conscious mind and the enormity of it almost crushed him. Spence wiped his hand over his mouth trying to reel in from the sensations and memories swimming in his head any line of thought that would help him understand what to do now

164

and how to help Marty. "Marty, I—" His cell phone rang and flashed an image of Rian his mind.

He put the phone on speaker and answered it. "Spence, I called to warn you. I think you already know that, but the men who tried to take Marty yesterday are going to try again. In fact, I'm afraid they're coming your way now. Please get Marty out of there. Spence? Can you hear me?" Spence hit the end call button and turned the phone off.

"How does Rian know that?" Dorel breathed, wringing her hands.

"Because she works for them," Spence said and swung around to the Roshi. "How can you keep them from finding Marty?"

"We monks are very good at losing ourselves in meditation. And so lost in the infinite, one may not be found. Martin recalls the old ways. He will not be found. We are intent upon this. You must also be intent upon this and forget your sadness at his departure. Guard your thoughts, keep them filled with happiness." The monk inclined his head in a slight bow to Dorel and Mike.

"Michael, it's started again? Oh my God. What are we going to do?" She put her fingers over her trembling lips, fighting for composure.

Mike released a heavy sigh and picked up his son. "Okay, you're going with Roshi. I'm trusting that you've made the right choice and that he will take good care of you. We'll get this all straightened out and then we'll come get you, okay?"

Marty looked at him solemnly. "Help Spence remember quick, Daddy. Then you and him take Momma and go hide somewhere. You gotta do it. Promise."

"I promise. Now give your mother a kiss." Mike handed the boy to Dorel who hugged him to her. "I guess you're already packed, too. I'll go get your bag."

"Momma, you're squeezing too tight," Marty squawked and squirmed out of her arms.

Spence scooped him up, and nose to nose with him, said, "Come see me in my dreams again, M-Man. We'll go flying." Marty gave him a big wet smooch on the nose and said he would.

They followed the Roshi and Marty out to a late model Volvo station wagon and put the boy's backpack and bag in the back. The monk helped Marty strap himself in the passenger seat and then turned to them, closing the door. "If you will be so kind now as to enjoy yourselves watching a sporting event. Perhaps a tape of Martin's last soccer game. This will present a happy diversion and give us an opportunity to arrive at our destination unobserved."

Dorel frowned. "I don't understand—"

"It will be fine," Mike cut her off and thanked the Roshi again.

As the monk drove down the gravel drive, Marty stuck his bear out the window and dropped it. "Oh, no. Stop!" Dorel cried and ran after them, grabbing the stuffed animal out of the dirt and waving it at the car. "Come back. He's dropped his bear."

The Volvo kept going and Mike walked to her, putting his arm around her shaking shoulders. "Don't cry, Dorel. He'll be back."

"Why didn't he come back for his bear?" Dorel sobbed into Mike's chest.

"He left it for you, to keep you company," Mike said, kissing the top of her head.

Spence followed the couple back into the house, appreciating Mike's facile lie to make Dorel feel better. Marty dropped the bear, strongly imprinted with his energy, so they couldn't find him. Very smart.

Now, were they going to be as smart protecting themselves against these guys, and Rian?

The bad guys didn't arrive like Rian said they would. Mike cued up a soccer DVD as the Roshi had suggested, which would have been fine if Rian hadn't kept showing up on the big flat panel screen and on the one in Spence's mind.

"Why did we have to do this?" Dorel asked, tearful. She got up and paced in front of the French doors.

"Let's go for a walk and get our minds off on something else." Mike led her out to the deck where they stood in a quiet embrace, comforting each other, then walked down the path.

Spence closed his eyes against the isolation rolling in on him and leaned back, trying to snag a happy memory that didn't involve Marty. Best keep the boy out of mind or packaged in a memory loop that a viewer couldn't trace without a lot of effort. That's how it worked! Since his experience last night, he'd been trying to put some order or meaning to the scramble of targets and protocols. It seemed that he could do something that the others couldn't, now he knew what. The Roshi had tipped him to it. Manage your thought, construct in your mind what you wanted someone to perceive and keep it running on a closed loop. A viewer would eventually break through it, given enough time, but by then you'd have built several others they'd have to wade through with laborious protocols.

What he couldn't remember was how to direct his mind without the protocols or how to make sure he didn't misinterpret the data. That was a tough one, because his biggest problem at first, he recalled, was analytic overlay—projecting meaning upon the raw data based upon his own misconceptions, background and experience. Ian had always ragged on him about that.

Mike and Dorel came back in and Spence roused up, rubbing his eyes. They exchanged a look and Dorel left them alone to talk.

"Dorel's brought me up to speed. But what we don't get is Rian, and you, I guess. What's up with that? The bad guys are Datascape, I take it," Mike said in a low voice and rubbed his hands together. "Another thing. You're coming online but it isn't working too good, is it?"

Spence shook his head, trying to focus on Mike and keep his mind from chasing down every stray thought or impulse coming in.

"Okay, here's what we need to do. We've got to build a blueprint of this thing. View the big five—who, what, when, where and why. First, have you remembered how you used to shield? You were the only one who could do it."

"I think so. I construct a bogus or decoy scenario opposite of my frequency and that cancels mine. And I'm just puking what I'm thinking, because I don't understand most of this."

"I'll be your monitor and put you through a couple of protocols, then when you're in the MAW—"

"What's that?"

"Mental Access Window, frequency range within the broad bandwidth, remember?"

He did remember, but maybe it was what Mike had told him a few days ago. "Yeah, okay."

"When you're in the MAW you'll remember how to construct your shielding. Once you do that and get some practice, you can view Datascape and find out—why they want you and Marty."

Mike's expression fell. "I can't let myself even think about that."

"I know. They might want him a whole lot more than they do me. Dorel told you about the hooked tool, right?" At Mike's nod, he continued, "It has something to do with the sword. Datascape baited me with it, then gave it to me. Mike, what if they somehow got the sword, but don't know how to use it? And need me to fix it or tell them how to use it?"

"You don't know either of those things. First, you aren't a swordsmith. As far as I know you weren't able to completely decipher the inscription on the blade or the tang. I was the only one to use the sword—for several lifetimes. So, I ask you, why wouldn't they come after me?"

"Who says they aren't?"

Mike's eyes rounded and he jerked back. "Son of a bitch."

He told Mike about handling the tool and hearing the voice. "We need to find out what that tool really is, where it came from. We need to establish a chain of custody, that's right, isn't it?"

"Yes. You trace the tool through all those who've possessed it, to who made it and where."

"The Forge of Balance. That's where it was made, I'd stake your life on it," Spence said with a wry grin.

"I bet you will. Where is this forge you said the voice told you to return to?" Mike stopped and shook his head in exasperation. "Look, we're getting off track here. We've got to get you up to speed quick so between the two of us, I at least can shield while you target. Are you ready?"

Spence took a deep breath. "Let's do it."

"Let's start with getting you in the MAW. Sit at the dining table. I'll be right back," Mike said and headed down the hall. After a couple of minutes he returned with a tablet of paper and pencils. He put a lined sheet in front of

169

Spence. "Hold this pencil. I'm sure as you do this everything will come right back. Okay, now the object is to relax,
holding onto the pencil and when you are so relaxed that
the pencil drops, that's a signal to your consciousness that
you're in the MAW and ready to go out of body. Out in the
ether you get what you think. That's the way you do anything. You think it. If you fear something, you'll manifest it.
So you have to control your thoughts, discard prejudices
and don't project meaning upon anything. Take some deep
breaths and clear your mind of everything but the thought
of your shield and let it come to you."

Spence breathed several times, but tension still sat on his
shoulders like a yoke. He stretched his neck, rolling his
head side to side and tried again. He inhaled to the count of
eight, held his breath for eight beats then exhaled to the
same count and repeated the process. He began to feel
lighter and disconnected as if chains that were holding him
down broke loose one by one. His chin dipped, eyelids fluttered, the pencil dropped to the paper and he lifted out of
his body. With the speed of light, his astral body shot into
space. Free of his earthly body, it all came back in a dynamic rush of enlightenment and power.

He had only to think a word or a concept and he experienced it, the same with his shield.

"Spence, come back," Mike called.

Spence popped back into now and blinked open his eyes.
"Got it all back, didn't you?" Mike proclaimed. He nodded,
still a little woozy and out of sync.

"Good. We'll start with some coordinate remote viewing
of blind targets to give you some practice. I'll get Dorel to
come up with some and put them in sealed envelopes."
Mike left Spence and went down the hall, returning in a few
minutes with five legal size envelopes and a pad of paper.

He held them out to Spence.

He selected one and started to open it. Mike stopped him. "I open it. Okay, the coordinate is D8240-57. Now, clear your mind, take some deep breaths and see if the protocol for acquiring a target comes to you."

Spence took the breaths, but his mind got noisier than ever. He scrunched up his closed eyes, willing himself to remember.

"No. No. Relax. Just float with it."

The protocol came in a flash and Spence initiated it. "Hey, I see the cabin. Man, the wildlife has been in there again. Torn things up," he said and opened his eyes.

Mike laughed. "Use the pad. Sketch out your impressions. I know you don't need to but it gives you a translating point. Now I'll ask you the questions."

They spent the next hour working through the envelopes until Spence made his last sketch. Mike called Dorel to bring the targets out to them. In a couple of minutes she appeared with five envelopes and Mike asked her to read the coordinate number first on the front, then open it and read the target written on a slip of paper inside.

She read the first. "D8240-57. The cabin."

Mike looked over Spence's drawings and the sensory impression words he'd written around his doodles. "That's a hit."

With every targeting confirmation, Spence felt his intuitive skills strengthen and amplify. There was nothing and no one that he could not see. Anytime. Anywhere.

"You got them all," Mike said with wonder. "I made myself forget just how good you were." He and Dorel congratulated Spence, but he felt their fear of him, too.

"Now let's go to work," Mike said. "We've got to find

out what we're up against. Dorel, unless you want to, you don't have to stay."

"I'll just sit here with you if that's okay. I don't want to be alone," she said with an embarrassed glance at Spence.

"It's great by me. I want you here," he said and meant it.

Mike scribbled targets on the pad while Spence generated a shield of thought energy like a huge mirrored bubble around himself. The sensation of his personal and unique electromagnetic frequency that he was able to isolate from all the others in and around his body translated to a particular feeling. He created the exact opposite feeling or frequency and projected it on the shielding bubble.

It was as if he'd turned flood lights on in a dark room and he realized that the dark spots or lower vibrations he'd sensed were viewers targeting him or parasitic other worldly entities hooked up to his energy field, sucking it off. He looked out of his sparkling shield at Dorel and Michael and saw the dark energy like malignant growths attached to their energy bodies. Spence extended his shield and drew them into the light.

Mike and Dorel didn't recognize what Spence had done, but they perceived a resurgence of vitality and well-being that he saw in their auras.

"Feel that?" he asked his dearest friends. "It's freedom. Sanctuary. Remember how this feels and you can reinstate it, create it around you anytime you need it."

"Now, you have got to find out why Rian is doing this to us," said Dorel with resolve. "I'd hoped that she was in love with you. I don't want to believe that she's capable of killing us all to get what she wants."

"Believe it," Spence said, preparing to target Rian Farsante and use whatever skills he had to stop her.

Chapter Eleven

Rian closed her eyes again, took three deep breaths and tried to project her consciousness into the ether. But the low frequency of panic interfered with her energy. That had to be why she couldn't find Marty. Spence, on the other hand, was shielding. He'd bounced her right out of his field, along with everyone else. Only they were still trying to hook up again to an illusion.

Spence hadn't gotten the shield up in time. She'd viewed them sending Marty away. The rogues did too, and would be looking for him. Gabrielli and Spence both had to know that there was no hiding from an experienced remote viewer—unless of course Marty was being shielded by Spence right there in the house. And perhaps Mike was able to shield as well. The whole messy separation scene might have been a little pseudo drama like she would have shielded with—at least, she hoped it had been. Otherwise, Marty was as good as caught already.

Spence had hung up on her and wouldn't take her subsequent calls. The Gabriellis weren't answering the phone either. The three of them had to be making plans and coordinating their remote viewing efforts if they were smart, and they were. However, Mike wouldn't be effective now. Six years had passed since he'd actively viewed during the Inada case. She'd been assigned to monitor him right after Inada had cancelled his contract with Datascape. He'd viewed very little and then not at all.

Though Ian had never shown any real interest in Gabrielli or his family and friends, he insisted that she relocate to Seattle from the Denver home office last spring to get closer to them. She continued to file her reports and live her life until she was tasked with bringing Spence back in. Then everything went to hell.

Rian blew out the focus candle and stood, kicking the meditation pillow out of her way. Ian had to know how much these rogues were screwing this up. Datascape could stop them, so why weren't they? She put her shield in place and dialed his private number. For the first time ever, she got his voice mail instead of his picking up on the first ring.

"Call me," she snapped and hung up.

The doorbell rang and she queried the system as she walked into the living room. "Who is it?"

"Your neighbor from downstairs," a male voice said over the intercom. "We've got a bad leak in our ceiling and we think it's coming from your place."

"Did you call maintenance?" She stopped in front of the fireplace and directed the system to give her a visual of zone one. The monitor went blank.

"Yeah, he's on the way."

Ice prickled into her stomach. The maintenance man was a woman named Ginger. Rian spun around, sprinted to the bedroom, grabbed her purse and bolted out the terrace door. She stepped on the edge of the large potted dwarf plum and boosted herself over the privacy screen to the terrace next door. The door was locked, but she could see through the sheers that someone was inside. Rian rapped her knuckles on the glass and heard an excited mumbling. The sheer was pulled back about an inch and an eye peered at her. "What are you doing out there?"

"I'm Rian. Your next door neighbor. Can you help me, please? I'm locked out." She heard her terrace door open. "Please, I'm a doctor." That got action every time.

The door opened wide enough for her to squeeze through and come face to face with a frightened elderly woman holding a very big gun.

Rian put on a friendly smile. "Thank you so much, Mrs. . . ."

The woman lowered the gun a bit. "Radmacher. You're a doctor?"

"Yes. I have an office in Bellevue in the Towers." Rian reached behind herself and locked the door.

"Dermatologist?"

"No, I'm a psychologist."

She lowered her gun. "Too bad, I need a new dermatologist. Come on through. I'll call Ginger to let you in. And maybe you can look at this mole on my back anyway."

While Mrs. Radmacher made the call, Rian stood in the center of the living room so she could see down the hall. She crept to the front door and peered out the view hole, but could see no one. Taking a deep breath, she reached out mentally, scanning her condo. Three male energies. She had to chance it.

Rian opened the front door a crack and looked toward her condo. Seeing no one, she opened it far enough to see the other end. She jerked open the door and dashed to the elevator. The doors opened with a chime, revealing an empty car. Rian leaned in, punched the button for the top floor and jumped back out as the doors closed and ran for the fire exit stairs. Ten flights later she exited the stairwell into the parking garage, scanning the area. No unfamiliar cars. No one lurking. Rian hurried to her car and drove out into the rainy late afternoon, headed for the Gabrielli house thirty miles south.

What she would do when she got there remained to be seen. And by now, Spence was focused trying to view

175

Datascape, not aware she was on her way to him. She was the last person in the world he would want to see, though he was the one she had to see. Rian fortified her shield and sent Spence and the Gabriellis an image of her coming to them and their welcoming her, because it would take several viewers to blueprint Datascape's elaborate and far-reaching operation, if indeed they could. If this were going to go right, without the rogues kidnapping or hurting anyone, she had to convince the Gabriellis that Spence needed her help if he were to avoid the reclamation team, even though she knew he would do everything in his power to make sure they didn't.

Besides, if she had no access to Ian, did that mean she was out in the cold? Why? Some unbidden whisper at the edge of her consciousness suggested that she might entertain the possibility that all she trusted and knew about Datascape was what she'd been conditioned to believe. Not true. Not real. She began to wonder if Ian weren't ever-present and available to assuage her fears, reinforce her prized protégée status, and pay for the lifestyle he'd taught her to require, what the hell would she do? Who would she be?

Dorel and Mike had decided that Spence should stay with them at the house so they could work together and shore up their defenses. Dorel was troubled that they weren't coming up with a concrete plan and Mike assured him that she always reacted that way to a problem. The woman had lists!

Dorel telephoned the world, rearranging their schedules and giving clever excuses about their taking Marty on a spur of the moment trip to Europe. She began to prepare the house like they were in for a long siege. Mike teased her about not cutting up the new Ralph Lauren sheets for bandages. She didn't take that in her usual good-humored way and they began to argue.

Spence took that opportunity to borrow Dorel's jeep and duck home. He threw a few things in his flight bag, including his .45. As he made a sweep of the living room, he saw the wrapped tool on the seat of Slack Ass. He didn't remember tossing it in the recliner or even bringing it upstairs. Again, the feeling that it was some sort of key to this whole mess clicked with him. He grabbed it and rode downstairs to the office.

"Spence! Where have you been? You've missed all of your appointments," his OA exclaimed, waving a handful of pink message slips at him. "The Datascape production team came all the way over here to get you when you didn't show at the convention center this morning."

He took the messages out of her hand and sorted through them. "What did you tell them?"

She gave him a baffled look. "What could I? I didn't know where you were either. I was worried you'd had another accident or something."

"No, everything's fine." He gave her back the selected messages with action instructions and tossed the rest in his briefcase.

She saw his flight bag and asked, "Are you going somewhere?" She slapped her forehead. "Oh my gosh, Miami! JET called. The airplane is ready and the airline wants to make the transfer early as scheduled. But you haven't told me when you and Mike want to travel so I can get the tickets."

Spence groaned. "Something's come up. Hey, I'll take care of that myself. It's late. Go home."

The woman old enough to be his mother grimaced and

gathered her bag. "Thank you, sire. And may I add that you look terrible? See you tomorrow?" She came around the desk. "That was a question, Spence. Are you coming in?"

"No, not for a couple of days. Get Ethan up to speed with the remaining action items and tell everyone that I'm sick or something," he said, walking with her. The other offices and shop were emptying quickly as they passed through toward the parking lot.

"Can do. They'll believe it too. Want to tell me where I can reach you?"

"I'll call in," he said and dropped his bags on the Jeep's back seat.

Sharon shrugged. "Okay, then. See you when you . . . get back, I guess?"

"Yeah, and remember—"

"Trust no one?" she cracked, deadpan.

"Good idea. See you, Sharon." He backed out of his reserved parking slot and headed for I-5. As he drove south the rain picked up and the commute traffic slowed down. Forming out of the mist in his mind was a filmy intellection—Rian playing her flute at Mike and Dorel's front door. He stepped on the throttle and commanded his cell phone to call the Gabrielli home. The call went right to voice mail.

"Mike. Dorel. I'm about thirty to forty-five minutes out. Rian's coming your way. Shoot the bitch or whatever you have to do. Just don't let her in, man."

But they did. Her white convertible was sitting in the driveway behind Mike's gold QX4. Spence wheeled the Jeep in behind her car, blocking it. Now that she was here, no way was she going to get away until he finished with her and maybe not even then.

The front door was locked. Rather than ring the bell, he

eased around back, sidled along the house and sneaked a look in the window. Rian's face was the only one he could see. She sat on the couch with Dorel opposite her. Mike stood, arms crossed over his chest, a little in front of his wife's left side with his right side turned to Rian.

Rian glanced toward the window and Spence pressed his back against the house. The French door opened on the deck and Mike leaned out. "Better come in."

"I phoned to tell you not to let her in," Spence said, staying where he was.

"The message must have gone to voice mail. She showed up. Dorel thought we needed to get it straight from her."

"Are you crazy? You let her into your house, knowing that she'll bring them down us any minute."

"She's out in the cold, Spence."

He hesitated, thinking that one over. "Then she confirmed she's a Datascape operative?"

"Yes, but they've cut off access."

Spence shook his head. "A confirmed Datascape operative tells you she doesn't work for them any more, and you believe it? I thought you were smarter than me."

"What she's been saying feels legitimate—"

"Sure it does. She's a freaking hired gun hypnotist. Remote influencing is what she does, for crissakes," Spence countered, agitated by his friend's unusual thickheadedness.

Mike stepped outside. "I think she means or at least believes what she says. We've got to know what she will tell us about Datascape. There's bound to be a kernel of truth in there somewhere that we can target and save ourselves a lot of viewing time. You have to figure that if we were conditioned, she is, too. Of course she's believing what Datascape tells her. We did."

179

"She's not us, Mike. She's one of them—with weird-ass talent not to mention unlimited spec ops resources we don't have. Get her the hell out of there. She's dangerous."

Mike narrowed his eyes and shrugged. "You've already made up your mind and *that* is dangerous. It will only close you down so you're not open to all the data. I think you should come in and at least sense where she's shielding while we talk to her. Or stay out here in the rain and do it. I don't care." He ducked back in the house, leaving the door open.

Spence took a deep breath, squared his shoulders and, against his instincts, followed him inside. He leaned against the arched doorjamb separating the living and dining rooms and let his gaze glide over her as she talked in earnest to Dorel.

"He told me that a reclamation team would intervene if I couldn't help Spence. Then my control pressured me to bring him in quicker because he was in danger from rogue viewers," Rian said, shaking back her hair and pushing up the sleeves of her white knit top that fit closely like a dancer's leotard tucked into black tights. Her feet were bare, one sole unconsciously rubbing the top of the other foot as if she were trying to warm it.

"But what's this got to do with them trying to kidnap Marty?" Dorel asked.

Rian flicked her gaze to Mike. "I don't know. I'm not certain they're trying to—acquire Marty."

"Liar!" Spence bellowed. "I heard Marty ask you not to let them get him, or me. He also said that you knew why they were trying to take him."

Mike narrowed his eyes at Rian. "Is that true?"

"Well, yes. Dorel had asked me to talk to him and that was one of the things he mentioned. But he could have been projecting, transferring the trauma of his near abduction to Spence. Children often speak tangentially about their fears. There's always a lot of incidental material mixed in with the essence of the problem," Rian lectured, her professional therapist persona in command.

Dorel leaned forward. "*I* know how children think, how they act. *I* know what I'm talking about because *I* have a child. You don't. But if you did, if you were a mother, you wouldn't be putting me through this hell with your platitudes. Now, if you care anything about my son at all, you help us. Tell me who and why they are trying to get Marty."

Rian blinked and studied her hands. "I haven't been able to view it, but in light of all the other developments, it seems that the rogue viewers may have tried to abduct Marty." She brought her gaze up to Mike. "But it could have been a mistake, too. My control—"

"Ian Stoddard," Spence interjected and moved closer, keeping his right side to her.

She nodded and continued, "Ian said the rogues were trying to bring Spence in, and they did break into his apartment the night before. They might have been the ones who made a grab for Marty in order to draw Spence out."

In unison, Mike and Dorel turned incredulous stares on Spence. "Yeah," he said with a shrug. "I forgot to mention that to you. Sorry."

"So, tell me now," Mike ordered.

"Three guys in tactical came in through the shop's rollup door I'd forgotten to close. I ran them off. Which was way too easy since they weren't carrying weapons, even though the mind spy chick there thought I ought to shoot them."

"I didn't know they weren't armed," she shot back.

"Why the hell not? Too busy *working* me?" Spence sneered.

181

"Do you think they were the rogue viewers or that reclamation team you were talking about?" Dorel pushed Mike, who was now standing almost in front of her, out of her view of Rian.

"I don't know for certain, because I can't view into Datascape as I said. I've never tried before this. Haven't ever had the desire," Rian responded and glanced at Spence. "Can you?"

He nodded. Mike told her what Spence was sure she knew very well—that Datascape conditioned their viewers *not* to view inside the company or its operations and business unless assigned to do so. Then it was a double blind coordinate viewing exercise so neither the viewer or the monitor knew if the unconfirmed data gained was a training exercise or a real mission.

"If you can overcome and breach the deprogramming, you can remote view anything," Mike added and sat on the arm of Dorel's chair, opening himself rather than protecting his field from Rian's influence. She even sent him a grateful smile.

Stupid ass, Spence huffed. What else was Mike going to do, hand her the house keys and tell her to make herself at home? They wouldn't be so goddamn trusting if they knew her like he did. "Oh, I think Rian can do just about anything she sets her mind to," he chipped from the sidelines. "She doesn't need our help." He directed a hard look at Mike.

"I don't blame you, Spence, for your suspicion and your distrust," Rian responded. "You must understand that I thought I was helping you. It's my job and—"

"I vas joost followink orders." Spence clicked his heels and gave a straight arm salute.

She turned a baleful gaze on him. "Speaking from experience, perhaps? When I was assigned you not only did I hope to help you, I prayed it was in time to save some innocent lives as well."

Spence glared back at her. "If you can't view inside Datascape, how did you know that they were coming here this morning? They didn't, by the way. Bad intel, any way you cut it."

"I made an assumption. They'd just broken into my house and at the time their energy seemed similar or negative intentioned, at least," Rian said. "Since Ian wouldn't take my call, I had to consider that they might be the reclamation team looking for you."

"Why not save everyone the time and trouble and bring them on down here to get me, huh?" Spence smirked.

"If they're coming here and you haven't known from the moment they decided to do it, then you haven't shielded properly or corrupted the view with an adulterated AOL."

"Analytic overlay," Mike answered Dorel's unvoiced question.

"Hold it, time out. So, do we all agree that Marty isn't in danger from these rogues or reclaimers or whatever they are?" Dorel asked, looking from one to the others.

"I think Datascape wants him," Spence said with finality and Mike agreed with him. Rian didn't respond.

"Rian?" Mike asked.

"Until we can get more information and are more certain that it's safe, I think it's best that he stay away," she rejoined, holding Dorel's gaze.

"Who gives a goddamn what you think?" Spence blustered. "There is no *we* as far as you're concerned. I bet the first thing you did was try to acquire him, wasn't it?"

Rian raised her chin in defiance. "I wanted to be sure he was safe. I couldn't find him, so he is safe. And I don't want you to tell me anything about where is he. Just do as you have been and no one else will find him either—if they were trying to. And I'm not certain they are, unlike Spence."

"Rian, don't get me wrong, but why do you care this much about a little boy you've known for a few months?" Mike asked.

"She's going to give you some crap about being his sister in a past life. But I think that's just something she latched onto during my regression," Spence groused, wanting to hurt her, but wished he hadn't when her eyes misted and she pressed her lips together. When she brought her sad gaze up to Spence, Meredith looked back at him.

"Yes, I believe I was Meredith Everly in my past life. She was a good woman who loved well and honestly," Rian professed with pride.

"You were my Aunt Meredith?" Dorel said with wonder, staring at Rian as if trying to find her great aunt in her olive-toned features. She turned to Spence with a sly smile, "Well now, Romeo, doesn't that just put a different spin on things?"

No one spoke for a few moments, the air charged with their cautious processing as they tried to make some sense out of all this. "So, what now?" Spence asked.

"I think it's a given that Ian has dispatched the reclamation team," Rian said to Spence. "They will track you with last known location delineation constantly updated by a large team of viewers targeting you twenty-four seven. You, actually we, will have to augment and vary our shielding, change our actual locations."

"I was afraid of that. Why do they want Spence back?" Dorel asked.

"I was told I have no need to know when I made the mistake of asking Ian that. Datascape viewers and operatives are given enough information to get the job done. Nothing more, and if you ask, you flag yourself as having inordinate curiosity. Not healthy," she said, a frown marring her forehead. She looked tired and vulnerable, her smokescreen of elegant sensuality and smooth sophistication fading.

Mike stood and settled a loving gaze on Dorel. "I swore I would never allow anyone or anything to drive me out of my house again. But she's right. We've got to go. I'm sorry, babe."

Weary, Spence wiped his aching hand over his face. Where in the hell could they go and for how long? He hadn't even taken a vacation in two years, now he was supposed to take off and let Integrity run itself? Mike had gotten the time off from TransAsia with no problem, but what about their aircraft leasing business? They couldn't afford to hire a crew to fly that Miami airplane to the mod center . . .

"Mike, can you give me a hand with my stuff in the car?" Spence asked, giving Mike a pointed look and starting for the front door. Mike caught up with him outside.

"Okay, what's up?" Mike asked behind him as he pulled his bags out of the car. He handed Mike the flight bag.

"You know that bird in Miami?" he asked and grabbed the wrapped tool off the seat.

Mike's eyes lit up and he grinned. "Hell yes. That's a damn good idea. We'll go get her."

"JET says the airplane is ready to go now. All we need are the tickets. We need to find a redeye going out tonight and buy the tickets online. Get one for Dorel, too."

"That's too trackable. Why not just leave a note on the front door and tell Datascape where we've gone. We can't go commercial and Rian comes with us even if we have to persuade her pretty hard. Remember that old saying—keep your friends close and your enemies closer."

He agreed with Mike on one count—Rian was an enemy. "We could kill her," he ventured. "Okay. She comes with us, but I'm not driving across the country playing license plate poker with her." He thought a moment. "You know that near derelict Metroliner Barnes keeps at Renton Field? He says he's going to scrap it out, but still flies it. Offered it to me several times, just put fuel in it. No one will pay any attention to an old Metroliner. We'll need to make one fuel stop, and at three hundred miles an hour, that will put us in Miami in about eight or nine hours."

"You think that piece of junk will get us down there?"

"Sure. You know what they say, it takes only two things to make an airplane fly—money and airspeed," Spence said, waggling his eyebrows.

"You never miss an opportunity to thrash me with those prehistoric clichés, do you, smart ass?" Mike nodded toward the parcel in Spence's hand. "Did you bring me a present?"

The parcel weighed heavily in his hand. "Dorel didn't tell you about this?"

Mike shook his head. "I don't think so. Wait, yes, something about a tool and the sword. Let's go in. It's too wet to be standing out here. Give Barnes a call and ask if the Metroliner is available and if he'll get it ready for you." Spence agreed and they hurried back inside.

"You brought it," Dorel exclaimed when Spence set his bag and the parcel on the floor by the sofa. "Show Mike."

"He's got to make a call while we talk about a couple of things," Mike said.

Spence pulled out his cell phone, listening to Mike fill the women in on the plan as he called Barnes.

"I can't do that. I'm not flying to Miami," Rian objected

and picked up her bag. "I'll take care of my own security. You are free to do as you wish."

"Our security dictates that we take you with us. You understand why, so don't argue about it," Mike told her.

Rian sent a challenging glance Spence's way. He hung up and stuck the phone in his pocket. "Hell, stay here. I believe dragging you along is a mistake."

"Rian's coming with us, even if I have to chain you both to the bulkhead. Dorel can fly the second seat if she has to, can't you, babe?" Mike said with affection and turned back to Rian. "Do I need to tie you down now, or can I trust you to help us?"

"Honestly, I don't know," Rian said. "I'm so emotionally exhausted by this mess I can't think straight, much less keep my shield fortified. I'm afraid they can target me now no matter where I am. And that means they can target Spence if I'm around."

"They won't get through Spence's shield," Mike countered. "Dorel, can you pack a couple of bags for us and call the dog sitter to ask if we can drop Katana off? I've got some stuff to take care of real quick. Spence, you've got this leg of the Rian watch."

Before Spence could protest, both Dorel and Mike headed out of the room, leaving Rian and he scowling at each other.

"I've got to leave, Spence, you know that," Rian said, softening her expression.

He took a seat on the ottoman as far away from her as he could get and still be in the same room. "Dorel and Mike are kind, good people. They don't deserve what you've brought down on them. I may. They don't. If you want me to help you go against what they think is the right thing to do, forget it. You'll get no traction with me."

"I'm not looking for traction. I'm just asking you to try to separate yourself from your fixated devotion and guilt to perceive the truth. You're being ham-strung by your emotions like you were when you blindly got involved with Michael's problem with Inada."

His throat constricted and his heart pounded. A wave of rage carried him into a huge holographic panorama of existence where his present life intersected with Mike's. He experienced every event and detail in a split second.

Spence took a deep breath and snapped back into his body, bringing his focus to bear on Rian. She shrunk back, her eyes wide and fearful.

"You viewed for Inada. You helped him find the sword. And you helped him find Dorel and Mike. He didn't kill Dorel because of some spiritual intercession. You remote influenced him, made him leave, because when Datascape discovered the value of that sword, they decided to take it themselves." He let a harsh laugh escape. "What a mind blower than must have been when the sword disappeared in a flash. And you viewed it, didn't you?"

"Yes, but I wasn't working for Inada. Ian assigned me coordinates and I blueprinted them. I didn't interpret the data. Ian or someone higher up did that. I viewed targets until Ian asked me to remote influence Inada and I did."

He regarded her without emotion just like she'd urged him to a couple of minutes ago. She didn't appear to like the result. "Then you've seen the Defender's sword."

She nodded warily. "I ran a chain of custody on it."

The back of his neck prickled. On a hunch, he picked up the chamois-wrapped package and opened it. "Do you know anything about this?"

Rian brushed a trembling finger across the inscribing on the tool and gasped. "Oh my God. The *aptet!*"

Chapter Twelve

Hidden deep beneath the majestic protector lion-god Aker, the jackal-headed god Anubis stood watchful over their secret labors.

The powerful magician Seta's bare torso shone with sweat as he struck life into the malleable metal, each blow of his hammer casting white-hot stars into the darkness of the underground temple. His queen Kalūkah, a great sorceress, sought his help to defend Egypt from its many enemies without and within.

The god Anubis had bestowed a mighty alchemy upon Kalūkah's lover Seta. Only here in the Forge of Balance did Anubis share his mysteries with Seta and teach him to craft a potent aptet for working magic upon earthly things.

Seta plunged the glowing tool, hooked on one end to catch the power of the heavens, into the deep basin of water. Steam effervesced, flowing around Seta's smooth, hairless body. He grimaced against the heat, turning his bald head aside, while intoning the sacred incantations of creation. When the steam drifted heavenward and the waters calmed, he withdrew the aptet, now inscribed with arcane markings of the omnipotent.

With great reverence, Kalūkah placed upon the forge two identical flat, thin strips of gold somewhat longer than Seta's strong arm. She, too, chanted magic spells, their voices blending in a harmony of conception that reverberated through the temple, ascending its apex, gathering strength. Kalūkah raised her open left hand to the spiraling sound above. Seta took up the warm aptet in his right hand and, clasping the right hand of his beloved queen with his left, touched the aptet to the twin bands of gold.

Undulating waves of sound overhead melded into a tight

spiral and shot downward, consuming the forge in an explosion of resonance and illumination. Seta and Kalūkah writhed in the torment of parturition but they did not waver in their sacred trust and held fast.

Roaring ebbed and brilliance receded. Upon the forge where bands of gold had lain, two identical long shining swords of strange alloy and plain appearance waited. Their handles, wrapped with straw-colored cord, held tiny golden goddesses. Their delicately curving blades were inscribed with the markings of their creator Anubis.

Seta released the aptet. Still joined by the right hand to his beloved, he and his queen each took up a sword, crossing the blades. Anubis spoke from the shadows of the Underworld:

Defender and Guardian blood mixes
Minds meld and both become whole
Eternal power shall be forged

Kalūkah released Seta's hand. With eternal love and unwavering acceptance of his fate, Seta knelt at her feet, holding the Guardian sword in his open palms.

"Be at peace and await me in the Underworld, my love," Kalūkah whispered and swept the Defender sword against Seta's offered neck. As his ka began its journey guarded by Anubis, his warm blood cooled upon the Guardian's blade that Kalūkah lifted from his hands.

Rian released a horrified sob. She covered her face with her hands and rocked with a soft keening. A strong pair of arms went around her and she leaned on him, allowing herself the comfort Spence offered. She listened to his heart's steady beat as she wept against his chest. He smoothed his hand over her hair and held her until her crying subsided.

She sat up, wiping her face with her fingertips, but she couldn't look at him. He caught her chin in his hand and tipped it up. "You okay?"

He didn't look okay either. "No," she sniffed and tried to pull away. He let her go and sat back, staring at her with an awkward expression.

"What? I told you I was exhausted. I've got to go home."

"You can't. Are you ready to talk about it?" Spence asked, narrowing his eyes at her.

"Sure. Why I can't go home?" Could he have experienced what she did or was he wondering what was up with her when she went rigid and vacant-eyed as her spirit catapulted out of body. She hadn't even heard of an *aptet* before the word tumbled out of her mouth when Spence showed her the tool. It was a conditioned trigger. The question was who anchored that memory.

"Rian?" Dorel dropped the sleeping bags she carried and hurried to her. "My gosh, Spence, what did you do?" Dorel clucked over her and asked if she needed something. Rian thanked her and said she was fine.

"Well, if you're sure you don't need something. Just rest here. I'm packing some sandals and clothes for you, too, since we can't go back for your things. They'll be big on you, I'm afraid." She patted her tummy. "I've never seemed to lose all that baby weight." Dorel started to walk away. "Oh, you don't have any pets that we need to make arrangements for, do you?" Rian shook her head and Dorel went down the hall, calling instructions to Mike.

"So, two swords, huh?" Spence said from the corner of the sofa where he sprawled.

"Two swords, huh?" she repeated, pulling herself into the same position as he and projecting a suggestion of him smiling and opening to her.

"This is about as open as I'm going to get, so you can stop your Jedi mind tricks or I'll go Darth Vader on your ass with the power of the dark side," he smirked and crossed his legs.

Without thinking, Rian started to match him and cross hers, but stopped herself. He'd caught her, knew exactly what she was doing. She smiled acquiescence and put her hands together, bowing. "You have learned well, cockroach."

"That's grasshopper, smart ass." He leaned forward. "Now, let's talk. When you touched the tool and went out, so did I, right along with you. I was there and like you say, seeing what I saw, hearing what I heard, feeling what I felt—"

"Then you think you were Seta in that life?"

"Hell no, you were!" he exclaimed, then settled back with a smirk. "It felt that way, yeah. What do you think?"

She chose her words with care. "I experienced the scene from an omniscient point of view. I wasn't in either body, but both, we'll say. That doesn't mean I couldn't have been one of them in that life. It seems to me that the importance of this experience to our present situation is knowing there are two swords, one of which is Dorel's."

Mike and Dorel appeared and set their bags in the foyer. Dorel rechecked the house and turned off lights and Mike ducked into his office for his pilot's case. Spence stood and looked down at her. "Time to go. We'll get this sorted out when we get in the air. We'll have a lot of time to figure out what it means."

"Figure out what?" Mike asked and shut his door.

Spence gave him an abbreviated recap of their mutual regression and ended with, "If we're to believe that happened." Mike's face went ashen and Dorel moaned, shaking her head.

"Good God. Two swords!" Mike exclaimed. "I thought

we ended it when we cut up the Defender sword and it disappeared. We better hope to hell that no one has the other one, if there still is another one."

"The Guardian twin," Rian murmured, her past of seconds, hours, millennia coalescing in a tangible enlightenment. "That's why Datascape wants you." Spence jerked back and frowned at her, confused. "Think, Spence. You can view Datascape. They can't shield from you. Now, this moment you can view right in there while they're so busy generating all that energy by trying to view you. You're targeting the sword. Do it!" she ordered.

Spence's eyelids fluttered and his body stiffened as his auric field expanded. Rian had to control herself to keep from being swept out of body with his strong energy force. Mike stood behind Spence, extending his own energy protectively around him. Dorel grabbed Rian's hand and sat down on the floor at her knees. Rian strengthened her shield and created a reflective energy force field around the four of them.

Many long, silent minutes passed before Spence sucked in a deep breath and opened his eyes. He rubbed his face with his hands and sat up. "It's called deep doodie, kids. They've got us. Even tried to hold me there with some kind of technology. We've got to get out of here now."

"I take it they've found out that you and I aren't enjoying ourselves at the Tacoma Dome," Rian muttered and picked up her bag.

"Yup, the unconcert is over. Let's go," Spence said, rewrapping the *aptet* and stowing it in his flight bag. He put a hand at the small of her back and propelled her toward the foyer.

Mike called the dog and they picked up the bags, exiting the house. Rian tried one more time to convince them that

193

she shouldn't go with them, but wasn't so sure. They couldn't deal with Datascape on their own. Spence's skills weren't reliable yet, because he was conflicted about his feelings for her. As she allowed them to insist she climb in the back seat of Mike's SUV with Spence, she resolved to help them no matter how they felt about her. The big Airedale hung over the seat, swabbing her neck and cheek with his drippy beard. As they drove away from her beautiful SL, she was gripped with sadness. It hadn't bothered her before to leave possessions behind. She'd had to many times and learned not to care much about them. However, driving that fast, pearl white convertible was like a magic therapy. She was a different person in that car. And almost the one she'd always wanted to be.

After they dropped Katana off at the dogsitter's, Spence suggested they use the drive time to the Renton airport to each construct vivid thought forms, keeping their minds and energy focused and more difficult to view or influence.

"Don't be afraid of thoughts of Marty," Rian advised Dorel when she mentioned that she was worried because she couldn't stop thinking of him. "Just let the thought come in like a breeze and flow through. Observe and let it go. Anything you're afraid of or resist gets bigger and more difficult. Just let it go."

Dorel decided to focus her thoughts on the Sonic Cruiser, engineering schematic by schematic. Mike said he would take a mind tour in Singapore with a large group of Japanese tourists. Spence formed a mental picture of his F-14 Tomcat and began to make night ops carrier landings, but he couldn't keep his mind off of Rian. Her sitting next to him became such a distraction that he suspected she was launching pictures of her naked body his way. He rolled his shoulders and squirmed in his seat, trying to get comfortable and concentrate. Didn't happen. By the time Mike pulled the QX4 into the Renton airport, Spence had crashed and burned his Tomcat and made wild love to Rian on the flight deck while the Yellow Shirts cheered.

They parked beside the Barnes Aviation hangar, leaving Rian and Dorel in the car. Mike instructed them to continue shielding while he and Spence got the airplane ready. Spence walked away from the car uneasy. Should they be trusting Rian like this?

After they'd gotten the Metroliner's door key from Barnes, who let them know he'd waited for them way past closing time as a big favor, and ordered the fuel truck, they walked around the building to the turboprop tied down on the parking apron. "What a piece of junk!" Mike exclaimed and unlocked the door. He pulled the handle and the door rotated down out of the fuselage, forming a stairway. Mike climbed inside while Spence began to walk the airplane as the fuel truck pulled up.

Spence finished his preflight and joined Mike in the cockpit to complete the cockpit check. "It may be a dirty pig, but I think it will probably get us there."

"Looks like it's ditto for in the cockpit, too. Go get the girls and we'll crank this thing up and get down the road," Mike said, flipping switches and checking lights.

"Where's the log book?"

Mike raised up in the seat and pulled the aluminum-covered book out from under him. "It's a clean book. I didn't see any open squawks or problems."

"Good. I'll pay for the fuel and go get them," Spence said and backed out of the cockpit. He paid the fuel truck driver and went to get the girls. They weren't in the car. Spence touched the .45 at the small of his back and glanced around the floodlit lot. Dorel and Rian walked out of Barnes' office, carrying cans of soda and small bags of chips.

"Your in-flight meal service tonight will include Dr Pepper and corn chips for the captain and assorted month-old cookies from the vending machine," Dorel said and handed off the stuff to Rian. "Take these. I'll help Spence with the luggage."

After they climbed into the airplane, Spence pulled up the stairs and closed the door. Dorel and Rian stood bent over in the middle of the empty plane with stunned expressions.

"It smells terrible in here," Dorel said, her nose wrinkling. "Where are we supposed to sit?"

Spence pointed aft to the two remaining seats in front of the lavatory's bulkhead. "Those don't look too bad, and they may even have seatbelts. Too bad they're back there, though. We'll get the lav serviced when we make our fuel stop. Here's some earplugs, you're gonna need them."

"We're stopping?" Rian said, an anxious frown turning her mouth down.

"Yeah, just once according to the flight plan." He set the sleeping bags and luggage on the floor against the cockpit bulkhead and started to duck into the cockpit.

"Spence, if you filed a flight plan, they'll be there when we land," Rian said and raked her teeth over her bottom lip.

"Yes, we filed a flight plan online, but we're going to make an in-route change. Trust me, they won't know. Or if they do figure it out, it will be too late. Better get buckled up, we're outta here," he said and ducked into the cockpit, squeezing into the right seat, and pulling on a headset.

"Go ahead and crank right number two," Mike said, after the tower had given them clearance to start engines.

Spence flipped the switch and heard the faint snapping of the igniter until the engine started, while he watched the gauges for temperatures, pressures and RPM. The turboprop engine turned up with a deafening combination of jet engine roar and propeller noise. He lit off number one and monitored it as it came up to match the parameters of the other engine.

"Thank you, tower," Mike said on the headset. "Metroliner Six Tango Whiskey is taxiing into position, runway five, for takeoff."

"Six Tango Whiskey, you are cleared for immediate departure as soon as you line up on runway five," the controller advised.

"Thank you, tower, Six Tango Whiskey will be making an immediate departure as soon as we line up on the runway," Mike repeated.

Spence leaned and looked back at Dorel and Rian and yelled, "Are you strapped in good and tight?" They gave him a thumbs-up and he settled back in the seat. Mike taxied toward Lake Washington and made the turn onto the active runway.

"Tower, Six Tango Whiskey commencing immediate takeoff, runway five," Mike said and pushed the throttles forward.

"Six Tango Whiskey, permission to take off denied. Please taxi back to your ramp position immediately," the controller ordered as flashing red lights raced down the taxiway toward them.

"Screw this," Spence growled. He laid his hand on top of Mike's and firewalled the throttles.

"Tower, Six Tango Whiskey unable to safely abort takeoff. Switching over to departure frequency," Mike said as the airplane rotated off the runway and flew into the rain clouds.

Four hours later they were setting up the airplane on final into Gallup, New Mexico. He and Mike had talked and argued about what to do now that they seemed to be wanted by law enforcement, with Datascape's encouragement no doubt. Mike griped that they could be the topic of this week's *Most Wanted* TV program. Spence had laughed and agreed, but they both knew the chances of their coming out of this with their money or lives was slim to none.

"What I let you get me into," Spence said, shaking his head and he dropped the landing gear. "Gear down and locked."

"Give me approach flaps," Mike said. "*You* got me into this, not the other way around. And this time you might just get us killed." Spence couldn't dispute that and stayed quiet until Mike called for landing flaps.

As they touched down and Mike reversed propeller thrust, Spence got instructions from the tower to taxi to the ramp. He half expected to see the taxiway blocked with police cruisers but there was no one around at 2:30 in the morning. They were going to have to hang around until six a.m. when the fuel dock opened.

He and Mike shut down the airplane. Dorel came forward in a stooped over shuffle, "What an incredible piece of crap this airplane is and it smells like it, too," Dorel yelled, then took the earplugs out.

"Are you speaking of this sewer tube otherwise known as a Metroliner or the condition thereof?" Mike asked and gave her a kiss on the mouth.

She jerked her head back toward her seat. "Rian's still sleeping. Hey, did you guys notice that the escape hatch is bolted closed?"

"Well, I guess you aren't going out that way, are you?" Spence scoffed, bringing the logbook up to date.

She looked out the windscreen. "Ramp services gone beddy bye?"

"Yup. We can either sack out in the back or see if we can catch a ride into town." Mike eased out of the seat, pushing his wife back into the cabin. "You decide. I'll tie the airplane down." He opened the door and dropped the stairs.

"Hmmm, Gallup, New Mexico at 3:00 a.m. or sleep in a flying toilet." Dorel held her hands out, weighing air. "I'm having trouble seeing a viable choice here," she said as Mike hopped down the stairs.

"Put those earplugs up your nose and let's get some sleep," Spence said, turning off the cabin lights to save the batteries and rolled out a sleeping bag on the filthy carpet. He unzipped it, glancing at Rian sleeping in her seat, and crawled in. His .45 was a hard rock under his back. He pulled it out, laying the gun on his chest, and closed his eyes.

Strident whispering woke him. Spence eased his fingers around the .45's grip as he peered through slitted eyelids towards the sound as his eyes got used to the darkness. Light streamed in the windows from the ramp illuminating shadowed forms that he recognized as Rian and Mike. They sat on the floor in front of the seats that Dorel was curled up asleep on, their backs against the cabin's curving wall. He couldn't make out what they were saying, but he sensed it was about him. Not good. Rian might have a hard time manipulating Mike, but she'd get the job done.

He sat up and stretched. "Is it time to roll?"

"Got an hour yet. Go back to sleep," Mike said and tipped a soda can up to his mouth.

"Is there a Dr Pepper left?" Spence crawled out of the bag and crouch-walked back to them.

Rian held out a can to him. He took it, eased into a

squat in front of the pair and popped the top. "So, what's up?" He slugged down the warm soda. It hit his empty belly hard.

"We're working scenarios and projecting strategies. In other words, we don't know what the hell we're going to do," Mike answered and crushed his soda can.

"We pick up the airplane. Take it to San Antonio," Spence said with a shrug.

"What then, Spence?" Rian asked, the worry in her voice hitting him like a dash of ice water. "They tried to stop us in Renton. We'll see them in Miami, you can count on it. We can't keep running from them."

"What do you suggest? That I just turn myself over to them? Is that what you want?" Spence argued. He wanted her to say no, but he knew that's exactly what she thought.

"Don't be a jackass. Of course we don't want that. It wouldn't solve a thing anyway. There's still the problem of their looking for Marty. I think the best way to handle this is to go on the offensive. I've never cared much for running." Mike rubbed his hands together and slipped them into his jacket's pockets. "It's getting cold in here."

"We can't forget that Datascape has a full cadre of specialists. You were one of the first remote influencers," she said. "And the best."

"Yeah. Mike was smart enough to opt out of the program. I wasn't . . ." Spence grimaced as the memories spooled up. He was an assassin—targeting personal frequencies and then broadcasting an interrupt wave that could result in nausea, disorientation, memory problems and, ultimately, death. That's all they wanted him for, killing people who never even knew he was coming after them. Datascape didn't care if they were deserving or innocent. If the client paid, Datascape delivered. Ian had loved to say his job wasn't passing judgement and advised Spence not to either. And then the breakdown, but the cause wasn't clear.

"There were no particulars in your file about the breakdown," Rian answered his thought. "It's possible that you opted out like Mike did. Couldn't take it any more, don't you think?"

"Maybe," Spence said and sat, resting against the wall. His eyes burned and his muscles were stiffening up.

"Back to what we're going to do," Mike urged. "I keep thinking that if we could get a hold of the Guardian sword ourselves we'd have some bargaining power. Maybe buy our way out of this."

"It's more complicated than that, I think," Rian countered. "Look at the elements of Datascape's plan that we know of—they've known about the Defender or Mike's sword—"

"It was Dorel's," Mike corrected. "Or as you viewed in the chain of custody, it followed us, brought us together through several lifetimes. But what's incredible is that you two viewed the creation of the sword or swords, I should say."

"We created them," Rian affirmed. "Datascape may not know about the Guardian sword, but I'm not sure. And when I consider my viewing for them since I first began, I think they've had the Defender sword in their hands somehow. Spence, why don't you target the sword now?"

Spence felt an odd resistance. Maybe because she was suggesting he do it, and he couldn't be sure she wasn't manipulating him. But it probably made sense anyway. Information was power. "Yeah, okay."

"I'll guide you, if that's okay. It's a little different than what you've been doing, but guiding you will allow me to support you with my energy as well as protect you," Rian said.

He nodded and her voice began to flow over him like silk. "Allow yourself to open to the protective light of love and protection. It flows in through the top of your head, fills your body and flows out through your heart in an endless cycle. The light forms a shield of protection around us, this airplane and expands across the world. In and out, expanding with our breath. Now allow yourself to follow that expansion out of your body, with your intent to become one with the energy of the Defender sword. You are instantly with it. That's right. Now, see its energy as it intersects with yours and go to the last time you held the sword in your hands and trace it forward in this lifetime. Bring it clearly into focus. Observing and remembering everything. And when you're ready float back to now. Into this cabin and into your body and open your eyes."

Spence's eyes popped open but his energy body hadn't synchronized with his physical body yet. He had a sense of being out of phase, a pervasive fuzziness and took some deep breaths.

"The viewers and other entities were out there, did you see?" Rian asked with excitement. "Nothing attached to you, though. You did a good job. Spence?"

He smoothed his hand over his moustache, trying to put into words what he just experienced. "I traced the sword to a room under the Sphinx. The Forge of Power, I assume. Then a bright light and I followed it to Denver. Ian had it in his hands. He also had the tool. The pieces were stolen from a secret dig in Egypt and Datascape bought both pieces on the black market. I worked on getting Datascape's intention surrounding the artifacts. It's not clear, but I think they're looking for the key to the sword's power. They know how Mike used it, but think there's more. And Inada had filled them in on what he knew about the sword." He glanced at Rian. "Were you assigned that?"

She shook her head. "No, I was assigned to you. Whatever or whomever came into your energy field, I blueprinted. Someone else had Inada."

"I don't think anyone at Datascape can figure out what the symbols mean. And they don't know what the *aptet* is either, but Ian's got some idea that I know or can remote view it, because they haven't been able to. At least that's the motivation I got. Though I could have a big analytic overlay going. Too close to home, you know?" he added with chagrin.

"What time is it?" Dorel asked in a sleepy voice from her seat and sat up. "I've got to get a double tall vanilla latte right now or someone's going to get hurt."

Spence looked at his watch. "They ought to be opening up in about ten minutes." He pulled himself into a half-crouch and added, "It's not only me that they want." He cut a guarded glance at Dorel. "They'd been watching Marty since he was born. Knew who and what he was. The plan was to snatch him one day and he'd be just another missing kid. They intend to build him into some sort of super viewer, like Rian."

"I swear I didn't know. I didn't know what they were doing with the reports I sent on the family," Rian cried. "They monitor all their former viewers. I was assigned to you. Nothing unusual about that."

"Marty's still safe, isn't he, Spence?" Dorel asked. "You saw that, didn't you? He's safe?"

Mike moved to the seats and gathered her into his arms. "Yes, he's safe. Don't worry. Remember, he's a hell of a lot smarter than all of us together. He knew the right thing to do and did it." Dorel leaned her head on Mike's shoulder and closed her eyes, silent tears seeping from the lashes.

Spence prayed Mike knew something he didn't and that he was telling Dorel the truth. He cleared his throat and took a breath. "There's something else. The sword is back at the forge. It disappeared from Datascape somehow."

"Guardian took him home after Daddy came back," Doral murmured. "That's what Marty told us, Spence, remember? I thought he was talking about his *Everlasting Warriors* game."

Connections snapped into place in Spence's brain. "Rian, does Datascape have a marketing research division?"

"Market Intel Group, why?"

"Dorel, is that the name of the company that gave Marty the game?" Spence asked, excitement edged with dread building in his gut. She nodded.

He slapped his forehead. "The sword in the game was an exact copy of the Defender sword. They could have thought that he could interpret the symbols on the blade. Hell, maybe he can, because he knows about the twin swords, too. When I showed him the hooked tool, he called it my key. Key to what? Datascape made sure I got the tool, so, that means . . ."

"Datascape knows there are two swords. And they know that when the swords are joined together according to the ritual, they will command the greatest power on earth."

They stared in horrified shock at Rian sitting against the wall, her eyes downcast to the dirty floor. "How?" Spence breathed.

"I'm afraid that I told them."

Chapter Thirteen

Rian steeled herself for the onslaught of anger, but she had to tell them. She'd already brought enough down on these people. The very least she could do was arm them with information, make them understand what they were truly up against.

No one said anything and Rian raised her gaze to them. "I warned you that I shouldn't come with—"

"Get out!" Mike popped open the door and jabbed a finger at the outside. "Get your ass out of my airplane."

She gathered her bag and stood, sending a furtive glance at Spence. He stood immovable, a cold murderous glint to his eyes. "I can't believe I let you con me again."

"I know that's how it seems, but it's not." Rian turned to Dorel. "Please, let me explain. I can still help—"

"Get the hell out and consider yourself lucky that you're still breathing when you do," Mike growled.

"Wait, Michael," Dorel said. "She didn't have to tell us. I think we ought to give her a chance to explain herself. Spence, can you be okay with that?"

"I don't want to hear anything she has to say. If you want to let her lie to you, go ahead. I'll be outside," he said, refusing to look at Rian and started for the door. Mike put a hand on his chest, stopping him.

"Hang on. I'd like to hear what she comes up with," Mike said.

They were talking about her like she wasn't there. Convincing them she was telling the truth and getting them to act on it was going to be very difficult. And with Spence's

10820088008806

0806 text:

raw hatred-stoked opposition, it might be impossible.

"I just put this together as I was guiding you. I didn't think they targeted me during our mutual regression to the forge, Spence, but they did. I hadn't shielded properly and was open, vulnerable," Rian explained, then added, "I didn't control my emotions and they followed the strong low frequency or vibrations right to me. They perceived what we experienced as an echo, but that's all they needed."

"That's why you didn't want to come with us," Dorel said, giving her an empathetic pat on the arm.

"She said she didn't want to before that," Mike reminded his wife, still looking unconvinced. Spence glared at her but there was something else in his eyes, too. "And you said they didn't know about the Guardian. Now you change your story, why?"

"I didn't want to come with you because I was worried this might happen, that I wouldn't be able to control my emotions and Datascape would track us, following my energy trail like a road map." She caught Spence's gaze and held it. "Because it's been a very difficult few days, life altering, you might say between Spence and me." He snorted and looked away. "But I believe whatever that was isn't a factor any longer and won't interfere with my ability to help you."

Mike pulled up the door and shut it. "Sit down, Rian. You might save yourself from a long walk home yet." She lowered herself to the floor with a shiver as the cold light of day cracked the horizon. Dorel cocooned herself in a sleeping bag while Mike sat on his heels opposite Rian. Spence defended his position in the corner opposite the door, his tall frame hovering near the ceiling like an avenging angel.

"So, help us," Mike dared and crossed his arms over his chest.

She hugged herself, rubbing her arms and ordering her thoughts. "During the flight I considered what you said about Datascape viewers being conditioned to not view within the company. I was determined to overcome my conditioning, if there was any, and remote view their intentions regarding us and the swords. It took me several attempts to locate the junctures in the past where my conditioning was installed. Once those were breached, I saw that Datascape, or Ian, really, had begun my conditioning from the moment I volunteered for the psych experiments at college."

"Where was that?" Dorel asked.

"Whitworth College in Spokane. I was there on a music scholarship—"

"Can we cut the Rian retrospective and get to the point where you help us," Spence groused. "I want Mike and Dorel to see just how creative you can get."

That stung, but she projected thoughts of toleration and kindness at him and took a fortifying breath. "What I didn't realize was that during my graduate work when I was also training in hypnotherapy I was regressed more extensively than I remembered to a very deep amnesic state and instructed not to remember. However, once I was able to break the conditioning, I accessed the material from the regressions. Ian selected me to bring Spence in, knowing that we have a deep connection that would prevail because of our past life together as Paul and Meredith and as Seta and Kalūkah. So Ian learned about our Egyptian life and the swords long before we did."

"Ian again," said Mike. "Was he with Datascape when we were?"

"Yeah, but I don't know if you met him. I remember now that after you left Ian was like my mentor. He was a good friend," Spence said, a bit of yearning in his voice.

"Ian said you were the best he'd ever seen. He was proud of you like a good son," Rian disclosed but didn't reveal how jealous she'd been when Ian raved about Spence. She hadn't realized then that Ian manipulated her through her need for approval. His ceaseless comparison of her performance against the Datascape legend whom he appeared to love more than her had hurt terribly. But Ian never loved anyone. She'd realized this the hard way and was able to grow out of her dependence on him. Spence helped her do that, because she came to know him so well in her researching and viewing. Spence was a much better man than Ian could ever be.

"I asked Ian once why you left. He alluded to some sort of breakdown. A few months ago he professed to be so worried about you that he wanted to bring you back in. He was afraid that if your deprogramming breached you would harm yourself or others. Then he restated the situation and said that rogue viewers were after you. I believed him because he framed the whole scenario around my repressed feelings for you and my subconscious desire to be with you again. He knew I would jump at the chance to work with you. I'd been programmed to trust him. As you said, he was my mentor and like a father to me."

Spence sniffed and cleared his throat. "Yeah. Well, I guess he wasn't such a good guy after all. So what's this got to do with the problem at hand?"

A fuel truck stopped outside the airplane and Spence moved to the door. "I'll get him going." He opened the door and directed the driver to put on a full load. "How do we want to pay for this?" he asked Dorel. She told him to charge it to the company card. "Do we want to leave a paper trail?" Spence asked.

"I'm going to make the assumption that our lives and

our business aren't always going to be on the edge of a stall. This is a business trip and I want receipts," Dorel returned with a buttoned down crispness and dug in her bag. She handed Mike a credit card to give to Spence.

Spence gave the driver the card. "He says the café is open. Let's go get some breakfast."

"I want to hear how she's going to help first," Mike said and both Spence and Dorel groaned. "We'll have time, don't worry."

Rian continued with a sense of urgency, "This is huge and risky. Datascape has massive financial exposure with mobilized personnel and commitment of resources dedicated to this operation. In effect, Ian has bet the company and his life is on the line here. He's lost Marty, but he cannot fail to bring you and me in, because we are the forgers of those swords. He made a mistake when he gave you the key to the Forge of Balance. And even though they're going after the swords, they cannot retrieve them without the key."

"The *aptet*," Spence said with awe and slapped his hand over his mouth.

"Yes. The Egyptians figured the chamber had been breached and wanted to get rid of the evidence, because disclosing that a samurai sword had been found there would have made them a laughing stock. Once the *aptet* and the Defender's sword were offered on the antiquities black market, Datascape traced the chain of custody to a member of the archeological team that discovered the samurai sword. Datascape discovered that he also had a digital map of the chamber. They *employed* him, to put it nicely, to interpret the hieroglyphs and other pictures on the walls that tell the story of Queen Kalūkah's wielding the twin swords to gain incredible victories over all the enemies of Egypt during the course of her thirty-year reign."

The sun rose above the horizon, beginning to warm the clear high desert air. A freshening breeze drifted fumes of aviation fuel in the open doorway that Spence guarded. Rian coughed into her fist and continued, "Ian ran all the various pieces of data—what I'd reported when Mike was using the sword, the legends, the interpreted hieroglyphs, our past lives in Egypt and more. He now had the Defender sword, broken and useless, and that strange hooked tool the glyphs suggested was a key."

"Ahhhh. I get it. Ian figured since I or Seta made the *aptet* that we used to create the swords, I could fix the sword I'd also cut up," Spence added.

Rian nodded. "More importantly, Ian knew there were two swords, but he only had one. The Egyptian swore that they didn't find it in the chamber. Ian believes that you will be able to find it."

"How about the symbols on the sword matching the tool, don't they mean something? Maybe how to find the other sword?" Dorel asked. "Did you see what those mean, Rian?"

"Spence will confirm this, I believe," she said, hopeful he would. "It wasn't just the *aptet* alone that created the swords. It was magic."

Mike snorted and stood. "Come on, Rian. Give us something we can work with."

"She's right," Spence confirmed. "During the regression I felt the power of the words Seta was saying. The queen was chanting too. The words or the ritual, combined with the *aptet* created the swords."

The fueler knocked on the side of the airplane and handed a clipboard up the stairs. "Here's your fuel slip and card. Sign right there and you're good to go." Spence pulled the slip and signed.

"I'll take that," Dorel said with her hand out as the fuel truck rumbled away. Spence stepped between Rian and Mike to give them to her. "Rian, hurry up and finish the story. I mean it about the coffee, guys. I'm getting cranky."

"Give me the short form, you two," Mike said. "I'm feeling pretty cranky myself."

Rian held Spence's gaze. His expression warmed under her scrutiny and a small ripple of accord flowed between them. "Somehow the Guardian sword took the Defender sword from Datascape. Both are back at the forge under the Sphinx in Egypt. Is it possible that these swords have a consciousness of their own and can operate independently of whomever is using them? I have so many questions, the big one being why are they samurai swords when they were forged in ancient Egypt? Are they only used by us or are there others?"

She saw the recognition on their faces. They'd wondered, too, but were so focused on the swords and their own experiences with them that they'd pushed these peculiarities to the backs of their minds. She hadn't viewed anything at Datascape to explain the questions either, but they had to be working on this, too. "If the swords have a consciousness, could they take whatever appropriate shape to match the culture of the wielder?"

Spence frowned and looked impatient. "I don't think now is the time to worry about this." Dorel and Mike nodded.

"Okay then, Datascape wants the swords and is coming after us and the swords with everything they have. If Ian gets the swords, he will discover how to use them. Then he will have no further use for us. He will be unstoppable," Rian finished.

"So what are we supposed to do? Go to Egypt and get the swords first?" Mike asked with a smirk.

"Yeah," Spence urged. "I think we should. If we've got 'em, then we're the big dogs and call the shots. And Datascape Systems International is out of luck."

"Oh, Spence," Dorel gasped, a fearful expression lining her face. "You don't know what you're saying. The sword changes you. When you have that sword in your hand, the lust for power consumes you and draws pure evil." She turned to her husband. "Please, Michael. Don't do this. Don't throw away our future. I can't lose you again."

"Don't worry, babe. We pick up the four seven in Miami and take it to San Antonio, that's all," Mike assured her.

After the four of them walked through brisk morning air to the airport coffee shop, Spence and Mike spent the thirty minutes of breakfast time arguing about going to Egypt. Dorel said very little, but she looked frightened and that worried Rian. She tried to comfort her with reassuring words reinforced with thoughts of bravery and victory. They needed to be united in courage and intention if they were going to survive when they got to Miami, let alone Egypt.

They touched down in Miami before noon. As the luggage was unloaded into the waiting courtesy van and Mike buttoned up the airplane, Spence phoned Barnes back in Renton to tell him where the airplane was and make arrangement to have it ferried back.

"Naw, just leave it sit," Barnes said. "I've sold that bird to a guy from Columbia who needs a small freighter. Leave it unlocked and put the key in the visor. The guy will pick it up."

"Are you sure? Stuff gets broken into and stolen all the

time. You're making it pretty easy for them by leaving it unlocked." Spence glanced around the transit parking apron
stacked with planes of every type lined up wing to wing.

"I'm not worried. Either way, I come out okay. Hey, I
hear you had some trouble with the FAA or was it the cops
on your way out of here last night? Someone reported the
Metroliner was being stolen. Sorry about that."

Spence rubbed his moustache. "Huh. Don't know anything about that. We didn't have any trouble. Thanks for
the loaner."

"Sure. And when you get back, I need that Bell of yours
for a little cruise to the San Juans," Barnes said and hung
up before Spence could tell him hell no. There was a big
difference between asking to borrow a ten million-dollar
twin jet helicopter and a derelict Metroliner that you hoped
some drug runner would steal.

"Why did you tell him where we were?" Rian asked at his
elbow as he clicked end call. "I thought you said no one
would know where we were."

"It's his plane. I had to tell him where it was. And what I
said was we could deviate from the flight plan so Datascape
couldn't get someone in place to grab us when we refueled.
But once you go instrument flight regulations, which we
had to, everyone knows where you are. No getting around
it."

"Then Datascape knows we're here despite all the
shielding I did the last five hours," Rian pointed out and
leaned against the side of the airplane, shading her eyes
against the hot sun with her hand.

"If they can get the FAA to kick with the plan, yeah. And
they may have because of that little problem last night with
our being denied takeoff at the last minute." He shouldered
his flight bag and added, "Thanks to your shielding they

won't know where we are if we get out of here quick enough. Though they probably have a team on the ground by now. They may know that we're here, but not what for if we keep our thoughts occupied elsewhere and keep moving. Let's get going."

They rented a car and drove around until they found the largest hotel they could near the airport. At check-in Dorel registered for two connecting rooms under the Avion International Aircraft Leasing corporate account, then turned with an apology to Rian as she handed the key to Spence. "I'm sorry we can't get you a room of your own. Please understand that it's not that Mike and I don't trust you, but . . ."

"I understand. Spence has a right to feel the way he does," Rian assented, but Spence caught the rueful cast to her expression before she turned away.

A king size bed took up most of the small room. Rian began to unpack the bag that Dorel had brought for her without comment. Spence unlocked his side of the adjoining room doors and knocked. Mike opened theirs and said he was going for ice.

Spence watched Rian for a moment. "You want me to call down for a rollaway?"

She carried toilet articles to the bathroom. "There isn't room for one. I don't mind sharing the same bed if you don't. And if you do, there's always the tub."

"Sure, if *you* want to sleep there, I don't mind," he answered and hefted his flight bag to the table, unzipping it. The chamois-wrapped *aptet* lay on top. He shifted it to the bottom and piled his clothes back in the bag, laying the spare .45 magazines on top.

"Aren't you going to unpack?" Rian said behind him.

He shook his head and slipped off his leather jacket, removing the .45 at the small of his back in his Levi's waistband and laying it beside the magazines. He and Mike were going back to the airport to check on the 747 and he'd never get through security with that. "Nope. I travel all the time. I never unpack, just live out of my bag."

Mike poked his head in the door. "Ready?"

Spence told him he was and turned to Rian. "You've got my cell number and Dorel has the numbers at the airline if you need us. What I want you to do while we're gone is put a thought form of us in every room in the place just in case someone is looking in, okay?"

"That will take the rest of the afternoon," she said with a perturbed glance at Mike as if hoping he'd disagree with Spence.

"You've got the time. We'll be inspecting the airplane until late," Mike said. "We'll try to make it back for dinner about 8:00 p.m. if you want to wait. Besides, Dorel's working right next door. When you two get finished you can go to the pool or whatever."

"Let's do massages," Dorel called. "I'll see if they have a massage therapist in the beauty shop." She appeared behind Mike, grinning. "I should have my items worked in a couple of hours and the funds transfer ready to go for Monday. How long will it take you, Rian?"

Rian shrugged and picked up the hotel directory sheet. "Let's see, there are 400 rooms. It's 3:00 now. I'll be done about 6:30, give or take a week," she said with an impish grin that made her look like a happy teenager.

"See you later and call if anything comes up," Spence said as Mike gave Dorel a long kiss. He glanced at Rian who was watching them, too. Her expression was mild but the wave of longing from her heart hit Spence like a punch.

Rian stretched out of her cross-legged meditation position while taking deep centering breaths. She eased off the bed and moved through several yoga postures until all the tightness released from sitting stationary for four hours. At home she would have played music after a session like this. Making music was the best therapy for her, but she'd had to leave that behind.

She became aware of the sounds of the hotel and heard the TV in Dorel's room. Rian poked her head in the open doors between the rooms. Dorel lay on the bed, the remote control in her hand, asleep, her red mane spread across the stack of pillows behind her head.

The lioness sleeps. A rash impulse to make a run for it and escape swept over Rian. She quickly backed out of the doorway into her room. Where would she go? She wandered to the windows and looked out at the busy airport across the street, watching the constant stream of airplanes taking off and landing. Rian looked down at Spence's bag on the table and saw his gun sitting there. He must trust her more than she realized if he left a loaded gun in plain sight and where she could get it. But she would never use it.

Rian zipped up the bag and carried it to the little closet where she put it on the floor, covering it with her empty bag. "Dorel," she called. "Are you ready for that massage?"

"What time is it?" came her sleepy reply. "Oh, we're too late. Want to go for a drink instead?"

Ten minutes later they had ensconced themselves in a booth in the tropical motif bar off the lobby. They ordered white wine and watched a mariachi band stroll from table to table in the adjoining restaurant for a while.

The cocktail waitress appeared with their drinks and, hungry for new customers, the band stopped at their table. The portly guitar player bowed to them and asked if they had a request.

"*Quando Salí de Cuba*," Rian requested in flawless Spanish.

"*¡Cómo no!* It is an old song but one we know," the guitarist said with a wise smile. The violin player counted the band in and they began the beautiful song of longing for what was forever lost.

"What does it mean?" Dorel asked with awe.

"When I left Cuba. It's one of my favorite songs. It always makes me cry," Rian said and blinked back tears, washing them down with a sip of wine.

Dorel was sensitive enough to listen until the band finished before she spoke. Rian dug in her purse and gave them twenty dollars, waving them along as they struck up another Cuban folk song, reluctant to leave a well-tipping patron.

"Thank you, Rian. I enjoyed that very much. You are Spanish, then?" Dorel took a sip of wine, watching her over the rim of her glass.

"My mother was an undocumented Mexican worker in the Yakima Valley. And my father, well, I don't know any more than he might have stopped in Yakima once, but that was enough," she said, deadpan. No matter how many times she told the story of her ignominious origin to those she wanted to put off balance, she always enjoyed the look of shock on their faces.

Dorel, however, laughed. "Poppa was a rolling stone, wherever he hung his hat was his home," she sang, snapping her fingers and weaving like the Temptations.

"Nice," Rian said with a grin, bobbing her head in time with Dorel's performance. "I thought it was pretty good not having a father, really, because when the other kids were stuck with drunks and losers for fathers, I'd just make up one that suited whatever situation and believe that he was coming to get me. It was great."

Dorel sobered. "What about your mom?"

"She went back to Mexico when I was four. And I got to stay here because I'm a U.S. citizen, don't ya know," she said, fluttering her eyelids like a starlet. "She could have stayed too, but she didn't. Everyone had a different story about why she left—men, missed her family, she was sick. Whatever."

"Where did you get the name Rian?"

She winked at Dorel. "You'll love this story. My mother named me Ana. When I was in junior high I was desperately in love with this kid Ryan. So, you know how you write all over your notebook, Ryan plus Ana or Mrs. Ryan something or other? I noticed how really cool our names looked together, especially when I changed the y to i, so I made everyone call me Rian from that day on."

Dorel laughed and shook her head. "Girls! I'm so glad I've had a boy. I understand them because I was raised like one by my grandfather . . ." She looked at Rian and blushed. "Your brother, once."

Rian nodded, joyful memories of a long ago childhood in a loving family warming her. "Wish I'd remembered that life when I was little and my mother left."

"Yikes. Who did you stay with?"

"Foster care until I was sixteen. The best thing that ever happened to me was one of my foster dads taught me to play guitar. Then I enrolled in the Running Start program at the community college where I finished high school early and got the scholarship to Whitworth. And that, as they say, is the story of my life. Now what about yours?" Rian asked, finishing her wine and motioning to the cocktail waitress for two more.

Rian enjoyed listening to her even though she'd studied

Mike's file as well as viewed his and Dorel's discovery of each other in this life. She envied that they'd been able to make it work against such incredible odds.

"Do you think we're going to live through this, Rian?" Dorel asked, her solemn gaze on the wine reflecting gold in her glass.

"If we choose. And I'm not being flip, honest. It is a choice. I can view endless possible outcomes that have been created or projected, set in motion by thought. If I view a particular outcome and decide that it is the future and apply my focus positively or negatively through fear, it will manifest—for me. I'll be responsible for creating it. What most of the world doesn't realize is that our future is in our hands. We don't need to fear the future or think we are subject to it. We have to change what we believe about it and the future becomes that. Our thoughts alone create and control our reality."

"You viewed the future, didn't you, when you said Datascape was coming after us?"

"Yes, one particular outcome—the one Datascape is creating with their thought and actions. I believe that I don't have to be subject to it if I can control my fear and use the information, the data I view to create the outcome of my choosing. I need to see what they're doing, so I know what to protect myself from and how. I don't have to help them do it to me by scattering my focus and fearing them. I must focus on what I want to happen," Rian said with a sharp jab of her finger.

Dorel sat back and gauged her. "Can you do it? Can you help us by thought alone?"

Rian nodded. "Don't mistake this as detachment or being passive. I'm engaged. Focused. I have input, data bombarding me every second, just as everyone has, except

I'm more aware of it, which can make it difficult to focus. But Datascape trained me very well. Spence and I are fully capable of bringing this off. We just have to decide what we want to do."

"And that would be go to Egypt, wouldn't it?" Dorel crossed her arms, narrowing her eyes. "If you think like Spence does—that your true motivation is saving the world from Datascape by getting the swords before they do, you're kidding yourself. It's the power calling to you, seducing you again. It killed Mike and love brought him back. But you and Spence? He gave his life once so you could have that power. Where's the love that can bring either of you back this time?"

"Regardless what you fear will happen or what my motives are, I believe the way for us to be free, for you to get your son back, is if we have the power to do so. Possessing the swords is the greatest power I know of. And yes, I wielded that power once and saved a nation. Now, I want to save a little boy and his family. And the man I've loved through time. How can that be a wrong use of power?"

Tears glistened in Dorel's eyes and she warned, "If power isn't tempered with love it's destructive. I haven't seen anything between you and Spence that seems like love. With what you're both proposing to do, and Spence will no doubt talk Michael into, you're going to need to love each other very much to help each other survive. Michael and I have that love. We'll sacrifice ourselves for each other or our son, and Spence, too. Can you say you would do that?"

Before she could reply, Mike and Spence walked toward them and slid into the booth. "Hey, it's looking pretty serious in here," Mike said, ducking his chin to look in his wife's downcast eyes.

"What's going on?" Spence asked, squinting at Dorel

then back at Rian. She shrugged, staying quiet and letting Dorel say what she would.

"We were just chatting about life, kids and world domination. The usual stuff," Dorel said with a game attempt at a smile.

Mike wasn't buying it. He turned a calculating gaze on Rian. "Did you put up the no vacancy sign?"

She nodded and raised her glass to him. "Yes, I did. The hotel's got a full house for as long as needed. Any idea how long that will be?"

"The airplane looks pretty good," Spence said to Dorel. "There are some open squawks or action items and we'll be there tomorrow to make sure they're worked off. The attorney will make the funds transfer on Monday morning. If everything comes together right, we'll go wheels up about 1 p.m."

The three of them continued to talk business while Rian observed their interaction. They were a team, all right, closer than blood relatives. They hadn't closed ranks against her, but they didn't include her either. Dorel was a concern because she loved them both and was very protective. While she tried to be fair with Rian and would work with her, even be a friend, she would never trust her as she once had. And she opposed going for the swords because of her fear. She was afraid of her own power and so would deny the need and desire for power in others.

Rian had known power and been without it. It was far better to have power and, contrary to what Dorel preached, love and power weren't separate or opposed.

Love was the supreme power.

Chapter Fourteen

Spence let himself in the room trying not to disturb Rian who had excused herself before dinner, saying she needed to get some sleep more than she needed food. He moved quietly about the room, not turning on a light as the drapes were open to floodlights illuminating the outside of the building. He stripped down to his shorts and started to close the drapes.

"Please leave them open," Rian's sleepy voice said from the left side of the bed.

"Sure," he said and got in the big bed, careful not to touch her, which would have been a trick since she was hugging the other edge. He lay down on the wrong side that was as bright as facing landing lights and tried to get comfortable without a lot of moving around. Impossible.

"Are you going to be okay with this?" she asked, flipping on her stomach and looking at him. Her shoulders were bare. That meant the rest of her was too. He rolled on his side facing the window and prepared to get a sunburn on his eyelids.

"Yeah." No. She was naked on his side of the bed. Where he should be.

"Well, I'm not. I think we need to talk."

Spence groaned. Talk was the furthest thing from his mind. He sat up and propped the pillow against the headboard. "Okay, go for it."

"You first." She rested on her elbows, the sheet slipping off her back.

"I'm not the one who needs to talk. I've got to get some

sleep," he said, trying to keep the gripe out of his voice.

Silence. "You're right. I need to talk. And to that end all you have to do is pretend to listen, okay?"

"Sure," he said and crossed his hands over his belly, settling in for a long night. Maybe he could sleep with his eyes open.

"Do you believe in our past lives together now?"

That caught him flatfooted. "Believe? Yeah, but I don't know that it's a belief as much as an experience. I've experienced these past lives that feel real to me, but do I believe in them like a person believes in God or the American way? I don't know."

"Do you believe that we've loved each other in the past?" she asked, her tone soft and hopeful.

"Yes." He didn't really know he believed it until he said it.

"Will we love like that again?"

"I don't know, Rian."

"Goodnight," she said and rolled to her side, her bare back to him.

Spence was gone when Rian woke up the next morning. She ordered room service and enjoyed breakfast while she channel surfed, settling on headline news. After she'd showered and dressed, a knock came on the closed door between the rooms. She opened it and found Dorel dressed, ready to go into town.

"I've already talked to Mike. They're in for another long day. There's a shuttle to the beach or we can get a cab to Little Havana. Get some lunch and shop a bit, if you want to."

Rian felt uneasy at the prospect. "Do you know Miami? I haven't been here before."

"Yes, we've picked up an airplane coming out of service here before. We all came along on that trip. Ready?" Dorel asked. She was consciously trying to keep her thoughts off Marty. Good girl.

"Sure, I'll get my purse. Let's go to Little Havana and I'll try out my Mexican-American West Coast Spanish on these Cubans."

As they rode into town in a hot, dirty cab, Dorel made a call to tell Mike where they were going. They found a shaded sidewalk Cuban restaurant in the heart of the district and ordered lunch, then watched the colorful mingling of locals and tourists on the street.

Rian rolled her shoulders against the tension creeping into them. She kept her gaze moving, surveying diners and passersby, uncertain of what she was watching for. Then she saw him. Ian Stoddard, in a white polo shirt that made his skin look all the more tanned, sat across the street at a café table under a green market umbrella. His lean face broke into a sardonic smile and he squinted over the top of his sunglasses at her when she made him. He pointed to the empty chair opposite him and inclined his head in invitation.

Rian's insides churned, the rum and coke she'd just had curdling in her stomach. She glanced at Dorel who was oblivious to the danger just fifty feet away and enjoying her food. Real fear jangled through Rian. What was she going to do? Her cell phone rang and she knew who it was before she answered it. She looked at Ian. He had a phone to his ear.

"Hello?"

"Hello to you, my dear. Isn't it a beautiful day?" Ian's voice wormed through the phone.

She put her hand over the mic and told Dorel it was a

patient calling her. She got up from the table and moved deeper into the restaurant where she could keep an eye on Dorel and Ian as well. "Did you just pick up your voice mail?" she asked.

He smiled. "I got your message, don't worry. Perhaps you're wondering why I'm paying you this little visit."

"No, I'm not. Why don't you tell me why you sent the team to my house?" Anger bubbled under the fear and she gritted her teeth.

"I didn't. It was the rogues. You misunderstood the situation. And you will be happy to know that those undesirable elements have been dealt with," he lied without any change of tone that would betray his intention. Why hadn't she heard that deficiency before? What she took for father-like concern and friendship was cold, emotionless manipulation.

"So, what about the reclamation team?" She turned her head, looking for them in every face in the restaurant.

"Yes, unfortunately it's in their hands now. This is a courtesy call, my dear. I assume you're still on the team?" He waited a moment then continued. "I don't want my best viewer to get hurt when they complete the transaction."

Sweat rolled down Rian's back under her tank top and she shivered. "And when will that occur?"

He laughed with delight. "Let's just say that we feel things will go easier if we have some trading material or inducements."

"Such as?" She wove through the tables toward Dorel, drawing a bead on the two men at the table behind her and closest to the street where a van stood waiting at the curb. Rian raced to the table and stepped in front of the man making a grab for Dorel. She pushed her sideways off her chair and brought the cell phone up under the man's nose with a sharp jab, slamming the heel of her sandal on his instep.

Dorel scrambled to her feet, cussing like a sailor and started pummeling the other man with her fists. The waiters came running and nearby patrons joined the fray. The men broke off and jumped over the planter boxes bordering the sidewalk and ran for the van. The door slid open and they dove inside. The van squealed away and disappeared around the corner.

Rian glanced across the street and Ian was gone.

After they refused treatment and gave a detailed account of the attempted mugging, Dorel and Rian got a ride back to the hotel with two very nice officers who suggested that they wait to see the sights of Miami with their husbands or on an escorted tour. By the time they got back to the room, Rian tried to call Spence and discovered that she'd broken her phone on the operative's nose. She threw it in the trash and lay on the bed, listening to Dorel talk to Mike.

"They're coming right home," Dorel said, leaning in the door. A couple of buttons were missing from her shirt and her khaki pants were torn and ripped in the seat. "What the hell happened?"

"Let's wait until Mike and Spence get here." She sat up. "You did great, by the way. And where did you learn to swear like that?"

Dorel blushed. "The engineering pools at Boeing. When I get really scared or pushed, I just revert. Horrible isn't it?"

Rian grinned. "I think it's pretty darned creative. You soccer moms can fight pretty well, too."

"So do you. I guess you learned that at Datascape?"

"Yes, and growing up, too. Learned to defend and fend for myself at a young age. Isn't it gratifying to know that those old antisocial skills are still as valuable today?" she said with a rueful laugh. "Ow, I'm going to get in the shower before I stiffen up."

"Thanks, Rian. I really appreciate your helping me today," Dorel said, adding with a wink, "You're going to make me trust you yet."

Ten minutes later, Rian soaped herself and rinsed under the shower of warm water. She turned the temperature up and rested her forehead against the tile as the hot stream beat her aching body. The bathroom door banged open, the shower curtain was thrown back and Spence lifted her out of the tub in a crushing embrace. He held her, brushing kisses across the top of her hair and forehead. "Rian," he groaned. "Why did you do it? Why risk yourself like that?"

Her arms locked around Spence, holding onto him as if he might disappear like the steam evaporating on the cold air spilling in from the open door. Open to whatever he could give, she pressed her wet face to his and whispered, "I had to."

He pulled back and looked down at her. "Why?"

Rian put her hands on his cheeks, bringing his face down to hers. "Many reasons. From this life and the others. We've all been together before. We are bound to each other, helping, teaching, learning, loving." She dusted her lips across his lips and over to his ear, nibbling the lobe.

Spence pulled a towel off the rack and rubbed it over her back. He wrapped it around her like a mummy, his fingertips grazing her skin as he tucked the towel's end in between her breasts. "Does that include me?"

"Especially you." She began to unbutton his shirt, laying a soft kiss on his chest at each opening. "I believe there's someone special for everyone in each life. And you're the one for me. Again. We've come across vast reaches of time and other dimensions to be with each other again. We may look different in each life, taking other roles in dramas we

227

play out. But we know each other in our hearts. We've loved and lived together in the sun baked deserts of Egypt and the steamy South Pacific and so much more we've yet to remember. We are bonded together throughout eternity." She stared into his glittering eyes that were filled with love for her. "You'll never be alone."

"Nor will you," Spence promised and picked her up. She snuggled against him as he carried her to the bed. He laid her down, his mouth on hers. The tender kiss sent a jolt through every cell that awakened the memory of soulmates across millennia. A revitalizing thrill vibrated through her body as if her soul was jarred back to life. Did he feel it, too?

Spence undressed and lay beside her. He cradled her bare body and stroked her back, crooning little endearments into her ear that encouraged a feeling of intimacy, of allowing her deep inside him. She promised herself and him that she would never betray the trust he was once again investing in her.

There was no part of her awakening body that he didn't caress with great tenderness, each touch igniting memories of sensation and images that heightened to desire. And as she received, she gave back to him with greater love and passion until the climaxing waves of sound and color rolled through Rian as she came with Spence in an intense crescendo of love that they cried out for each other.

Lying in each others arms in a sweet afterglow, Rian stroked his hair and admitted, "I was afraid that you wouldn't forgive me and I would lose you before you could even remember that you loved me. Sometime soulmates don't recognize each other, or one feels the bond but the other doesn't. I couldn't stand that, but no doubt that's happened to us before."

He nodded against her. "Umm, maybe."

"Are you sleeping while I'm trying to get you to tell me you love me again?" She ducked her head to look at his face lying on her chest.

He raised his head and shook it. "Nope, and I love you again."

"Hey!" yelled Mike on the other side of the closed door. "How long of a shower are you guys going to take?"

"Oh my gosh!" Rian yelped and dashed for the bathroom to turn off the shower. Clicking the lock in place, she answered Mike through the door, "All done now. Was there something you wanted?"

He laughed. "If you guys can tear yourselves away, I think we better talk. Think we can risk some dinner downstairs?"

She looked at Spence on the bed, his hand behind his head. "Tell him we'll be down in about an hour," he said, patting the bed beside him and giving her a come here look.

Rian conveyed the message and swung her hips back to the side of the bed, just out of arms' reach. "Something I can do for you?"

"Yeah, bring me a beer and turn on the game, will you?" he said with a devilish grin and grabbed her. She fell laughing into his arms.

Mike and Dorel had been waiting in the bar for over an hour and were way ahead of them, pretty much wrecked. Rian and he joined right in, catching up, the four of them celebrating still being alive, Spence figured. He tossed back a shot and grimaced, closing one eye against the burn.

"What time is it?" Mike demanded, casting a bleary eye at his watch.

"Dinnertime," Spence said. "I've got to get some food."

He glanced at Rian sitting beside him. Stray pieces of dark hair had fallen out of her sleek, dark ponytail. Her cool, keep your distance sophistication had long since melted into a sexy, very touchable—lush. God, the woman could drink. While he was about on his chin, she chatted perky as hell with a slight Spanish accent at Dorel, who was almost slack-jawed wasted.

"I need to use the little girls' room," Dorel advised and asked Rian to join her, then told Mike to get them a table in the restaurant. The two women were quite a contrast to each other as they wobbled off to the restroom—Rian, velvet midnight to Dorel's fiery midday.

"I didn't want to worry Dorel more, but Datascape got us pretty quick, don't you think? Right down to the god-damn restaurant. Either they had people on the ground here already, targeting us from the time we landed or . . . it's something else," Mike said, sobering. "I think we better come up with a plan."

"You're wrong if you're thinking Rian is still feeding them intel." Spence tried to hide his anger as he pushed the empties aside and leaned on his crossed arms toward Mike. "Our only option to win this thing is to go for the swords. Take that bird out of here on Monday and head for Egypt, that's what I think." He gave a sharp nod and sat back, waiting.

Mike shook his head and stood, throwing some bills down on the table. "That is not as easy as it sounds, and you know that. The fuel alone would set us back over two hundred grand round trip, then there's the landing permits, visas and all that crap. JET would charge us a fortune to ar-range an international flight. Then there's the TFRs to worry about. There are always temporary flight restrictions across the Middle East and Africa. It would be easier and cheaper to go commercial, if we were going at all."

"We can't go commercial. They'd pick us up before we got to the gate. If we took the 747, they wouldn't expect that and they couldn't stop us. It's our plane once the funding clears. We can take it where and when we want." Spence pointed Mike toward the restaurant and followed.

The hostess seated them in the back of the restaurant in a corner booth. They started to talk again but a waiter interrupted, asking for their drink order.

Spence stared eye-to-eye with Ian Stoddard. "What do you want?" he growled, palming the table knife.

Mike looked from him to the middle-aged man. "Ian, I take it," he said and moved to slide out of the booth.

"Hold it, Michael, my boy. I've got my little persuader on you." He pulled back the towel over his hand to reveal the tip of the barrel. "Let's not cause any undue annoyances to the other diners. I'm just here for a friendly chat to see if we can't settle this among old friends without anyone being further inconvenienced."

"Where are Dorel and Rian?" Mike glowered, still poised to leap at Ian.

"In the ladies' room, I expect. I believe Mrs. Gabrielli is rather discomposed, but will soon be feeling better and return. That in mind, I suggest we conclude our business. Do sit down, Michael." Ian didn't take his eyes off of them or lower his gun.

"There's nothing to discuss. I'm not coming back," Spence said, inching toward the end of the seat as Mike lowered himself to the seat's edge.

"Of course you are. You will come back into the fold and save your friends a lot of trouble. You need our help, Spence. My help in particular, for I know which triggers will fire the anchors in your subconscious and set you on an unfortunate rampage, as it were, against your fellows. And only I know how to remove them. In return you will do a bit of interpreting for us just like the old days when you were active," Ian said with an oily smile.

"You deprogrammed me. I don't work for you any more," Spence said and flicked a glance at Mike. "We're out of it."

Ian laughed. "We don't allow anyone to leave the program, not really. The deprogramming has proven unreliable and ineffective as you two have shown. But then we never were so foolish as to depend solely on that. Each of you has a tiny little piece of silicon under the skin on the back of your necks." He turned his head and pointed at the base of his skull, "Just there. We always know where you are, so your projections and attempts to shield from us are quite ineffective."

Spence put his hand on his neck then dropped it in disgust. "Sell that to your new recruits who are ignorant enough to believe Ian Stoddard is the great father of scientific remote viewing he claims to be. You know what scares you the most? We can do this stuff. You can't. And here's another one for you—how do you know you're actually talking to us right now? We may be a projection in your mind. And I may *not* be about to flush you like the piece of crap you are without even touching you. Scientifically remote view that if you can, Ian," he said and stood up. Mike got out of the booth with him. They glared at Ian. He began to back away, motioning with his gun for them to follow.

"You're mistaken about that particular ability as well, Spence. It's a myth. Remote influencing and assassination are the stuff of legend. Your believing you can kill people with your mind is a fantasy we gave you. It's a screen memory just like most of your supposed skills. The only thing you've ever been good for is classified and you'll never know. We will catch you one by one," Ian included Mike with a glance, "and when we are finished with you, we will kill you. You are nothing to me."

Mike's fist hit the inside of Ian's wrist. The gun dropped. Ian scrambled backward, dodging Mike's chopping sweep and Spence grabbed the gun. They chased Ian through the kitchen and he charged out the exit door. Mike started after him, but Spence hauled him back inside. "No, man. He'll have backup out there."

"What now?" Mike asked, straightening his clothes, then rubbing the side of his arm.

"Get out of here and keep moving until we fly on Monday. Here come the girls. Let's go." He jammed Ian's pistol in his pocket and composed a bland expression. They guided the protesting women back out into the lobby.

"Something's come up," he told Rian as he propelled her to the elevator.

She looked deep in his eyes. "Ian." He nodded and leaned in the elevator, checking it out before getting in. Spence did the same at the room then Mike brought Dorel and Rian in, locking the door behind him. They scrambled to pack and fill the women in on what happened in the restaurant. Dorel insisted on taking the time to use the quick checkout on the TV, while they decided what to do.

"Won't they wait and follow us in the rental?" Dorel asked, clicking through the checkout menu.

"Good point," Mike said and looked at Spence and Rian. "You think they really did install tracking chips in us?"

"That is news to me, but I can check," she said, glancing around.

"What are you looking for?" Spence asked with a frown.

"Something to use as a dowsing rod. Then I can scan you with it and see if it picks up anything." She walked to the closet. "No wire hangers."

"Don't you need a forked stick and doesn't it have to be from a certain kind of tree?" Mike asked, watching her from the door.

"No, you can use anything. My grandmother used L-shaped rods, but she used a five foot crowbar, too. She'd walk along with it balanced across her fingers and when it found what she'd programmed it to find, it would dip. Worked very well." She rubbed her hands together and blew into them. "I can't find anything that resonates with me so I'll just use my hands." Rian closed her eyes, shaking her hands out for a few moments, then walked to Mike.

"Turn around. Clear your mind and just allow me to access your energy field," she said, raising her open palms to the back of his neck about six inches from the skin. She held them there with her eyes closed, then opened them, shaking her head. "There's nothing there. Spence, let me check you."

He felt the heat from her hands spread across his shoulders and down his back like a deep massage. She laid her hands on his shoulders and he turned around. "Nothing. You're clear. That means I'm the one."

"Why should any of us have a tracking chip? We can't trust anything Ian said. He wanted us to think there was no getting away from him," Spence countered and tried to pull her into his arms.

Rian put her hands on his chest. "Spence, I've been feeling something, a foreign energy at the back of my neck since, well, that night in your house. Because that's the most vulnerable place for attachment by negative entities, I thought perhaps I was being psychically attacked and protected myself. Now I know what it is."

"So what are we supposed to do? Leave you here?" Spence asked, agitated and tightening his hold on her. "Not an option."

"I could wear a tinfoil hat," she said with a smart ass grin.

Mike and Dorel laughed, but Spence began thinking. If the chip sends a signal that signal has a signature, a wave pattern. It can be interrupted. "I think I can take it offline." He told her his idea and met with resistance. "It's better than digging around in your neck with a pocketknife, don't you think?"

"Yes, all right. Go ahead and try," Rian said, a doubtful edge to her voice.

Spence took three deep breaths and expanded his consciousness on the third exhale. His energy field expanded and he extended it toward her. Her aura outlining her body in a rainbow of bright color opened at the back of her and there he perceived a small spot of black emitting a long, low frequency wave. His energy surrounded the dark blemish the size of a kernel of rice and began to bombard it with an opposite frequency disrupter wave. The dark spot began to lighten in color until it disappeared in the band of surrounding color.

Spence took a deep breath and opened his eyes. "It's gone." He looked at her closely. "Can you feel it?"

Rian stretched her neck and rolled her shoulders. "Well, something's different. It feels lighter there."

Spence grabbed their bags. "Let's hope it works. I guess we'll see soon enough, huh?"

They caught a cab to the airport and hurried into the main terminal, checking behind them as well as maintaining mental surveillance. Dorel rented another car and drove around the airport twice before finally picking up each of them at different airlines.

They took turns driving and sleeping from Miami north up the coast to the Georgia line and back south along the Gulf. It would have been like a vacation if they hadn't watched their backs for bad guys trying to grab them or shoot them at the many rest stops, beaches or gator farms along the way.

On Monday morning they sat on Miami Beach drinking coffee and eating warm bagels as the sun rose over the Atlantic. They'd argued it back and forth, up and down the state, and now the decision was made in silence as they stared east across the ocean.

Dorel turned on her wireless laptop and keyed in their corporate user account password to access JET Aviation Services' website. On the international flight services page, she applied for landing permits, visas and completed other paperwork, then filed the flight plan. She directed JET to re-cater the airplane, put on a full load of fuel and have everything ready for them when they arrived at the airplane.

"I need your passports for the visa applications," she said. "Mike, mine's in the side pocket of my briefcase where I always put it. Could you get it for me, please?"

Spence opened his flight bag in the trunk and took out his passport. Did Rian have hers with her by some miracle?

Rian shook her head, worry creasing lines over her eyebrows. "I don't carry my passport. I can't get into the country without it. What are we going to do?"

"We'll influence them. Convince Egyptian Immigration that they've already processed you when they do us, or we can make you invisible. Which suits you?" He grinned at her.

She gave him a kiss. "You are a god. I worship you. I'll

take the first option, Obi Wan. Convince them they don't need my papers," she advocated and returned to Dorel sitting on a sleeping bag on the sand.

Spence leaned against the front of the rental with Mike and watched the beach come to life with joggers and walkers enjoying the freshly groomed sand. "So, you think we've got a shot?"

Mike nodded. "Maybe. There are more contingencies than I like. I'm not a seat of the pants kind of guy."

Spence agreed, but they didn't have any other option than to go for it. "Yeah, I know. If we can get out of Miami, I think we've got a good opportunity to pull this off."

"Well, he's shown up every place so far that we didn't expect." Mike swirled his coffee cup and took a drink. "He knows about our company and about the airplane. Guess I'm expecting a surprise of some kind at the airport, because they tried in Renton. That's what I'd do if I were Ian."

"We'll make it. My problem is Egypt. Never been there. And how the hell do we get into the Sphinx?" Spence crushed his empty cup and laid it on the hood, watching Rian walk toward the water. "Looks like I'm taking a walk," he said and jogged to catch up with her.

Chapter Fifteen

The morning breeze kicked up whitecaps and swirled her hair around her face. She braided it in a long, single plait as they walked and tucked it in the back of her white T-shirt. They strolled hand in hand, checking over their shoulders on Dorel and Mike back at the car every now and then.

"Remember when we walked on the beach together before?" she asked, slipping her arm around his waist. He put his around hers and pulled her closer.

"When was that?" Then he smiled. "Oh, yeah, Hawaii. Paul and Meredith."

"That's right. Does it feel the same to you?" Though the memory of that day was bright, the love wasn't as tangible as now.

"No, not the same. We were different people and hadn't been through as much as we have. It was probably better in that respect," he allowed with a hint of sadness in his voice.

She agreed. They weren't the same now, but at the essence of their being they were. Now that they were remembering the eternal love that they had for each other, these would soon prove to be the best times that they would remember when they were old and still happy together—if they had much of a future together.

"Spence, when we get back to Seattle, what then? I won't be working for Datascape, but I'd still have my practice and that's very important to me. What about you?"

He shrugged. "You're assuming that we're going back to Seattle?"

"Well, yes. Do you have other plans?" She hoped they included her.

Spence stopped and turned her to face him. "If you're wanting to know if I think we have a future together, yes, I think so. How long that future is remains to be seen. You know as well as I do that it doesn't look good whatever we do. We can't go back to our lives as they were before. Dorel and Mike might be able to, but then what about Marty? My security company was built on Datascape business. Could I survive without them? I don't know. Would they let me? I don't think so. Do you think they'll let you out? Ian said they don't let anyone go, did you know that?"

She dropped her shoulders with the weight her fear confirmed. No, they wouldn't let her go. "And did he share what he intended to do with us?" She looked into his eyes and understood. "Oh."

"As the four of us have argued back and forth until we're ready to kill each other, the viable option is to retrieve the swords, reforge them and use the power to defend ourselves. Then we call the shots and Ian will have to run from us," he dictated with a hard edge to his tone. "Hell, we could even go after Datascape's market if we wanted to and blow them out of the water. No one could touch us."

Dread crawled up her spine. The change in his energy was disturbing and she didn't like the cold cast to his features when he talked about the power. "Do you want that kind of power, Spence?"

He frowned and shook his head. "What?"

"The power of the swords. Do you want it?"

"I'll take all I can get, because it sure beats the hell out of being without it like we are right now," he scoffed and dropped his arm off her.

She grabbed his hand and began to pull him along.

"Maybe the swords aren't for us to use or for anyone else. They could be pieces of ancient metal that two people put all their hopes and dreams into and were galvanized to action. Perhaps there's no more power other than what one invests in them and believes?"

"No, you saw like I did. There's a power, a magic we don't understand or remember now, but we did once. And we'll have to remember if we're going to make this work."

He hadn't even heard her. She had to change the subject, get his mind off the swords, because he looked so dangerous and predatory right now, so un-Paul like. There was no love in his eyes, the doorway to his soul. "Tell me something about you. Something fun that I don't know."

Spence's scowl melted and he quirked his mouth, thinking. "Man, that's tough. I figure you know everything about me. How about you? Tell me something weird about you."

"I said fun, not weird," she teased, swatting his arm. "Well, I worked food service when I was in high school and that was both fun and weird. The fun part was earning money of my own and the weird part was working in one of those mom and pop fast food and ice cream places in Yakima. Working for that family really taught me a lot about people. The mister was a short, round man whose favorite pasttime was re-dipping his ice cream cone into the chocolate topping. His big tall wife had a giant nail on her baby finger like a paring knife that she used to open boxes with. I was very impressed and terrified. Then there was the allergy-ridden daughter. She was the most inventive. She made all the frozen ice cream bars out of soft serve ice cream that was put in molds, frozen then dipped in topping and refrozen on waxed paper covered trays. Problem was the bars would stick to the trays, so she gave each and every bar a big juicy blow to warm them up and pop them loose. I'd watch customers eat those blown-on ice cream bars and chocolate dipped cones that I won't eat to this day and think, suckers! It may have been that experience that put me on the path to wanting to know all the secrets and becoming a psychic spy, do you think?" she said with a knowing smile and nod.

Spence grimaced in disgust. "I loved those chocolate dipped cones. Ugh. Never again. Jeez, why didn't you tell me something good weird like you've got a sexual fetish that we could both enjoy?"

She stooped to pick up a half of a clam shell, brushing the wet sand off of it. "Hmm, there is that thing with a rubber band, six maraschino cherries and a peacock feather. No, I'm over that," she said, aiming an evil grin at him.

He hauled her close and swung her around. "Are you sure?"

Rian laughed and hugged him tight. "I'm sure I love you. That's fetish enough."

"Yeah, you're right." He looked over his shoulder. "Looks like they're ready to go."

Dorel and Mike had the car packed by the time they returned, because she wanted to turn in the car and be at the airplane to make sure JET got the paperwork cleared. At 11:00 a.m. they stood under the left wing of the 747-400, Dorel dictating instructions to the attorney on her cell phone while the money transferred. Rian stood beside Spence and Mike, projecting a shielding energy around the airplane as they suspected that they were being targeted.

Hyper-aware of every tug and truck going by, Spence and Mike divided their attention between the crew readying the airplane and completing the buy on the airplane.

When the transaction was complete, they shook hands

all around and signed the purchase documents. Dorel and Rian boarded the airplane while Spence finished his preflight walk-around and Mike began his preflight in the cockpit.

The air stairs truck pulled away and a tug began to push the 747 back toward the taxi apron. Rian sat in the right jump seat behind Spence, because he'd told her that they maintained a quiet cockpit during takeoff and landing. She extended her excited, loving energy around him like a warm embrace. Dorel strapped herself in behind Mike and advised Spence that all the doors were armed and checked.

When they were airborne and reached altitude overflying the Bahamas they all breathed a little easier.

"I kept expecting to be stopped at every opportunity by the FAA, DEA, PTA or Future Farmers of America, whomever Datascape could manage to lie to like they did in Renton," Dorel said. "Thank God, that part is over. Let's just hope they don't scramble fighters out of Pensacola to shoot us down over the Bermuda Triangle. Wouldn't that be a fitting end to this whole escapade, though."

"You're such an optimist, babe. There are other little tricks they could have pulled," Mike said over his shoulder. "Catering didn't put on chicken or fish, did they?" He winked at Spence and brought up engine parameters on the flight management system's screen. "Hmmm, number four seems to be running a little hot."

"Really!" Dorel leaned forward, grabbing the back of his seat.

"No," Spence said. "He's just screwing with you. Everything looks good."

Dorel whacked Mike's shoulder. "Jerk!"

Mike flinched and said to Spence, "Number One, get the fire axe, we're under attack in the cockpit."

"I'll make sure Spence gets the meal without the botulism," Dorel jibed and leaned back.

After a couple of minutes, Mike said, "You have to wonder, though, at how easy it went."

"Easy?" the three of them cried and began to talk at once.

Mike ducked and held up his hand to ward off further verbal assault. "Come on, think about it. Datascape was pretty aggressive about showing they were after us. Then Ian is in Miami when we are; again, a couple of effective demonstrations to give us added incentive. Yet, there were several opportunities to stop us if he'd wanted to . . ."

"Yeah, but maybe it's as simple as they aren't able to track us electronically now. We know it takes a whole team of viewers working around the clock to view and work up a detailed, coherent blueprint of a single target. We've been pretty good, I think, at putting a lot of mental flack out there to shoot them down. What do you think, Rian?" Spence asked, turning in his seat.

Her expression was pensive. "Yes, I think that's effective. Also, I do feel that whatever that was in my neck, you've affected it somehow, and they can't track us that way. Since it takes the ordinary viewer more time and effort than it does us, we might want to consider that Ian has others like us available to him. I always thought he could do what I, and you, did. He trained us, after all. When you told me he couldn't, I have to admit it was like learning there was no Santa Claus."

Spence patted her knee. "He used to mean a lot to me, too. Now I'd like to off the son of a bitch and save us all from further problems."

"Don't screw up your karma. Datascape is a multinational vehicle, a shadow from which the gray men of the world exert faceless power," Rian said. "Ian is the face we know, but he is a stable master, a minor functionary."

"That sounds like a conspiracy theory that you'd hear on one of those late night talk shows," Dorel said with a raised eyebrow. "People call in and say they saw Elvis get out of a flying saucer at Wal-Mart."

"That's crazy," Mike snorted. "Everyone knows Elvis only shops at The Gap."

Spence hooted and slid his seat back, putting his feet on the footrest under the instrument panel. Mike listened a moment to his headset, then repeated, "Roger, Miami Center, Seven Uniform Alpha making course correction to a heading of three zero."

"I think we're a little off topic, here," Rian asserted. "Perhaps we need to discuss our concerns, whatever they may be, so that we don't keep channeling energy in that direction." She looked to Spence for agreement.

He sighed and nodded, groaning inwardly. Spence looked at his watch. "Sure, let's talk. We've got eleven to twelve hours with nothing else to do." He bounced his eyebrows and suggested, "There's a big empty airplane down there, not to mention the first class sleeper seats behind us. Oh, and the crew rest bunks. Can I interest you in a tour?"

She laughed. "Tempting. But don't you have to fly the airplane?"

"Nope. It's all set up flying itself. Boring as hell. Nothing for us to do but talk about money and women," Spence said.

"I could use some of that coffee," Mike said, turning in the seat to Dorel.

"Yes, Captain." She gave him a kiss. "Anyone else want something?" They said no and she left the cockpit, heading for the first class galley.

Spence waited until she was out of earshot, then said to Rian, "I don't think we need to upset Dorel with any more of the grisly details about Datascape, okay? I agree with Mike. We got out of there too easy. Feels like we're being herded in the direction Datascape wants us to go. I wouldn't be surprised if they met the airplane in Cairo."

Mike took off his sunglasses and gave Rian a serious look. "I'm with Spence. Could be the plan all along was to get us to go for the swords. Then they swoop in, grab them and us. Ian's probably in Cairo already."

Rian frowned and thought a moment. "That's possible, of course. We haven't viewed anything to confirm that though, have we?"

"Maybe this is fear talking then, is that what you're saying?" Spence lifted his chin toward Dorel coming in with a tray behind Rian. "Good. I was hoping you'd had them put Dr Pepper onboard."

"There's a case of the wretched stuff, and nothing else but bottled water." She handed Mike his coffee and sat cross-legged in her seat, looking out the windscreen. "It's beautiful out there, isn't it?"

They agreed that it was and sat in silence for a few minutes. Spence reached behind and squeezed Rian's leg. "Too bad you didn't bring your guitar, you could have led us in a sing-along."

"Oh, goody. If that isn't every musician's dream, I don't know what is," she griped and pushed the back of his seat.

"Yeah, you'd rather play that weird stuff, wouldn't you. It's a good thing you don't have that flute along. It would probably take the ICAS offline," he said, jerking a thumb at the computer on the console.

"That's pretty harsh, Spence. I like flute and I'm sure Rian plays beautifully," Dorel said.

"Thank you, Dorel. He's just jealous of my special skills," she said.

"No, ma'am, I deeply appreciate all your *special* abilities." He leaned out, turning to look back at her and winked. "Just not that weird music that takes my systems offline."

"What kind of music is that?" Dorel asked.

"Well, my own—"

"You said you got that music from a guy you'd regressed to a lifetime in Egypt . . . Oh," he sighed, realizing the truth. "That was part of your conditioning me." He didn't like remembering that she'd played him, moved him around like a game piece. He let go of her leg.

Rian caught his hand and gave it a squeeze. "Yes. Playing the music had nothing to do with the system fault. I did that with an interrupt projection. Jason had said that your company had installed the system at the Bagel. I decided that was a good place to meet you, besides I like playing at the Bagel. It's fun. As to the music, it's possible that it is Egyptian and I *remembered* it from our life then. The skills and interests people have in this life are often a carryover from a previous life. Take General Patton, for instance. He believed he'd been a warrior through many lifetimes. In our case, Paul was a pilot and Meredith a nurse. Airplanes are an important part of your life today and I'm a therapist." She held up her palms with a cringe. "Yes, yes, I know—when I'm not being a psychic spy for a secret quasi-government agency."

They were quiet a moment, then Mike asked her if she'd ever been part of the remote influence program at Datascape.

"There is a group, but I never worked with them," she answered.

"What's remote influence?" Dorel asked.

"Assassins," Mike answered and checked the breaker panel over his head. It got real quiet and Spence wished to hell Mike had kept his mouth shut. Mike did, too.

"If you can affect machines with mental projections and convince people they see things they don't, then you could, what, convince them to hurt themselves or have an accident?" Dorel persisted.

When no one else spoke up, Rian answered, "When trained to do so, one can perceive someone's frequency and then project the exact opposite to them, which would have varying degrees of effect, depending on the intent."

"And you can do it, can't you?" Dorel threw an inclusive glance at Spence. "Like he can."

Rian's blue eyes darkened. "Yes."

Dorel stood up, her fair skin reddening with anger. "Then why in the hell haven't you two taken care of this Ian, instead of acting like he's some sort of god you can't touch?"

"That's out of line, Dorel," Spence started in, but Rian stopped him.

"We haven't *taken care of* Ian, as you say, because we aren't murderers," Rian began in reasoned tones. "In defense of myself, I do try to heal people, help them in my practice. And I always believed that I was doing work vital to national security with Datascape. I've viewed every sort of target, and influenced some, too, for the military and corporations, and received thanks for my help. But never once was I asked to kill someone. Was I naïve about what Datascape was into? Apparently so. I may not be able to *take care of* Ian any more than I could kill anyone, but I would do everything possible short of that to stop him from harming you, or me," she finished, breathless.

Doral cut a wide-eyed questioning glance at Spence. "What she said," he answered, jerking a thumb at Rian.

He couldn't tell Dorel that unlike Rian, he had killed by remote. He wasn't going to do Ian that way, like some unseen angel of death. It would be face to face; he owed Ian that much. If it came to that. And it would, he felt it in his gut.

Dorel dropped her shoulders with a resigned sigh. "Okay. It doesn't seem that these people are at all reluctant to use whatever power they have on us. But you know what? I'm not going to worry about this anymore. I'm going to go run it off."

Rian raised an eyebrow. "Where?"

"Up and down the aisles. Sit anywhere I want. A childhood dream realized, because I always wanted to do that, but my granddad wouldn't let me. Spence, want to come?"

He dropped his feet off the rest and got up. "Sure, lead the way."

They made several circuits of the lower level, then up and down the spiral staircase. Spence worked up a sweat, running in the opposite direction from the girls. He turned around and dropped in behind Rian. At the lav bulkhead, he grabbed her hand and dragged her into the corner by the exit door for a quick kiss that became full-blown Mile High Club foreplay.

"Hey, guys," Dorel yelled from somewhere forward. "Mike says he wants to eat and then catch a nap. Come on up."

Rian pulled away, trailing her finger from his lips, down his chest and zipped up his pants. As they walked to the stairs, she tucked her T-shirt back into her jeans and ran a hand through her hair. Spence enjoyed the telltale flush that spread over her chest and neck that she wouldn't be able to hide.

At Dorel's insistence, as they ate reheated lasagna airline meals, they began to discuss what to do once they landed in Cairo.

"How many days will we be there?" Dorel asked. "Our ramp parking fees alone will cost over $7000 a day plus any other fees they can levy."

Mike and Spence looked at each other. "I figured in and out in twenty-four, if we could. We get a cab to the Sphinx, bribe someone to let us in and grab the swords. Sound like a plan?" Mike said, grinning like an ass.

"Minimalist, don't you think?" Dorel said to Rian who agreed and asked if they'd been to Egypt before.

"No. But we have friends who went there on a cruise ship. They treated us to an endless video of their docking in Cairo and the armed guards everywhere. They took a bus to Giza. They said it was about a three and a half-hour trip, didn't they, Mike? I think we watched every unedited hour of that bus trip. The one almost interesting part was at the Sphinx. They were doing some kind of archeological work behind the canvas enclosures. The entire thing was roped off. They were only allowed to walk on one side of it on a catwalk, but a privileged few VP types got a private tour of the Sphinx. She was furious about that. I have to admit I would have been, too."

"Don't worry, babe. You'll get your private tour," Mike said with a cheeky grin.

"The circumstances won't be entirely conducive to a tour, Michael. The way I understand it, you're talking bribe someone to let you in, find the right chamber, steal the swords and run back out. First, bribing someone won't be tough, but the right someone who knows the chamber may be a bit more difficult. We'll need lights, something to put the swords in . . . oh yes, provided the Defender sword is there as you believe, how do you find the Guardian? That's been bothering me."

Spence held Rian's gaze, an unspoken agreement passing between them. He cleared his throat. "I have the key to unlock the Guardian."

Mike and Dorel stared at him. "Okay," Dorel said. "I'll trust you on that, but how?"

"The *aptet* is the key. We'll figure out the how when we get there," Spence said with more certainty than he felt and looked to Rian.

"As to the other arrangements, Spence and I can influence people to help us as we need. Don't worry about it, Dorel. There are things we can plan for and others we can't, but it will work out, we have to keep that foremost in our minds. It will all work out," Rian predicted.

"I'm going to get some shuteye. You've got it, Spence," Mike said and got out of the captain's seat. "Wanna come? You look like you could use a nap," he said to Dorel. She grabbed his hand and he pulled her out of the seat. They went into the crew rest bunk area and closed the door behind them.

"Want to get some pilot in command time in a 747?" Spence asked Rian, jerking his thumb at the empty seat. "Don't touch anything, though."

Rian leapt up and took the seat, settling in with a happy smile. "This is awesome. I think I'll be a pilot in my next life."

"Why not this one?" He liked watching her lean this way and that, checking the gauges and the sky outside. She was beautiful and she loved him. At this moment he couldn't ask for anything more out of life.

"I like what I do." She shined a gorgeous smile on him. "I love my music and my practice. As I get further away from Ian and Datascape, my connection, my past there fades. Soon it will be as if it never happened."

"We'll see them again, you know," Spence cautioned, then wished he hadn't said it. Why couldn't he let her go with her illusion?

"I know, but for right now I'm going to pretend I'm living the kind of life I want." She shrugged. "I'm always telling my patients that they're creating their future with every thought. So, I've decided to create what I want. Why don't you create with me? It's a wonderful way to pass the time." Rian turned a hopeful gaze on him

He leaned over the arm rest and kissed her. "I can think of a better way."

"Mmm, I agree but you have watch the gauges or something, don't you?" She took his face in her hands. "You could regale me with little Spence stories or were you a Jonathan back then?"

Mom called him Jonathan. He hadn't thought of that in a long time. "My dad called me Jon." There was a good reason to go by another name.

"When did you become *Spence?* It's so virile and edgy sounding. Goes great with the goatee, too," she said and trailed her finger down one side of his moustache to his mouth. He caught it between his lips. She pulled it out and he kissed her fingertips.

"Mike started calling me Spence when we were in flight school together and it stuck. He was fresh out of Annapolis. I'd graduated UW with a degree in electrical engineering and wanted a commission in Naval Intelligence, but the officer candidate board selected me for flight instead. I was disappointed and thought it was a bad match until I climbed in that T-34 trainer the first time. And when they assigned me to Intel, I thought that was a bad decision and it was. Put me on the wrong road, but maybe I was always headed there, who knows?" It didn't pay to think should have beens. Uncomfortable, he shifted in the seat and checked the engine temps. "Destiny is a delicate thing, isn't it? You think what if I'd done this or not done that, would my life be different today? Opportunities, taken or missed. I've come to believe what my patients report in their regressions that before they incarnate again, they experience incorporeal life between lives, what some traditions might call heaven or the afterlife. They tell me that before they incarnate again, they get together with those who will incarnate with them as a spouse or lover and plan how they will meet in the new life. They say we work out signals to awaken our *soul* eyes to each other, almost like at the appointed time I'll have a red carnation behind my ear and you wear a blue hat turned around backwards."

She smoothed a stray stand of hair back into its ponytail and laughed. "One couple had what turned out to be a very fun signal. They'd each been through several relationships which hadn't worked. One day at a business meeting during a round of introductions, a high powered executive looked across the table at a man who said he was an aircraft mechanic. She said the words aircraft mechanic blasted her and that man immediately became the most interesting man she'd ever met. She invited him to lunch and when she dug into her bag for her wallet her bikini fell out on the table."

Skeptical, he lifted an eyebrow and narrowed his eyes. "Bait, huh?"

Rian laughed at him. "No, she was going swimming that afternoon. Anyway, when the man saw that orange bikini tumble out of her purse he said it was as if he'd been hit between the eyes with a hammer. They were married four months later. Isn't that a wonderful story?"

He chuckled and agreed that it was. "So, does everyone have a prearranged signal?"

A frown furrowed her brow. "I think so. Since this is a free will zone and living in the body isn't the easiest thing to do, we can catch the signal and welcome our soulmate into our life again, or we might miss it because we're so blinded by our own stuff. Take Mike and Dorel, for example. I think their soul signal, if you will, is the sword. It's brought them together over many lifetimes—"

"Then the sword or I should say swords are our signal, too. We created them and they've brought us together again." Made sense. Felt right. End of story. But the vibe he picked up from her didn't agree.

"Perhaps, but they don't feel like a soul signal to me."

He lifted their armrests and swiveled to face her. "I think you want the romantic bikini, aircraft mechanic kind of soul signal, don't you? How about this?" He took her hands and pulled her into a deep kiss. She slipped her arms around his neck and moaned against his lips as his hands explored her.

Rian pushed away a little and looked with such love into his eyes that he was humbled by the infinite scale of it. "Whatever our signal, we're together again. That's the point of living. Everything else is the journey."

Rian watched over Spence's shoulder as he flew the final approach into Cairo after twelve plus hours in the air. The runway looked like a skinny white ribbon off the end of the 747's nose. It floated toward the ground and Rian's stomach sank. How had he learned to fly something so huge and land it on a tiny and short strip? He'd said landings were the most interesting to him. From this perspective *interesting* was a horrifying understatement. She didn't even feel the wheels touch down and didn't realize they'd landed until Spence called for thrust reversers and stepped on the brakes slowing the mammoth airplane.

They held on the taxiway, waiting for an escort to the transit parking area. Mike turned in his seat and told Dorel and Rian, "They're sending an Egypt Air tug to tow us to the parking area. The tower says Egyptian customs agents will meet us there. No one is allowed on or off the airplane until Customs finishes with us."

"Rian, that's your gig. Make a pretty picture for our Customs friends," Spence said over his shoulder and reached behind his seat.

She put her hand in his and gave it a squeeze. "It is a thing of beauty even as we speak." She released his hand, relaxed back in her seat and extended an energy field around herself like a mirror-skinned bubble. At the same time she would direct a suggestion at them not to see her. Their senses would perceive her, but they would ignore the input. She would be invisible to them.

Rian was aware when the tug arrived and towed them to transit parking. She stayed in her seat while Spence finished updating the logbook and the Egyptian customs agents boarded the airplane. Dorel dealt with the paperwork while Mike followed the agents around the airplane. When one came in the cockpit to check Spence against his passport, Rian saw Mike and Dorel hesitate at the door behind him. They needn't have worried. The agent didn't see her as he poked around the cockpit, nor did the others when they came in.

Spence and Mike escorted the agents off the airplane, then supervised the refueling. Dorel watched the customs agents drive away and shook her head in amazement. "I wouldn't have believed it if I hadn't seen it. I was so worried they were going to be pointing those guns at us when they discovered you. I'm sorry I let my fear get in the way and didn't support you with my thoughts."

Rian patted Dorel's shoulder with true affection. "You did great. Everyone is afraid. Fear, like any emotion, is energy that you can make work for you. You redefine it, intend it to produce a different reaction or result and direct it as you desire."

Dorel gave her a hug. "You make it sound so easy and natural, like everyone can do what you do. But you've got to know that we can't. We don't have these powers that you do, and that may be a good thing."

Chapter Sixteen

Cairo was a large, fairly modern city. Unlike Seattle, drivers were heavy on the car horns and mixing it up with pedestrians and even a few donkey carts. At noon the heat wasn't too bad, about 80 degrees in the unairconditioned cab.

Mike asked the driver about taking them out to the Sphinx, but the driver refused, saying something about not having the right permit. He insisted on taking them to a hotel that the girls refused without getting out of the car.

"I am not staying here. If we can't go to Giza now, take us to the Hilton," Dorel ordered and Rian agreed.

While they checked in, Spence spoke to the concierge and arranged for a car and driver early the next day. He picked up some brochures and a free map of the tourist sights at Giza. The concierge told him that the archeological work was ongoing at the pyramids and the Sphinx, but tourists were now allowed to walk around it. He waited by the elevators where he could survey the lobby. Everything had gone pretty smooth at the airport, but Ian and his team would be around.

They made sure the suite was secure for Dorel and Rian, then made a run to the gift shop to pick up flashlights, bottled water and sunscreen for Dorel. Mike found the leather bag hanging on a rack at the back of the store and called Spence over.

"This should be long enough to fit the swords." He put one end to his shoulder while holding on to the other. The bag was about three inches longer than Mike's arm.

When they returned to the suite, room service had arrived. Spence wasn't as hungry as he was tired but didn't want to sleep and wake up at 2:00 a.m. with jet lag. The plates were cleared away and they sat at the table with paper, pencils and the brochures to placate Dorel's desire for a plan. Spence and Rian had already decided how they were going to take the swords, but they understood that Dorel needed to talk it out.

"The chamber is about one hundred feet underground. This is where the opening is," Rian said, pointing between the Sphinx's front paws on a brochure. "It doesn't show the digs or their enclosures, but I've map dowsed this and believe that is the spot."

"Map dowsed?" Dorel asked, writing on her sheet of paper.

"I have in mind what I'm looking for, then move my hand over a picture or a map. I can feel the energy of the item if it's there. The swords are right there," she said, tapping the picture.

"Both of them?" Mike asked.

"Yes," Rian said, looking at Spence. "Don't you agree?"

"Yeah. The Defender is on the forge and I get the impression that the Guardian is inside something. I'm betting it's hidden inside the forge. And I think the *aptet* really is a key that can be used to either open a secret compartment or fit in a hole of some kind and the sword drops out. At least that's what I've been able to view."

"You know what amazes me about the swords is that they seem to move through time and space on their own. How? How do they do that? Magic?" Dorel asked with a frown.

"In our regression there was a sense of magic in the creation of the swords," Rian said. "The ancient Egyptians had a cult of magic. What I've put together from our regression to the forge and my viewing of the chamber is that it is a temple of Anubis, the jackal headed god. The Forge of Balance is there, and I've been wondering, forging a balance of what?" She shrugged and frowned at Spence.

He shrugged. "Got me. The Egyptians were pretty advanced in their understanding of wave physics and energy. It could be that their chants and magic were manipulations of sonic waves that produced a given result. Maybe the waves have to balance somehow in order to create."

"I think so, too," Rian asserted. "When Seta and Kalūkah were making the swords, they chanted constantly, the tone, modulation and pitch changing. That combined with their intent and the special shape of the chamber, oh, and with the *aptet* which could have some special properties, made and powered those swords. It was alchemy in reverse, I guess, because they started with pure gold and produced swords of a common alloy."

"Not common," Spence corrected. "I was never able to determine what Dorel's sword was made of. At first glance it looked ordinary enough, but it wasn't as we all know. And when I cut it up, it shrieked. Remember that, Mike?"

The memory transformed Mike's expression to one of pain. He nodded. "There was nothing ordinary about that sword. You just had to hold it in your hand and you felt the power. Nobody could defeat you. Nobody."

Rian stared into space as if she were entranced and nodded. "That's exactly how it feels."

"Well, I held it and didn't feel that way," Dorel snapped. "It fascinated me at first, but not enough that I didn't try to sell it. Then I came to think of it as nothing but evil. I hate to think what having two of them could do."

"That's why we can't let Ian or Datascape or anyone get their hands on them," Mike said forcefully. "We've got to get in there, get the swords and hide them."

"And they'll go right back to the forge," Spence said and slapped his hand to his forehead. "Good God, they brought us here! Ian could get both of them, take them back to Denver and the swords would disappear again. Zip. Right back to the Sphinx."

Rian, still with a faraway look in her eyes, nodded. "Guardian brought us here to perform the ritual. To remake Defender, to make him whole."

"And when the sword is whole, as you say, what then?" Dorel asked, looking askance at Rian.

"Then they are ours to wield," Rian said in an odd flat voice.

A shudder rolled through Spence and he pushed back from the table. "Can we forget about our world domination fantasies for a minute, please? We're here to get the swords, whatever condition they're in, before Ian does. Save our asses and the world, hopefully in that order." Dorel gave him a thumbs-up, but Mike wouldn't look at him.

"Spence, you said it yourself, the swords will keep coming back to the forge until we reforge them. They've drawn us here and we have to do it."

"Or we can leave them here and let Ian chase them back and forth," he said, cutting a glance at Mike, who was staring at his clenched hands on the table. Uh oh. No help there. He was struggling with wanting the sword's power again.

Tired and frustrated, Spence rubbed his face and sat back down, trying to think.

"The problem with that idea, Spence, is that Ian knows. He won't just chase the swords as you say. He will have us one way or another. We will be made to perform the ritual and when the swords are whole and energized, if you will, he'll have no use for us," Rian said. "And he'll have the power. He won't even need Datascape. No doubt that is his plan."

"Okay, so saying we find the swords and perform the ritual tomorrow. Then whose power is it?" It was a trick question and Spence watched their expressions. Mike tensed and glanced at Rian then him. Dorel cut her anxious eyes to Mike. Rian held Spence's gaze, unblinking.

"Whomever needs it, I suppose. Mike and Dorel need the power to bring their son home and insure their safety. I don't have such a need. And you? Do you need the power, Spence?" Rian asked.

Not so long ago he learned that he had been living a lie, that everything he'd done and built had been enabled by a huge entity that seemed to have tentacles in every part of his life. Did he have a need for real power of his own that Datascape didn't dispense as they deemed necessary to bind him with golden handcuffs? Hell yes, he needed power.

"We don't have the swords yet," Mike gruffed. "You said that in your regression you and Spence chanted. If you're going to do the same ritual tomorrow, how are you going to know what and when to chant?"

"I think the *aptet* is more than the key to Guardian's hiding place. Also, the swords will help us, if we're to believe that they brought us here to do this, then they've got to help us do it," Rian said with conviction.

Spence had to agree. A kind of knowing had centered within him. The more he thought about the swords, the more he seemed to understand about them. They were communicating with him. Were they with Rian, too?

Dorel stood, shaking her head, tears in her eyes. "I wish we'd never come here. There is no way that this can work, but we're here and it is what it is." She leveled her sorrowful gaze on Spence. "If I don't make it out of this and you do, please don't go anywhere near my son. He deserves better than you."

Mike muttered an apologetic goodnight and followed Dorel to their room, closing the door. Rian reached for Spence's hand and brought it to her lips. She closed her eyes and cupped his palm to her cheek. He rose and pulled her into his arms and they held each other in a meld of comforting stillness.

Later, after they made love, they lay awake long into the night.

She lay with her head on his shoulder as he stroked her silken hair. "Mmmm, I like that," she purred and snuggled closer.

"Me, too. Your hair is beautiful. Have you always worn it long?" he opened, wanting to know everything about her like she knew him.

"It's easiest long. I'm quite lazy in the fixing up department and never into the makeup and clothes thing." She traced a fingertip around his nipple.

"I guess it's lucky that you're a drop dead gorgeous natural beauty then, huh? Don't have to worry about those things."

"I don't know about that, but there have been drawbacks from my lack of interest in those things. I didn't have a lot of girlfriends when I was growing up and that's carried through." There was a tinge of regret in her voice.

Spence squirmed and grabbed her hand. "That tickles."

She laughed and kissed his chin. "It's supposed to. What about you? Lots of girlfriends growing up? Today?"

"Don't you know?" he asked, watching her turquoise eyes.

"Yes, I suppose I do," she said with a crooked grin.

"And you know all about me."

"No, I don't. I haven't had a chance to get in there and dig around." He tapped her forehead and she batted his hand away. "Besides, every time I tried, I'd drop in on Paul and see you as Meredith. Not a bad thing, but it's not Rian."

"That's a nice surprise. Meredith is a much better woman than I, I'm afraid. You just keep that in mind."

"But Rian is the sexy mysterious woman I've got in my arms. I want to know all about you." He pulled her into a soft kiss that she deepened, lighting him off with a slow burn. "Where did you learn to do that?" he breathed.

She pushed away a little and gauged him. "You're not going to give up on this getting to know me thing, are you?"

He shook his head. "Tell me."

"From a married man. Satisfied and horrified?" she asked and lay on her back beside him.

He propped his elbow, head on his hand. "Nope, weirdly stimulated. Go on."

"When I was at Whitworth I won a summer internship in the psychology department to study the effects, if any, of certain types of music upon children diagnosed with attention deficit hyperactivity disorder. A visiting professor was very supportive of my work and we became involved. I knew he was married, even met his wife when she visited that summer. A nice woman, and I felt very bad about that, but not enough to stop seeing him.

"He treated me like a child, wanting to control everything I did, and I usually let him, because I was absolutely mesmerized by him. We battled most of the time, but the makeup sex was phenomenal. When he went home, I realized that he was as addicted to causing me pain as I was getting it from him."

"Yeah, okay, but tell me about the phenomenal sex," Spence teased, trying to lighten the mood.

Rian chortled, but she was regretting having told him. "He was an adept in the art of seduction, using sex to manipulate and control. I don't really believe that he ever really got into it. For him, sex was all about making someone else give up their power. And as I said, I was willing. I thought I loved him. They say you always love your first."

"That's crap. I have no feelings for that hooker at all," he said, blinding her with his smart ass smirk.

She laughed and pulled him on top, her arms around his neck. "Well, thanks. I can forget about that then."

"So, did you see him again?"

Rian nodded, her expression becoming solemn. Uh oh. His gut went cold and he pushed up on his elbows. "Do you still?"

"Yes." She slid out from under him and got out of bed.

Spence sat up. "Do we need to discuss this?"

She whirled on him. "Why? Do we have a future together?"

"You tell me."

Rian put her face in her hands and turned away. "I love you, Spence, but there's no future in it."

He got out of bed and embraced her against him. "Okay, I know we haven't talked through what we're going to do when and if we get out of this, but I assumed it would be together. Am I wrong?"

Rian nodded against him, then turned in his arms, her eyes downcast. "It was Ian."

His hands dropped off of her and his knees went weak with the cold betrayal worming in the pit of his stomach. He dropped to the side of the bed and sat. Rian moved to him and hugged his head against her belly.

"I was seventeen when I met Ian. He was very clever in his handling of me and presented a blank canvas for me to project my need for a father, a lover and a friend upon. Because I'd tested in the broad bandwidth range and had no messy family ties, I was an ideal candidate for Datascape. He used sex as part of my conditioning to bind me to him. Our relationship wasn't sexual anymore after he recruited me. Then as part of my training, he began to teach me how to use sex the way he did."

"I thought you were viewing for God and country," he muttered and set her away from him. "Why would you need to screw the information out of targets, unless you got off on it?"

Her expression was sad, but she didn't retreat. "You know the intelligence game, Spence. Liars, cheats, thieves and murderers."

It was true. And if it were also true she'd been recruited at such a young, impressionable age, could she really be blamed for what she'd become? "You said you loved me. How do you know?"

"Because I've always loved you. From the first moment I read your file, something shifted inside me like a beam of pure white light in a dark room. Then when I began to view you," she shook her head, tears forming in her forlorn eyes, "I felt you, experienced your life as you did and I wanted more. I watched you with Marty, Dorel and Mike, and felt your love for them. I wanted that love shining on me—" Her voice broke and she pressed her lips together, wringing her clasped hands.

He wanted to tell her he was okay with her past and that he loved her. Did he still? He felt something for her, but a part of him worried the feelings might be more of her manipulation. What the hell did it matter now if it was? They only had right now. Tomorrow would come soon enough and if they lived through it, they could deal with their issues then.

Spence embraced her and kissed her hair, then tipped her chin up to him with his finger. "So, how does it feel?"

"What?" she asked, her eyes glittering, wide and hopeful.

"My love shining on you."

Her smile was like the sun. "Much better than I had any right to hope for. I love you, Spence."

The day didn't start well. While they stood by with their luggage, on the look out for Ian and friends, Dorel spent almost two hours settling the hotel bill because the credit card was denied. She had to talk to the bank personally to explain that representatives of Avion Aircraft Leasing were indeed in Egypt and would continue to use the card for fuel and other charges. The bank agreed to authorize.

Dorel strolled over to them, looking frazzled. She stuffed the paperwork in her briefcase. "We're good to go. Did the driver show up yet?"

Mike shook his head. "Concierge checked on it. He's had an accident but will be here in a few minutes." He looked at his watch. "That was an hour ago."

"We could make other arrangements. Rent a car, maybe? I could check," Rian suggested.

"Go ahead, but the guy will probably show any minute," Mike said and leaned against a marble pillar.

Rian dropped Spence's hand with a squeeze and walked to the informational brochure kiosk next to the concierge's desk. As she squatted to look at the bottom shelf, her white blouse rode up out of the waist of her black jeans. She pulled the shirttail out completely, tossed her hair back and picked through the brochures.

Spence joined Mike and asked out the side of his mouth, "Where did you put Ian's gun?"

Mike nodded toward the pile of luggage. "In the backpack with the flashlights and stuff. I'll give it to Dorel in the car. I've got mine on. You?"

"Same," Spence said, feeling the .45 against his back. Like Mike, he wore his shirttail out to hide it.

"Mister Mike. Mister Mike," called a short, dark Egyptian in western dress circulating through the lobby.

"Over here," Mike answered and the man approached with a fawning smile.

"I am your driver, Habib. Forgive that I am late, please. We will go now. These are your luggage?" he asked with a frown.

"Yes. Didn't the concierge tell you that we wanted to go to the airport afterwards?" Mike asked, picking up bags.

"Yes, yes. But we do not get to the Giza until three, maybe four hours. We do not see the many pyramids or we are in dark when we return. This is okay?" Habib took Dorel's briefcase and motioned her in front of him with a bow.

Spence sent Rian ahead and followed the group outside, taking one last careful look around, trying to assuage the sensation between his shoulder blades that they were being watched.

The ride to Giza was long, hot and uncomfortable. Habib gave up trying to interest them in the sights or stopping at every souk or market. He gave up and turned on the radio, singing along to the high pitched yammering of the Arab music. It put them all on edge.

From the time Habib parked the car at the Giza plateau, they were swarmed by aggressive souvenir sellers, pushing every kind of junk trinkets, beaded necklaces and canvas bags. Habib warned them to be alert because they had been known to surround tourists and rob them. Uniformed Egyptian security forces watched the vendors and patrolled among the groups of tourists that wandered inside and outside the sandy beige-colored Sphinx and the pyramid behind it. The early afternoon sun shown down warming the air that smelled of sand and heat.

Habib began his canned lecture at the front of the Sphinx. He nodded to a guard sitting on a wooden stool with his AK47 across his knees in front of a ten by ten canvas enclosure between its front paws. Spence moved behind Habib out of the guard's line of sight and surveyed the area. The tent's door flap was closed and there didn't appear to be any activity inside.

"Habib, they are working inside the chamber today?" Rian asked with an interested smile and moving closer to him.

He returned her smile. "Not today, Miss."

"Then we will see the chamber inside," she asserted as if there was no argument.

"It is not possible," he swept his open hand to the guard who looked bored, if not sleeping with his eyes open.

"My friends would appreciate anything you can do to help them have a look inside," Mike said, taking Habib by the arm and leading him away.

Dorel took off her backpack. "The flashlight, the *aptet* and case are inside. Do you need anything else?" she asked, helping Rian on with it.

Rian shook her head and focused a disrupting frequency on the guard. She and Spence eased toward the tent flap, while Mike kept Habib occupied. The guard rocked to his feet with a stricken expression and dashed away toward the toilets.

"You've got our six," Spence told Dorel and ducked under the flap with Rian.

Inside the sun-filtered enclosure, they looked down into a twenty feet deep excavation with a set of stone steps exposed at the bottom. Spence started down the aluminum ladder first, Rian following him. He pulled the flashlights out of her pack, handed her one, and with a deep breath, began his descent into the darkness.

He counted twelve steps down then entered a steep passageway that was barely four feet high. Breathing hard, Spence bent and started down, counting his shuffling steps. "Are you back there?" he called to Rian.

"Uh huh. Very close in here, isn't it," she puffed.

"You aren't claustrophobic, are ya?"

"Not till now. I can't wait to stand up in the light."

"I see the end about thirty feet ahead," Spence said, banging his head on the ceiling. "Hope Mike and Dorel have got it handled up top."

The stone door was closed with a tape seal across one side. Rian stopped beside him, gasping, and they both shined their flashlights around the edges of the door. "I don't even have a pocket knife," Spence complained. "Should have thought of that."

"Break the tape and push on it. It will open."

He cut a look at her. "How do you know?"

She smiled. "I remember."

Rian held both lights as Spence ran a thumbnail over the tape, then pushed on the warm stone. It swung open noiselessly. Spence shivered with anticipation and pulled it further open, Rian backing out of his way. She handed him a light and they both shone the beams into the blackness beyond.

They stepped inside.

The chamber came alive in their light, shadows fleeing to hide in the corner once the beams passed. Spence pulled Rian to his side and aimed his light to the apex some twenty feet above. Rian played hers across the hieroglyphics and pictographs on the walls. At the same time they turned their focus on the rectangular shape in the middle of the chamber.

"I'll get the *aptet*," she said, slipping the pack off her back. "We don't have much time." She handed him the wrapped tool and stood. Leaving her pack on the floor, she walked to the forge.

The tool weighed heavy in Spence's hand, and he was reluctant to unwrap it. He watched Rian move around the forge, pointing her light here and there.

"Here it is!" she exclaimed, her light fixed on the top.

Spence moved across the uneven floor to her side and looked down. The Defender sword lay in its black lacquer scabbard in a long canal in the top of the forge. His heart swelled and he reached for it, wrapping his fingers around the handle. Even mortally wounded the sword had life and jabbed a blow of power up his arm that centered in his chest, pumping a rush of ecstasy through his veins.

He opened his eyes to see Rian's wary eyes locked on him. "What's wrong?" he asked and laid the sword on the edge of the forge. He set the *aptet* on the forge and began to unwrap it.

"I saw the energy go out of the sword and into you."

"Yeah. Felt like that the first time I held it, too. Not that strong, though. It was just for Mike then, I guess." He picked up the *aptet* and another surge of energy boomed through him. He sucked in a breath and shook his head to clear it of the buzzing in his ears. "Wow."

"Spence, maybe I should handle the *aptet* and the

swords. This reaction doesn't seem what we need," Rian said, real fear showing in her eyes now.

"I'm okay. Look on the opposite side for any depression or hole about the size of this," he ordered, pointing to the hooked end of the tool.

"How do you know it's that end?" she asked, moving around the forge with her light.

"I remember." He threw her a smart ass glance that got lost in the dark. *Aptet* in his right hand and light in the other, he bent and searched the side of the forge.

"I don't see anything," Rian said and moved to the end opposite him. Spence continued to search but came up with no irregularities in the outside of the forge's stone walls.

They met back at the middle. Spence laid the tool down beside the sword, pressure to hurry beginning to burn in his stomach. "I don't know what to do. Have you got any ideas?"

Rian shook her head and flashed her light around the chamber then straight up at the apex. Spence's eye followed it down. The center of the forge was directly under the apex. He envisioned the two strips of gold lying side by side in the canal. He leaned over the side and pointed the flashlight's beam at the bottom of the canal, illuminating the symbols carved into the stone.

"There!" Spence handed her his light and grabbed the tool. He tried to fit the hooked end to the shallow rectangular-shaped symbol. It wouldn't seat.

"Try the other end," Rian suggested and he did.

Nothing happened.

Spence rotated the tool and again nothing happened. On impulse, he turned it counter-clockwise and heard a click, then a grinding sound as if gears were set in motion. A seam appeared on the canal's floor and began to widen, but the sides of the forge didn't move. The crack grew and Spence saw the cord-wrapped handle. He tried to jam his fingers into the crevice, but it wasn't wide enough yet. His breathing quickened and his pulse thundered through his body.

The grinding stopped. The twin lay in shadows, waiting for him. He slipped his fingertips inside and closed them around the sword's handle and lifted it out. There was no surge of power from the Guardian. He frowned and turned it in his hands, drawing the blade from the scabbard. It glinted in the light but did not warm to his hand.

The Guardian must be awakened!

Rian stood, shining both flashlights on him as he loosed Defender from its scabbard and laid the four pieces out, ends touching, across the bottom of the canal. He laid the sheathed Guardian beside its broken twin and picked up the *aptet* in his right hand. "Put the lights down and come here."

Rian did as he instructed and he stepped to her right, taking her hand. "You remember how they did it. Hold your left hand up. Yeah." He took a deep breath, forming his intention and touched the *aptet* to the swords.

Nothing.

"You said the chamber would help us. The swords would help us," he said, panic starting up his throat. "What's wrong?"

A strange hum vibrated down through Rian's upraised hand. Her vision went out of focus and she went rigid, grinding her teeth. Her *ka* or spirit rose out the top of her head and shot to the apex where it mingled with the gods and grew strong in wisdom again. She dropped her hand and turned to him. "The ritual didn't work because you aren't the creator of the swords. I am."

He gaped at her. "You, Seta?"

Rian nodded. "Yes. And now you remember that you were Kalūkuh. The swords were created for you in the magic of our hearts." She swept her gaze into the shadows. "These walls testify to that."

He dropped the *aptet* and reeled backwards, away from the light as the memories took ghostly form around them— battles, great victories, lands and wealth—all his bought with the price of sacrificed love.

"It wouldn't be that way now. We can have it all, to-gether," he cried to Rian. "Help me. We need this for Dorel and Mike. We can help Marty! Please, Rian. This is the only way we can stop Ian, if we have the power, you and I, together. If you love me, you'll do it," he pleaded.

She loved him more than he could comprehend, espe-cially now that the power had him within its grasp. The al-chemy of the gods was strong and she, too, was under its spell. She would perform the ritual and reforge the sword for him. And trust that he would use them wisely.

Chapter Seventeen

"I will remake the sword for you," she told him and basked in the love radiating from his eyes. She put her finger upon his lips, silencing his gratitude. "The swords are a manifestation of our desire for love and power. They are a symbol of how we achieve the power to love and defend it by force, implied or physical. If the Defender operates without the tempering influence of the Guardian, a violent imbalance is created. Power is pursued for power's sake, not in defense of love."

She swept her hand around the chamber. "This is a place of balance. That is why the swords were created here and why they return when they are not counterpoised. You and I have returned because we are not in balance. Here we shall find equilibrium, one in spirit and the other in the body."

His expression was eager as he listened to the gods speaking through her. "You must find the center of your desire and focus upon it. I will do the same. We will personify love and power, Defender and Guardian. And in doing so, the gods will work through us to manifest our desire. Bring me the *aptet*," she ordered, as music began in her head in an undulating swirl of rhythm and tone.

He bent to the dark floor and picked up the *aptet*, handing it to her. "You will speak of the center of your desire as I sing of mine. Our harmony will create your desire." She opened her mouth and the music spilled out, filling the chamber with beautiful sounds. He began to speak words she didn't hear but felt as a resonance pulsing through every atom of her being. She nodded to him and took his right hand in her left. He raised his left hand high to the gods and she touched the *aptet* to the Defender's broken blade.

Sound magnified and became light, blending with their harmony of creation and rising to the apex to be reborn in the alchemy of Anubis, the protector of the great beam of balance that weighs the hearts of the dead. Energy roared downward into his upraised arm, through his body, into hers and out the end of the *aptet* in an explosion of sparks that lit every corner of the chamber.

The sound stopped. The light receded and she let go of his hand as his left arm dropped. She pulled the *aptet* away from the swords and stepped to gaze upon them. The Defender's whole, unblemished blade glinted, cold and hard-edged, in the light. She took it by the blade and presented the sword, handle first, to him. His eyes locked on the sword, he took it from her and waited, turning it in his hands like a lover attending to his beloved.

She knew what she had to do—the final step to the forging of the sword. She must sacrifice for love, surrender her physical power.

Rian reached for the Guardian sword and her hand trembled. She grabbed the side of the forge for support, telling herself that this is what he desired. She promised to help him and he would do the right thing . . . with the power. She shook the image out of her head of the lust in his eyes as he grabbed the sword from her. Rian reached for the sword again, wrapping her fingers around the handle and managed to lift it out of the dark channel.

She lifted her eyes to Spence. For an electric moment they connected beyond time and space. They loved each other and would be together again. That was their destiny. This minor drama would pass into eternity and be forgotten, but they would always be bonded with eternal love and never alone. She could do this for him. And more, she wanted to.

Rian held the sheathed sword across her palms and lowered herself to her knees at his feet, struggling with the hope that Spence wouldn't strike and the impulse to defend herself if he did. She couldn't keep herself from gazing up at him instead of bowing her head.

He wasn't even looking down at her, but at the sword in his hands, then glanced at her with a frown. Understanding dawned on his face and he raised the sword over her head with reluctance. "I—I love you, but I can't . . ."

"Just do it," she cried, her heart breaking. She lowered her head and shut her eyes.

A battle raging within, Spence stared down at Rian kneeling in front of him. He had to do it. Had to accept her sacrifice or the power wouldn't be balanced. He had to kill her. She'd told him to do it. She wanted him to have the power that only she could give to him. No! Power was nothing if he didn't have her. But power was everything. He needed the power.

Tears streamed down Spence's face as he brought the sword back to strike. It seemed to swing itself with incredible force at her neck. He stopped it as Rian jerked back, bringing the Guardian up to block the Defender. She scrambled to her feet, jerking the sword out of the scabbard, blocking his sword with both. They stood face to face, the clashing swords between them, pushing against each other in a stalemate of equilibrium. She let the scabbard drop.

"I couldn't do it," she panted, still mashing her sword on his. "I'm sorry."

"I could, and I'm not sure I won't. The sword's power is

too strong." As if encouraging him, the sword grew hot in his hand, igniting a desire in him to use it. He gave Rian a strong shove, his sword against hers, and retreated as she fell back.

They circled each other in and out of the pools of light and darkness. The fear on her face tore at his heart, but another part of him was glad and wanted to take advantage of it.

"Spence, listen to me. You don't want power that I have to die for. You love me," she said, keeping out of his reach. Sweat glistened on her face and her hand shook. "You love me."

He shook his head. "Yeah, but if we don't do this, then what? We're going to die anyway. At least this will give one of us a shot at putting things right while the other one gets to go home. It's a win win when you look at it that way." He feinted a thrust at her and she jumped back.

"The sword's making you do this. You're not yourself—"

"No kidding," he spat and pressed her again. Jabbing her sword in front of her, she faded back toward the forge, groping behind herself with one hand.

Spence yelled and charged, swung at her sword. It shattered with a loud clang, the pieces clattering to the floor. Rian dropped the handle and dodged sideways, grabbing the *aptet* off the forge. She swung it with both hands. Metal attacked metal and both exploded into a dozen pieces that rained down on the stone floor.

Spence blinked and locked his gaze on a stunned Rian. He opened his arms and she walked into them, laying her head on his chest. He held her against him, closing his eyes on the dark chamber and opening himself to the great love enveloping them. She stirred against him then moved out of his arms, holding his hand.

"Is it over now?" she asked, glancing at the broken swords scattered across the floor.

"Maybe for us. I don't know what will happen now with the swords, do you?" A longing for power that he would never have again jabbed him, but he shook it off. That kind of power wasn't worth what you had to give up to get or do to keep it.

"I'm not feeling anything about the swords but relief. They're useless now and we can't forge them again, because the *aptet* is destroyed. Ian or whomever else finds them can have them. I don't care," she said and moved to gather their gear.

"Then we leave them here?" Spence picked up the flashlights, handing one to her.

"Yes. I don't ever want to see them again."

They took one last look around the chamber. Something seemed to be watching them from the shadows, but they turned their backs on it. Spence put his arm through the backpack's strap and stepped into the passageway, pointing his light ahead. He extended his hand back to Rian, leading her out of the darkness behind them. They'd ascended a few feet when they turned to look back at the same time.

The shadow of the god Anubis passed across the chamber's door erasing any trace of an opening in the solid rock.

The chamber had disappeared.

Spence hustled up the passage with Rian right behind him, feeling lighter and happier with every breath. He stood aside and let her climb the steps into the canvas enclosure first, then followed when she disappeared in the light above. As he hit the last couple of steps he thought he heard a muffled scream. A picture of Rian's frightened face flashed into his mind. He pulled his .45 out of his waistband and eased his head into the opening. Seeing no one, he ducked back inside the stairwell and listened, reaching out with his energy.

Ian. And five or six others.

He had no choice but to go topside. Spence stuck the gun in the backpack's side pocket where he might be able to get to it if they didn't snatch it away from him first and took the last couple of stairs to the top. Three of them were waiting for him outside the tent's door and grabbed him when he came through. A big guy patted him down while another went through the backpack and pulled out the .45, then they pushed him around to the back of the enclosure. There were no tourists or Egyptian Security Forces to be seen anywhere. Just sand, sun and two guys holding guns on Dorel and Mike.

Ian had Rian off to the side, talking at her. Rian's dislike bordering on hatred of her former mentor chafed Spence like a rubber suit in a sauna even before he reached them. Looking like a tired old man, Ian rounded on Spence. "She says the swords are gone."

Spence shrugged. "See for yourself."

Ian sent the two that had grabbed him down the stairway with a palm-size video camera. They waited ten minutes in silence before the men returned and the camera's playback confirmed that there was no evidence of a room. He scowled in Spence's direction then issued orders to his men. Those guarding Mike and Dorel released them and Ian motioned for them to follow him. Spence considered grabbing Rian and making a break for it and thought Mike was thinking the same thing, but Ian stopped before they could make their move.

"I'm letting you go," Ian said with a benevolent smile. "All I have to do is wait and watch. The swords will turn up again with the four of you somewhere, sometime. And when they do, I'll have them."

Spence took Rian's hand and led her past Ian toward the parking lot, hoping that Mike and Dorel followed. They reached the parking lot together and found Habib waiting at the car. He seemed relieved and a little surprised to see them. Mike and Dorel climbed in and fell asleep before the car got to the main road. The ride back to the airport was a little cooler and a lot quieter than the one this morning that seemed like a week ago. Rian slept on Spence's shoulder all the way back while he watched the sun go down and the stars come out over the desert.

They took off out of Cairo, climbing above the vast desert into the midnight sky. As they flew westward over the Mediterranean, Spence handed off the controls to Mike. Dorel took his place in the right seat and he went back to the first class cabin where Rian waited for him.

He slipped into the sleeper seat beside hers and pulled her into his arms, burying his face in her soft hair and reveling in being alive. They'd made it, but for how long? And what were they going to do now, go back to their lives as usual?

"You didn't tell Ian that both swords and the *aptet* were destroyed, did you?" he asked.

"No. I told him they disappeared," she murmured and snuggled closer.

"That explains why he thinks they'll come back," Spence sighed, relieved. "They won't come back, right?"

She sat up and took his face in her hands. "I don't want to know. I'm not going to view their future, their now or their past anymore. I only want to think about us. Let's create our future together, a future where there are no magic swords that people will kill for. We've lived that life. Now it's time to create a wonderful life for ourselves. Do you want to do that with me, Spence?"

"More than anything. But how? Are we going to ignore what's happened? Ian isn't going to let us do that. He'll always be lurking in the background, watching us. I think it's safe to say that my business is in for some tough times without Datascape. And how about you? Are you still on the payroll? Ian said they don't let operators leave—"

She put her finger on his lips. "Shhhh. You're trying to see the future by looking at the past. Are you and I trained minds with super psychic skills or not?" she asked with a grin.

He nodded.

"Well, then let's act like it. Let's create our future instead of living one we don't like by default. Let Ian lurk. Those swords aren't coming back, and he'll realize that eventually. And without Datascape maybe your business can take a new, more independent direction. As for me, I told you I love my practice and my music. Datascape doesn't want me anymore. Sure, they'll monitor us, but they aren't going to screw with us because they're afraid of our *powers*."

"What about Marty? Will they try for him?" he asked, worry gnawing at him.

"No. I think that was part of Ian's motivational plan. They may be interested in Marty when he's older. Until then they'll continue to monitor the family, waiting for the swords to appear again." She kissed the end of his nose. "Feeling happier?"

"Do you believe all that or are you working your Jedi mind tricks on me again?" he asked, wrapping his arm around her and lying back in the seat.

"Mind tricks, of course." She pulled a blanket over

them. "Believing. Mind tricks. They're the same thing, you know. Magic."

"Uh huh. How about we work some magic together and I introduce you to the arcane mysteries of the Mile High Club?"

"I knew you were going to say that," she purred, unbuttoning his shirt.

Epilogue

High above the earth the soulmates pledged to create a powerful life of love as they flew toward their future, the struggle to balance power with love behind them.

Far below the desert sands beneath the stone paws of the Sphinx, the jackal-headed god guided the dead in the temple of Anubis. He commanded each broken shred and shattered fragment of the Defender and the Guardian swords to gather on the Forge of Balance, and positioned them so that their hearts might be weighed. Then he summoned his father Osiris, ruler of the underworld and giver of life after death.

Osiris weighed the essence of Defender and Guardian and found the fractured pair worthy of life. Embodying the great magic of resurrection, Osiris passed the sacred ankh over the fragments and they became whole in a brilliant flash of rebirth.

The eternal apotheosis of power and love rose from the underworld into the ether to materialize once again in another time, a different place to forge and temper another pair of lovers.

About the Author

Melinda Rucker Haynes, M.Ed., is a certified hypnotherapist and neuro-linguistic programming practitioner with a hypnotherapy practice specializing in Personal Time Travel© past life regression therapy. She consults internationally as a performance enhancement coach and is the creator of Story Compass© personal development strategies. Her previous writing work has included published education research, technical, informational and entertainment nonfiction prior to *The Eternal Trust*, her first novel for Five Star Publishing. Her novels have won numerous awards and the praise of critics and readers alike. She and her husband enjoy working and traveling between the United States and Europe. At present, she's hard at work researching the next novel in her ongoing story that began with *The Eternal Trust* and is continued here.